"MAKE UP YOUR MIND, GARETH."

Margery strode toward him, hands on her hips. "Are you my protector, or my suitor?"

Gareth straightened, suddenly seeming as tall and wild as the Viking ancestors he resembled. "You hired me as your guard. Did you think—"

He studied her for a moment, and Margery began to think she'd miscalculated.

"I was worried my acting would not be skilled enough." He slowly looked down her body. "I've never had to make an effort to court a woman before."

Acting? A blush of mortification swept from her chest to her forehead. When he'd kissed her fingers, when he'd praised her beauty, he'd been *acting?*

"You asked me to hide my true purpose here," Gareth said calmly. "I'm going to pretend to be another of your suitors. What better way can I be near you, keeping you from danger?"

Margery remembered the heat of his gaze, the touch of his lips on her hand. Of course it was all an act. She buried the tiny pain that touched her heart, and smiled coolly.

Gayle Callen

My Lady's Guardian

AVON BOOKS
An Imprint of HarperCollins*Publishers*

This is a work of fiction. Names, characters, places, and incidents are products of the author's imagination or are used fictitiously and are not to be construed as real. Any resemblance to actual events, locales, organizations, or persons, living or dead, is entirely coincidental.

AVON BOOKS
An Imprint of HarperCollins*Publishers*
10 East 53rd Street
New York, New York 10022-5299

Copyright © 2000 by Gayle Kloecker Callen
Inside cover author photo by Tarolli Studio
ISBN: 0-380-81376-9
www.avonromance.com

First Avon Books paperback printing: June 2000

Avon Trademark Reg. U.S. Pat. Off. and in Other Countries, Marca Registrada, Hecho en U.S.A.
HarperCollins ® is a trademark of HarperCollins Publishers Inc.

Printed in the U.S.A.

WCD   10 9 8 7 6 5 4 3 2

Prologue

◠◠◯◯◠◠

England, 1475

Through his narrow window, twelve-year-old squire Gareth Beaumont watched the inner ward burn. The night was dark, lit only by the flames. The shrieks of women and children, the groans of men as they fought the blaze, filled the air.

He had *seen* this, in his nightmares and his waking visions. Everything had been muddled, but the fires had raged in his mind for days. He should have known it meant attack!

He wanted to bang his head against the wall to shake out these incomprehensible visions that haunted him. But he couldn't escape his legacy, the Beaumont Curse. Why did he have to be different from everyone else?

Now Wellespring Castle's stables and out-buildings were alive with flames. It was just like his parents' fate all over again: they'd died

1

three years before in a fire, leaving Gareth with nothing but painful memories.

But at least this time he could do something. He flung open the door to his room and raced down the corridor.

The inner ward was a nightmare of smoke and flames, and the screams of horses and men. The gatehouse held firm, keeping out the invaders, while fire illuminated the archers manning the battlements. At the stables, Gareth joined the line of men passing buckets of water from the well to the fire.

His eyes watered from the smoke, and his lungs ached with the need for fresh air. Although his skin was hot, a sudden chill of foreboding worked through him, and he wanted to groan aloud his denial. Not now!

The vision began as but a sound, a child's sob. Sometimes he could pretend he didn't see the visions. It made the headaches worse, but that was better than knowing useless information he couldn't understand.

But this time he knew who it was—Margery Welles, the eight-year-old daughter of the viscount.

In the mists of his mind he saw her impish face contort in a scream of terror. She wasn't with the women, as she was supposed to be.

He broke from the line of men and raced through the inner ward, dodging soldiers. He finally saw Lord Welles by the gatehouse. The viscount was a tall, broad man with gray peppering his dark hair, and a craggy face that always looked in control.

Gareth came to a stop before him, coughing from the smoke. "My lord, your daughter—I fear she's in danger."

The firelit ward retreated as he was caught in the formidable gaze of Lord Welles. They stared at each other, and for an instant, fear touched His Lordship's eyes.

"Gareth, she is with the women. Do you know otherwise?"

Before Gareth could respond, he heard a great rending of wood and a sharp crack.

Lord Welles caught his arm and dragged him away from the swarm of soldiers who rushed to defend the gatehouse. "Baron Hunter and his men have broken through the first doors. There will be a battle. Saints above, I wish my sons were here—but you will do. Get Margery away."

"But my lord, how—"

Lord Welles leaned into Gareth's face and spoke in a hoarse, urgent voice. "Take her into the undercroft below the great hall. You'll find a stack of barrels in the north corner, and a hidden tunnel beneath them. Lead Margery out into the forest and await my word."

"I'll find the women and take them all—"

"Margery first!" Lord Welles said, grabbing Gareth's arms and giving him a quick shake. "If you get her out to the forest before the castle itself is invaded, then you may return for others. I can't take the chance that Margery could be harmed. You must protect her. Promise me!"

"O-of course, my lord," he stammered.

"Now go!"

When Gareth searched the great hall and didn't find her, he knew Margery would go where she felt safest. He found her alone in her bedchamber, leaning out a window to watch the destruction below. He hauled her away from it and closed the shutters, weak with relief at having found her unharmed.

She looked at him solemnly, all dark hair and wide blue eyes. She wore white billowy nightclothes. "My father will win, won't he, Gareth?"

"Of course," he gasped, still breathing hard. He found garments hung on pegs and brought them to her. "But he wants me to take you to a safe place."

"You have to leave while I—"

Ignoring her protests, Gareth pulled her smock over her head. She was soon dressed and well-wrapped in a cloak.

He led Margery down through the levels of the castle to one of the entrances to the undercroft. He lifted the trap door, grabbed a torch off the wall, and descended into the darkness below the main level, holding her hand.

Wooden beams arched overhead, dripping cobwebs. Barrels of salted meat and foodstuffs were stacked high. He led Margery to the north

corner and had her hold the torch while he
started to drag barrels away.

"Gareth, what are you looking for? A hidden
treasure?"

"A secret tunnel." Above them, he suddenly
heard the pounding of many booted feet and a
distant scream. He threw himself at the next
barrel. Where was the tunnel?

He glanced at Margery. He could see tears
glistening in her eyes but still she held the
torch high.

As he dragged a fifth barrel aside, Gareth
heard the clash of steel over their heads. By the
saints, was the entire castle overrun? In despair, he realized he wouldn't be able to rescue
the other women. If he tried he would most
certainly be captured, and Margery would be
alone.

Lord Welles's words echoed through his
mind. *You must protect her.*

Gareth would prove himself worthy of his
lord's trust. He would never let any harm come
to Margery.

Feeling a sudden draft of cold air at his feet,
he shoved the last barrel aside and saw the outline of a trap door. When he lifted it, dust and
dirt billowed through the air.

He quickly took the torch and led her down
a short staircase. The tunnel was made of earth
and damp rock, carved out of the ground,
braced with rotting wood. When they'd
walked at least a hundred paces, tree roots be-

gan to poke through the ceiling. Soon all he had to do was push past the roots of a tree, and they were in the forest.

Gareth knew they were only a few hundred yards from the castle. He could hear shouts, weapons clashing, and the hissing roar of fire. He put his arms around Margery and led her back into the tunnel.

He used the sputtering torch to light a small fire near the entrance. Still kneeling, he turned and saw Margery gazing bleakly back down the tunnel.

Gareth didn't know the first thing about comforting a little girl. Feeling awkward, he held out his hand and she took it, crouching beside him. She stared into the fire as one tear slid down her cheek. Swept by a feeling of tenderness, he put his arm around her. She leaned into him.

"What else did Father tell you?" she murmured.

"He told me to keep you safe, and that he would send for you as soon as he could."

"You won't leave me?" She turned teary, pleading eyes up to him. "You're always trying to get away from me."

He hugged her closer, and pushed the tangle of hair from her eyes. "This isn't like our games," he said, feeling a stab of guilt. "I promise I won't leave you."

*   *   *

Gareth awoke to the chirping of birds outside in the forest as the sun rose.

With a gasp, Margery sat up straight. "Father?"

"Not yet," he said reluctantly. "Are you hungry?"

She shook her head.

"Of course you're hungry. Do you know how to fish?"

She looked at him out of the corner of her eye, and he saw some of her liveliness return. "I tried to follow you the last time, but you sent me home."

He sighed, feeling another ache of guilt. "Your voice scared away the fish. I'll wager you *still* can't be quiet."

She gave him a teasing glare and shoved him aside. "You just show me how to fish, Gareth Beaumont."

He dug his fishing hooks and string from the pouch at his belt, and soon they were lying side by side on the embankment of a small creek, dangling their hooks in the water.

Gareth pulled in a small, wriggling trout.

Margery lifted her chin. "I shall get a bigger one."

He barely kept from smiling. "I'd like to see you try."

And try she did. He was impressed, even as he cooked his own fish. She perched on the embankment, fishing mightily, ignoring him as he smacked his lips and ate his trout. He saved half for her.

He needn't have. Soon she caught her own fish, and it was bigger, just as she promised. She took it off the hook, learned how to remove the bones, and even cooked it herself, though she burned her fingers before she was through.

Side by side, they knelt at the edge of the brook and cleaned the fish smell from their hands. Something suddenly glittered beneath the surface. Gareth grasped the object and rose to his feet for the best light. It was just a gray stone, but imbedded in the center was a cloudy piece of crystal that caught the rays of the sun. Margery reached for it in delight, laughing.

In her haste, she knocked it from his hand, and it bounced along the rocky edge of the brook. As Margery picked up the two pieces of the broken stone, her breath caught on a muffled sob. Gareth knew that her grief had little to do with the stone.

"Margery, look, 'tis just as shiny as ever. And now there's a piece for each of us, so we can remember today."

She looked at the two stones, then gave one to him. When she lifted her face, he felt his heart give a painful lurch at the redness of her nose and eyes.

"I shall keep this always," he said.

A smile tugged at one corner of Margery's lips and she clenched the shining stone tightly in her fist.

Gareth's gaze rose over her head in the direction of Wellespring Castle and he tried to mask his worry. If he could keep Margery busy, she wouldn't have time to be afraid.

For three days, they waited for word from Lord Welles. They slept in a bed of leaves in the tunnel by night, and played games of survival by day. He taught her to snare rabbits, then how to cook them. They played hiding games in the forest, moving from tree to tree in an attempt to outwit each other. He made two pouches, so they could each carry their crystal stone on their belts. She was his first friend, and he pretended that someday when she found out about the Beaumont Curse, she wouldn't care.

On the fourth day, they heard soldiers riding through the forest. Gareth retreated to a little fort they'd built high in the trees and held Margery close. Hoarse voices called her name.

" 'Tis my brothers!"

He found himself rubbing the crystal stone in its pouch at his waist, and waited for her to climb down to her family, leaving him alone once more.

She took his hand. "Will you still be my friend when we go back?"

"Forever." The word reverberated through his soul like a blood vow. He had discovered what it was like to be a man, to take care of someone.

Margery descended from their perch and

into the waiting arms of her brother Reynold, only three years older than Gareth. James Markham, Earl of Bolton, not yet twenty, watched Gareth closely as he reached the ground.

"My lords," Gareth said, bowing his head stiffly. "I hope all is well at the castle."

They hesitated, and he knew in that moment that his visions, though unclear, had not betrayed him.

Margery pulled away from Reynold. "Father?"

Her brothers looked grim.

"Not Father!" she cried. "But where is Edmund?"

"He is fine," Reynold said as she buried her face in his tunic and sobbed. "He is with Father's body."

Gareth felt a tight ball of grief clutch his chest as he watched her tears. Reynold guided his horse out of the clearing, taking Margery away.

James looked Gareth over. "When we arrived home, we searched the castle for Margery and found the tunnel open. How did you know to escape?"

Gareth grew angry at the inevitable distrust. He would be forever judged because of his ancestors, not for himself. What could he say? That strange visions haunted him?

"Your stepfather told me about the tunnel, Lord Bolton. He asked me to keep her safe."

"Well, my thanks to you," James said grudgingly.

"How did your stepfather die?"

"An arrow. We lost five soldiers, and others are wounded—but Hunter will never bother us again. I shall go to the king with this treachery."

Gareth soon came to realize that Margery's brothers did not quite believe his story. Within a week he was sent to another household to finish his fostering. Surely Margery would tell her brothers that it was all a mistake, that Gareth was her friend.

But they never came back for him.

Chapter 1

June, 1487

Gareth Beaumont gasped for air and came up on his elbows, wide awake in an instant. He bumped his head on the tent pole, and a shower of water leaked inside to splatter across his face. He ignored it, staring into the murky darkness, the dream still fresh.

Margery.

The old bitterness welled up in his mind. She and her brothers had abandoned him, setting his life on a path of desperation and loneliness.

He breathed deeply, trying to calm his pounding heart. *'Tis just a dream, not a vision.*

But he knew better. A dull ache groaned to life behind his forehead, and his stomach gurgled with queasiness. It was a vision all right, of Margery Welles—whom he hadn't seen in twelve years.

She was in danger again.

Gareth sat up, resting his head in his hands. She was not his concern; she had brothers to take care of her problems. Besides, she must be married already, even have children.

The past was dead, and he could never go back to it. Why would he want to? He certainly knew early in life that he could count on no one but himself. At his final foster home, he'd been jeered at, called Warfield's Wizard because of the visions he couldn't control. To earn respect, he'd become a fierce fighter. It kept people away, just like he wanted, and it also kept him from starving.

But he had become too good at his craft, and the noblemen tired of losing. He'd been forced to leave England when he was no longer allowed to enter tournaments and no one would hire him. He'd done some mercenary work in France these past few years, but his name and his curse had followed him even there. He had no land of his own, no family, no money. He was so close to poverty that he could smell the stench. The only things he hadn't sold were his armor and his horse, because without them, he had no chance of earning a living.

By the saints, why did he have to be reminded of Margery after all these years? He wanted to ignore this vision of danger. She already had a family, and none of them needed Gareth.

He had a sudden memory of looking into the intense gaze of her father, Lord Welles. He was the one man who had ever treated Gareth fairly.

And Gareth had promised the old man he'd always protect his daughter.

With an angry curse, he lay back on his blanket. Lord Welles deserved his loyalty, but his children did not. Yet he would go to Margery and find this danger that awaited her. He would do what was necessary to satisfy his oath, and then he would leave.

The sun blazed down on the rolling hillsides and low stone walls of Gloucestershire. In the distance, Gareth could see the bright spires of a castle glittering atop a hill. Hawksbury Castle. As usual, Margery and her family owned the best. Resentment tasted bitter in his mouth, and he tried to put the feelings aside. His personal distaste didn't matter; only his oath to Lord Welles did.

Gareth was relieved when his horse plodded into the shadows of a cool wooded glen, and he could no longer see the castle. He glanced at Wallace Desmond, who for once wasn't eyeing him suspiciously.

Gareth had known it was foolish to approach this unknown danger alone, but he hated asking anyone for help. Desmond owed Gareth, though, for saving his life at a tournament. When Gareth called in the favor, Desmond had been willing to return to his homeland to help the woman from Gareth's past.

Though the day was unusually bright for England, Gareth felt a sudden cold chill move through him. He'd spent his whole life trying to ignore such warnings, but now he heeded it.

They were near Margery.

He pulled back on the reins, and his horse danced to a halt. He cocked his head, eyeing the woods all around them.

"Desmond, you go on ahead. Hawksbury Castle is not far."

Desmond leaned on his pommel and stared at him with narrowed eyes. "What is going on, Beaumont?"

"Nothing." Desmond was ignorant of his visions, and Gareth planned to keep it that way as long as possible. Not for the first time, he wondered why generations of a family had been cursed for one ancestor's crime. "I just need a moment to think on what I will say to Margery."

Desmond grinned. "Nervous about a mere woman?"

Gareth said nothing. The longer he traveled with Desmond, the more talkative the man had become, as if it was ever possible for them to be friends. Gareth didn't need friends.

"Very well," Desmond said. "I'll leave you to your peace. Who knows, the fair Margery might take a liking to me."

*   *   *

Margery Welles circled the clearing, keeping the stone bench between herself and a grinning Thomas Fogge. For the third time this day, she cursed her foolishness. Why ever had she thought he was different from all the others—different from Peter Fitzwilliam? Taking him to one of her favorite peaceful places had been the height of stupidity. Now she was forced to fend off his advances, when all she'd wanted to do was talk.

"Lord Fogge, I insist we go back to the castle."

"Mistress Welles—Margery," he said, with an ingratiating smile that showed his blackened teeth, "I am so enjoying our private visit. How else can you come to know me?"

"Then seat yourself, my lord, and we will converse."

Lord Fogge leaned one way. Margery went the opposite way, and found herself against his chest.

"Margery, I ache for one of your kisses. Just one."

She leaned back in his embrace and turned her face away, but felt his hot breath on her neck. She had been in this situation one too many times this last month. Why hadn't she learned by now that every eligible man in England considered her fair game? And yet, what choice did she have? The days were flying by at too fast a pace, and soon the king would need an answer.

Margery felt his mouth on her cheek and grimaced. Just as she was about to bring up her knee and end His Lordship's kiss with pain, Fogge abruptly released her. As she stumbled back against the bench, she realized that Fogge had not willingly let her go. He was caught in the grip of a stranger—a much larger, broader man, who punched him hard in the stomach.

With a groan, Fogge doubled over and staggered against a tree trunk. The stranger grabbed him again, and Fogge covered his head and whimpered.

"Let him go!" Margery said.

The stranger ignored her. His fist connecting with Fogge's chin snapped the man's head back.

"That is enough!" she cried, grasping the stranger's arm. She stumbled as his arm came forward again, but hung on grimly. "You've disabled him. He will not be so foolish again."

The stranger abruptly released Lord Fogge, who reeled sideways, blood dripping from his lower lip. Without a glance at Margery, His Lordship darted through the trees toward where they'd left the horses. But she soon forgot him when the stranger turned and looked at her.

She felt a shiver of fear. Her rescuer would have continued to pummel her assailant if she had not intervened. She could trust him even less than Lord Fogge. The man was tall and well-muscled, wearing a leather jerkin over a dark shirt. His bright blond hair was long and shaggy, as if he'd been traveling for some time. Then their gazes met, and Margery forgot to breathe.

She would recognize those intense eyes anywhere.

He was Gareth Beaumont, the boy from her childhood.

Shock and disbelief made her freeze. Not a week went by that she didn't wonder what had become of him. Almost without thinking, she reached for the purse hung from her belt, and touched the crystal stone through the fabric.

She'd never been able to forget the way his golden eyes seemed to glow with a light of their own. But now a coldness lurking behind those eyes made her realize he was no longer the boy she knew.

She stepped back, barely able to take in the man he had become. He was sun-burnished, golden, his nose straight and strong, his cheekbones as chiseled as if carved by a sculptor. He was so beautifully rendered, yet so male, that it made her uneasy. And in that moment, she felt small and dark and sinful, unworthy to even look upon such perfection. What would he think of her if he knew her secrets?

But this was foolishness. Gareth Beaumont needed to know nothing of her past. He was no longer her childhood friend, but a stranger passing through her land.

And then she remembered the ignoble rumors that had chased him from the country. He was said to be a vicious opponent in battle, who won at any cost.

He, too, was assessing her, staring into her face, then glancing down her body. The trace of his gaze left a burning path in her flesh. She was shocked and unnerved, aware of him suddenly as a man and not a memory. It showed what kind of woman she'd become, how easily the heat of desire consumed her.

But every man looked on her with a covetous bent, and she was disappointed that Gareth was no better.

"Margery."

She heard her name on his lips and she shivered. "Gareth Beaumont, can it really be you? I have not seen you in—"

"Twelve years." His voice was deep, rumbling, as unnerving as his face.

She swallowed. "What have you been doing for all these years?"

"I've been traveling through Europe," was all he said.

She hesitated, then asked bravely, "Doing what?"

He just stared at her in that cool way of his, and she didn't think he'd answer.

"There is money to be earned at tournaments, and noblemen to work for," he finally said. "It is as good a way as any to live."

She remembered then that his parents had died in a fire just after he'd come to foster at her father's castle. The king had taken the Beaumonts' land and possessions as payment for a debt. Gareth had no home, no family.

It was sometimes so easy for her to take her brothers' love for granted.

There was a long, awkward silence.

"Did you like Europe better than England?" she asked, then wanted to wince at her inanity.

"Yes."

She had heard that he had not left the country willingly. She had so many questions, but how to ask without inviting his own scrutiny of her life?

"Then why did you come here?" Margery finally said.

"You are in danger."

Her mouth dropped open in surprise and she sat down heavily on the bench. Fear shot through her, her hands started to tremble, but she forced herself to calm down. He could know nothing.

He remained standing, his hands joined behind his back, staring at her with his chilly gaze. He didn't look like he wanted to help her, or even be there at all.

"How do you know such a thing?" she whispered. She remembered the fateful night of her father's death. Gareth had come to her room when she'd been in danger then.

"I heard things in London."

Margery felt the doubts creeping into her mind. Where had he been? What had he been doing? He might have saved her life once, but she could hardly trust him now—she could trust no one.

She sighed. "Yes, I am much the talk at court."

"Why?"

"It is complicated. But I assure you, I am not in any danger." She tried to give him a bright smile, but was sure it looked forced.

"Then why was that man chasing you?" he asked dryly.

"For a simple kiss." She laughed. "Surely you have tried to steal a kiss or two from a pretty maiden yourself."

She thought he would smile. Instead, he raised one eyebrow. "I've never had to."

Her smile died. Of course he'd never had to. He was as beautiful—and as cold—as a statue of an angel.

In her brittle voice, Gareth could hear the truth: Margery was lying. She avoided looking at him for too long, as if he were beneath her socially.

Why was part of him disappointed? He knew what kind of family she came from: a family that rewarded kindness with banishment. What lessons had she learned from brothers such as hers?

She jumped up from the bench, and the sun slanting through the trees painted flickering patterns across her face and dress. Her steps were not delicate and ladylike; she paced like a woman with much on her mind. She was clearly trying to keep something hidden.

But still he was a man, and as she walked before him, he reluctantly noticed the grace of her movements. Her strides kicked her pale yellow skirts out before her, leading him to imagine the length of her legs. He broke into a sweat. This was not the way he meant to think of Margery.

Her waist was long and slender, cinched in fabric that molded upward to cup her generous breasts. Her collarbones arced out like the wings of a bird, and her neck had the unbending grace of a tall woman at ease with her height. Her long hair, dark brown, was pulled back from her face by a yellow ribbon.

And what a striking face Margery had. Her deep blue eyes flashed with intelligence above fine cheekbones. He stared at her mouth and told himself he was unaffected. But the little girl she'd been in his mind was gone, replaced by a woman—and she was as yet unmarried.

He suddenly realized she'd been talking. "What did you say?"

"I asked you to stop staring at me." She put her fists on her waist and leaned toward him.

Gareth kept his eyes on her face, and not her gaping bodice. "You have changed."

Her face blanched. She stepped backward, and her arms slid up to hug herself. She was frightened, and that made him even more suspicious.

"I have not changed much," she said coldly. "And neither have you. I recognized you immediately."

He pointedly glanced down her body. "I have changed a great deal—do not forget that. But one thing that hasn't changed is the oath I swore to your father. You need protection, whether you want to admit it or not."

"Gareth, I am fine," Margery said between gritted teeth. "But please come stay at Hawksbury and rest before you travel on."

He said nothing.

She looked over her shoulder. "My horse is beyond those trees. Ride with me back to the castle; you must be hungry."

As they walked through the woods, Gareth thought again of her startled face when he'd said she'd changed. She must have been so protected behind castle walls that she thought the world's cruelty could never touch her. How naive she was.

She came to a stop so quickly he almost bumped into her. He could see the road just ahead through the trees.

"My horse—" she began, then stopped.

It was nowhere to be found.

He quirked an eyebrow. "I assume it was tethered beside your suitor's?"

"Of course, but Lord Fogge wouldn't . . ." Her voice trailed off and she sighed.

"Your horse is probably waiting for you at the castle," he said.

She turned around to face him, wearing another forced smile. "I seem to need your help again. Would you mind sharing your horse?"

Reluctantly, he gave a low whistle, and his gray stallion came crashing through the underbrush.

Margery raised her eyebrows. "That is very impressive," she said dryly.

Gareth lifted his hands to help her, but she put her foot in the stirrup and swung her leg up over the saddle. As she sat down, her skirts settled over the horse like a blanket, revealing her lower legs encased in men's boots.

"Are you coming?" she asked, wearing what was obviously a smile of pride at her horsemanship.

He stood beside her leg, looking up into her face. Unwanted memories flooded through his mind, and he felt a momentary uncertainty. In a low voice, he said, "Do you remember the last time you rode my horse?"

Her forehead wrinkled with a frown. "Yes. My father had given you your own horse, and I wanted to ride it, too. The silly animal dumped me headfirst into the pond."

Gareth still had a vivid memory of Margery rising sputtering to the surface as he'd splashed out to rescue her. Every memory of her involved either rescuing her or escaping her.

"Well, that will not happen anymore," she

said, and with a dig of her heels rode off down
the path.

He watched as she bent low over the animal's neck. He grudgingly noticed the flare of
her hips and her competent seat in the saddle.
At least she was not a pointlessly dainty
woman; her brothers had done something
right.

She finally turned back and raced toward
him. He didn't move as she pulled up within
feet of him, haughty, proud of herself.

She shouldn't be, since she couldn't even
protect herself. She needed a man for that—
and maybe she needed a man to teach her a
lesson.

Without a word, Gareth swung up behind
her. He heard her gasp softly as he squeezed
into the saddle, bringing them in intimate contact. He rested his hands on her waist, feeling
the slight curve of her stomach against the tips
of his fingers.

She had to learn that most men were bigger
and stronger than she was.

But while he was trying to prove her frailty
to her, he couldn't help but breathe in the scent
of her hair. The warmth from her body melded
with his. The urge to trail his lips down her
neck was powerful, primitive, almost too com-
pelling to resist. He hated feeling out of control, pulled along by a woman's wiles. If his

thoughts went any further, she'd know exactly what he was thinking by the pressure of his hips against hers.

He quickly took the reins from her hands.

Chapter 2

E very roll of the horse's gait slid Margery deeper between Gareth's thighs. She simmered. She fumed. Her face burned with mortification, while he seemed unaffected, which angered her even more.

She sat as straight as possible, trying not to lean against him, but he was a large man. His clothing swayed against her, his chest touched her back when he breathed. His arms encircled her.

As he held the reins, she could see that his hands were large and tanned and scarred from training. The spurs on his boots were proof of his knighthood. He was a man with a history she knew nothing of. She didn't know what to make of him, except that he made her nervous. How did he know of her problems, especially the ones that stained her soul?

As Hawksbury Castle came within sight between swaying branches, Margery's discomfort grew. She didn't want to be seen riding so intimately with a stranger. Yet he wasn't a stranger to her, and she could hardly ask him to get down. He might rightfully take offense.

The dirt road grew steeper as they approached the castle rising from the hilltop. The curtain walls were whitewashed, with impressive towers jutting into the sky. They entered the tunnel of the gatehouse and came out into the inner ward, where people hurried between the barracks, the stables, the kitchen house. The castle residence itself sprawled with many wings and levels, with slitted arrow loops as windows on the lower floors, and glass windows above to let in the sun.

Servants and soldiers alike waved, and if they were curious, they hid it well. Margery tried to relax and experience the pride of owning such a wonderful home. Already she felt she belonged, though she'd been there only a few weeks. She looked back at Gareth, whose gaze took in everything but whose face showed nothing.

Just inside the gatehouse, they were met by Bates, the marshall of the horses. He was a large, robust man, bald but for a fringe of hair low about his head. His grizzled face relaxed into a smile.

"Mistress, yer horse came back without ye. I was gettin' worried."

She smiled, her teeth clenched together. She breathed a little easier when Gareth dismounted. "Just an accident, Bates. Where is Lord Fogge?"

"Inside. He told me to keep his horse saddled."

"I fear he's leaving," she said, and her smile became genuine. "Bates, this is Sir Gareth Beaumont. We knew each other as children."

The marshall looked Gareth up and down for a moment. "Nice to meet ye, sir," Bates finally said. "How lucky ye came along just as the mistress needed ye."

Gareth inclined his head. He put his hands around her waist, lifting her from the horse as if she were still a child. Margery stepped away from him, trying not to appear too hasty. Already she saw a group of dairymaids staring at him and whispering. They smoothed their aprons, adjusted their caps, and giggled.

Margery sighed. "Gareth, come inside. 'Tis almost time for supper."

She felt him watching her as he followed her into the great hall, and she knew she was too prideful by half. She wanted him to admire the tapestries on her walls, the gold salt cellars on the tables. All of it proved that she was a success in her own right, without marrying a man.

Then she felt guilty, knowing that his life was much harder than hers.

Margery called for ale to be served to her guest, then joined him beside the hearth. Though she asked him to sit, he preferred not to. She felt awkward standing silently beside him, but could think of nothing else to say. Gareth certainly didn't make conversation easy; he just gazed about him with an inscrutable expression. She found herself hoping that he would see how secure she was, and leave in the morning.

Lord Fogge trooped through the hall, followed by servants carrying his baggage. He kept his nose in the air, but his face betrayed him by flushing a vivid shade of red. He halted just before the double doors, and turned to face her.

"Mistress Welles," he said, bowing shortly. "I hope I will be free to call on you again soon."

What gall! She wanted to tell him her true feelings, especially about her horse, but she was wary of angering him further. Angry men thought of desperate deeds; she didn't need him seeking misguided revenge. Instead, she nodded and smiled. He bowed his way out the door, giving Gareth one last nervous glance.

Gareth sipped his tankard of ale and watched the servants set the tables. "I do not remember this castle as being in your family. Is this a dower inheritance?"

"No, it is a gift from King Henry and his wife."

He gave her an assessing look, but she just lifted her chin and refused to defend herself. It was none of his business.

"Your family left you no dowry?" he asked in obvious disbelief.

"Of course they did!" she snapped, struggling desperately to keep hold of her temper, and failing miserably. "I have several manors from my father, and some from my brother Reynold."

"You are truly fortunate, Margery."

His words were impassive, but she sensed an undercurrent of emotion that she couldn't read. Every moment she spent with him made her feel more and more like he was a stranger, a man whose motives were unclear to her. And yet, he drew her gaze in a way that unsettled her.

Margery forced herself to look away from Gareth's penetrating stare to watch the servants, soldiers, and guests file into the great hall for the evening meal. She led Gareth to the head table, where they were joined by Father Banbury, the castle priest, and Lady Anne and Lady Cicely Lingard. The girls each gave her a bright smile, and Margery's heart softened. They were her companions—her dear friends— and she hadn't wanted them to accompany her when she fled the turmoil of London, but they had insisted. In another year or so they would reach full womanhood, and have no problem attracting husbands. Margery comforted herself with the knowledge that at least she would be introducing them to future suitors.

Two of Margery's suitors arrived and bade

her sit between them. She was very close to telling them both she would not marry them, but she hated to hurt their feelings. And that was much of her problem. So she sat between Gareth and the priest.

Perched on her pewter plate was a small item wrapped in cloth. As her steward, Sir Jasper, appeared behind her, she said, "Another gift?"

"Yes, mistress."

Margery could tell by his warbling words that he was barely holding back a grin. She'd known him for only a few short weeks, but he had already included her as his seventh daughter, and took care of her just as well.

"Who is the gift from?" she asked.

"Sir Randolph White, mistress. He sent it with his regards."

"I see. It will be another brooch then. Please take it to the gift room."

"The gift room?"

Gareth's voice startled her, and Margery looked over her shoulder. She had forgotten he knew nothing of her predicament, and she wanted to keep it that way. He was sitting uncomfortably close to her, considering the table was only half full. He could hardly think she was in danger in her own home. But his elbow brushed against hers.

"I have been receiving so many kind gifts," she said, trying hard not to sound distracted. "Regretfully, I cannot make use of them all."

Anne and Cicely, twin sisters alike in looks but not in temperament, hid their smiles. Her two young suitors slumped in their chairs, and Margery leaned toward them.

"Please, sirs, I appreciate your gifts, too. Understand that I am grateful to be able to help those less fortunate than I. I use the gifts where they are most needed, whether in the castle or in the countryside. Your generosity is helping others."

She didn't look at Gareth. He must wonder why so many men were vying for her hand, but he would just have to remain curious. She would only feed him and house him and send him on his way—she didn't need anyone to solve her problems for her.

After the meal, Gareth spotted Wallace Desmond sitting alone at a table near the fire. When Gareth sat down opposite him, Desmond looked over the rim of his tankard, and slowly set it down.

"Am I allowed to speak with you now?" Desmond asked dryly.

"I do not understand your meaning," Gareth said. He nodded at a maidservant who blushed and bobbed a curtsy as she handed him a tankard. He waited while she backed away, giggling. He sighed—it had begun already.

Desmond leaned forward. "What is going on? I have not met Mistress Margery yet, but I can tell she is not all that comfortable with your presence. Does she need our help or not? I could be visiting my family right now."

Gareth sat back on his bench. "There is something wrong, but she is not forthcoming. I'll persuade her to reveal everything soon. Regardless of her wishes, I must protect her. Did you have any problems entering the castle?"

Desmond fixed him with a bland stare. " 'Regardless of her wishes'? It must be wonderful to know what's best for everyone."

"Did you have any problems entering the castle?" Gareth repeated sternly.

Desmond frowned. "None. My name helps." He glanced at Margery, who was smiling as she watched the jugglers. "She doesn't look like someone in trouble. She has beauty, wealth—and I assume intelligence?"

"Not today," Gareth said dryly. "I stopped a suitor from attacking her in the woods. It might have something to do with this danger she's in."

"I wish you had let me see the missive you received." Desmond studied him with a directness he found disconcerting.

"I shall tell you but once more," Gareth said, trying to keep his frustration at bay. "I don't know who sent the letter."

Desmond gave a mock frown. "How unusual! So, one of her retainers or family members sent a request for help to a man no one has seen in twelve years. Why you and not

Margery's brothers? And how did they know where you were? This is a puzzle."

Gareth shot him a dark look and Desmond raised a hand. "Forgive me. I know 'tis none of my business, but you've dragged me back to England. I can't help but be curious."

It was so hard to keep anything from Desmond, but Gareth wasn't about to reveal the visions he'd had all his life. He had learned not to trust anyone with that secret.

"How did you know she'd be in the woods?" Desmond asked.

Gareth took another sip of ale. "I accidentally stumbled on her."

"Did you now?"

There was a speculative look in his eye, so a distraction was called for. "How were the defenses when you arrived?"

"Careless. I rode up just as the guards were changing, and there was a good amount of time when no one was watching the road."

"What did you find out?"

"Well, since you insisted Margery was in danger, I did manage to speak with a few soldiers. They have a new captain of the guard. The last choked on a fishbone."

Gareth raised an eyebrow.

"Unpleasant, but not murder. The second in command took over but he's barely out of boyhood. Though he's doing his best, he has a lot to learn."

"Then I shall suggest to Margery that he learn it under you."

"What?" Desmond almost spilled his tankard. "Me, a common soldier? I thought she didn't want help."

"Her safety is more important than her wishes. I will convince her to accept my help. But do not mention this tonight."

Desmond's gaze focused on something behind Gareth. He abruptly stood up, knocking back his bench.

Gareth glanced over his shoulder and saw Margery almost directly behind him. He, too, stood, struck again by her beauty.

"Why, Sir Gareth," Margery said, "you have not introduced me to your friend. If I hadn't known you so long, I would think he is your brother. Your hair is almost the same color."

Though she was smiling, Gareth could see the skeptical curiosity she tried to keep hidden. "Mistress Margery, allow me to introduce Sir Wallace Desmond. He traveled with me from France."

"Desmond," she repeated. "I think I have heard mention of you."

Gareth tensed. He had known this was coming.

But Desmond only smiled as Margery sat down beside him. "I met your brother, Lord Bolton, last year. I knew his wife from her childhood."

"Did you know they just had their first baby? 'Tis a girl, Elizabeth."

"Then they are doing well?"

"Better than could ever have been imagined."

There was a softness to Margery's smile, or maybe it was wistfulness. Did she long to be married? Surely she had enough suitors to choose from, since he'd heard of four already.

Gareth made no secret of the fact that he was studying her. More and more she glanced at him with uneasiness, and soon she excused herself to join her ladies.

Desmond sighed and rubbed a hand across his face. "Well, you're just full of subtlety."

"She is lying to me. I'll use any means I deem necessary to find out what's wrong here."

"Even if she doesn't need your help?"

"She needs my help," he said gruffly, wishing it weren't true. Being with her dredged up all the old bitterness toward her family he'd long since put behind him, and there was no place in his life for useless emotion. He had enough trouble just trying to survive. "Come show me these pitiful defenses."

From the window in her bedchamber, Margery watched the setting sun reflect from Gareth's bright hair. She saw the looks her people gave him, wariness from the men, curiosity from the women. She could not blame them for their interest. Gareth would stand out even at court, where his stunning handsomeness would more than make up for his plain garments. He drew people's gazes, and it annoyed her that she, too, was affected.

He and his friend Sir Wallace were pacing through the inner ward, pointing toward the battlements or the barracks. Their faces were serious as they spoke. Surely they couldn't just be discussing the design of Hawksbury Castle.

No, they were discussing *her*.

It made her uneasy and anxious at the same time. How did Gareth know she was in danger? He'd been in London talking to people about her—what had he heard?

She had to know exactly why he thought she needed help. If she had to tell him part of the truth, so be it.

As Margery walked down the torchlit corridor from her bedchamber, she thought she heard a noise. Looking over her shoulder, she saw no one, yet she picked up her pace. At a corner tower, she began to descend the circular staircase. Immediately above her, booted feet made the same descent, almost matching each of her footsteps.

"Who's there?" Margery called, looking upward.

The sounds echoed away to stillness.

"Please identify yourself!" she said sternly.

Boots appeared on the stairs just above her

head, then a face peered down at her from the gloom.

"Mistress Margery, I did not mean to frighten you."

She recognized Sir Roger, one of her two suitors. She told herself to relax, but her body wouldn't obey. He was above her on the stairs, and one bad misstep could send them both tumbling to the base of the tower.

"If you didn't mean to frighten me, why have you been following me?"

"To spend a moment alone with you, mistress. I have not had enough privacy to declare my feelings for you."

He came down a few more steps, bringing his boots dangerously near her head.

"I will meet you at the bottom," she said, then quickly descended to the first floor. Her unease only increased when Sir Roger appeared beside her, blocking her way out of the tower.

"Mistress Margery," he whispered breathlessly, "your eyes shine like the sun—"

"Well, thank you, but—"

"Your hair is dark like the night—"

He came closer and closer, until her back was against the stone wall.

"Sir Roger, this is all quite lovely, but why the sudden need to woo me so . . . intensely?"

"Because I cannot stay any longer."

He put his hands against the wall on either side of her. She ducked beneath his arm and spun away—but toward the back of the tower instead of the door.

"Why can't you stay? I have been enjoying your company." The lies were starting to come too easily to her.

"Because I was told by Sir Humphrey Townsend to be gone when he and his friends arrived."

"He *and* his friends?" Her voice came out in a squeak of dismay. "How many?"

"At least a half dozen. But I had to be here first, to make you realize how happy we could be together."

He reached to touch her hair. Margery's thoughts were spinning through her head so fast that she let him. Men were coming—in a large group? And she was having trouble fending them off one or two at a time.

Sir Roger leaned toward her, his eyes closed, his homely face puckered for a kiss.

"Excuse me, I must leave," she said, elbowing him hard in the stomach.

He gasped, and his eyes flew wide.

"Oh, I am so clumsy!" she said, heading for the door. "Please forgive me."

Margery walked quickly through the great hall, imagining crowds of suitors taking up her time, eating her food, leering at her. She felt trapped, about to be besieged by men who thought of her as only a prize to win. How could the king do this to her?

Once outside, she took a deep breath of the

warm summer air, telling herself not to panic. There had to be a way to protect herself from such an onslaught.

She saw Gareth near the barracks, watching her with brooding eyes as if he knew everything she was thinking. And suddenly, he was the only answer she could think of.

Chapter 3

A lone, Gareth walked toward her, his eyes narrowed, his expression deadly—yet fascinating. She should be afraid of him, but she wasn't, and she didn't understand why. Though he made her uneasy, Margery could not forget that he had saved her life a long time ago. Now he was a tall, muscular stranger, rumored to be so good in battle that no one would fight him. He was just the man she needed.

In the center of the ward, they both stopped and looked at each other. She opened her mouth to speak, but the words seemed stuck. She had always been able to solve her own problems, and now she felt defeated having to ask Gareth for help.

He didn't make it any easier. He crossed his arms over his chest and studied her, waiting for her to make the first move. The dying sun seemed to light his hair afire. He was as remote and beautiful as the god Apollo. How would she ever make him understand?

She took a deep, fortifying breath. "I need to talk to you."

"What about?"

She looked around and saw that their unusual behavior was already attracting attention.

"Come sit with me." She led him to a low bench outside the garden, in full view of the ward. They sat down, she with her back straight, he leaning forward, his arms resting on his thighs. He turned to look at her, so that their knees almost touched.

"Are you going to tell me the truth now?" Gareth asked.

"Yes." *Well, part of it*, she thought, already resenting his superiority. "I told you that the king gave me Hawksbury. I had been spending a lot of time at court this past spring, and the king and queen grew fond of me." She tried to smile. "Together, Queen Elizabeth and I were less lonely. We spent many an evening side by side, while she talked to me of the joys and sorrows of her life. I don't think she had had many friends before me. I even kept her company through a long illness." She felt herself blushing. "Though they didn't need to, their majesties insisted on giving me a gift. Not just a pretty box for my jewelry or a new ribbon; they gave me wealth—manors and land."

Gareth stared down at his hands clasped between his knees, as if he couldn't even look at her. What must he be thinking? She was given easy gifts, while he risked injury and death just to earn his food. Embarrassment burned inside her.

"There is more, is there not?" he asked.

She glanced quickly away, knowing all her choices were gone. "In many ways, my life would be much easier had they not given me a second gift to complement the first. They gave me the freedom to choose my own husband."

He said nothing for a moment, then he sighed. "Margery, this does not sound like a terrible thing."

"Think on my words, Gareth. Most women are told whom they shall marry by their parents or their guardians. But since I alone control my choice, every eligible man in England has decided to petition me. Worse yet, the men try to—convince me."

She saw the exact moment he understood her dilemma. His head came up and he regarded her intensely, the depths of his eyes hinting at a danger that made her shiver.

"That man was trying to compromise you for his own purposes?"

She shrugged. "I know not. I only know that lately, men are resisting the word 'no.' "

They were silent for endless minutes, listening to the warbling of birds, and the barking of the dogs racing through the inner ward.

Margery tried not to think of all the things she wasn't telling him. And yet—

He had sought her out, claiming he wanted to help her. There was no one in her household she could confide in. Always, there was the worry that something would get back to the king.

But after all these years, could she trust Gareth to help her?

"Where are your brothers?" he asked.

"They are with the king's army in the north."

"Do they know of your problems?"

"How could I tell them? They would not be free to come to my aid, and that would only make them feel worse." Taking a deep breath, she blurted, "Gareth, you say you've come to help me. Would you stay and be my personal guard, at least until I've given the king my decision?"

This was just a temporary situation. She couldn't allow herself to depend on any man. For the rest of her life, she would have only herself.

The silence stretched out, and still he said nothing. He wouldn't refuse—would he?

"I know I am being forward, but Gareth, I am desperate. I promise that you would enjoy a stay at Hawksbury Castle."

"And how would you make this task easier?" he asked in a low voice. "There isn't much about you or your family that I have ever found enjoyable."

She was stunned by the bitterness in his voice, and the shock of pain that squeezed her chest. What had happened to him? And how could he blame her?

But she would deal with his problems later, if only he'd stay.

"Gareth, will you help me?"

He frowned. "A personal guard? 'Tis an interesting idea. I've done more than my share of such work."

"Then is your answer yes?"

"Where would a personal guard sleep?"

"You don't wish to sleep in the barracks?" she asked, attempting to smile. Surely he was trying to lighten the tension of their discussion.

He didn't smile back. "No."

She wanted to wilt at his seriousness. "Very well. I shall give you a bedchamber just down the hall from mine. I assume you are not going to sleep in front of my door; that would be a bit obvious."

"If I'm not to be obvious, then what do you expect of me? Why do you not want anyone to know that you have hired protection?"

"It is . . . complicated," she said, looking down at her clenched fingers. "The king must not know his gift is causing me problems."

"Are you afraid he'll take the gifts back?" He didn't even look at her as he said such cold words.

"No, I'm afraid he'll make me come to court,

where he could watch over me personally. All of my freedom would be gone then."

Margery forced herself to look into his penetrating eyes. "Will you do it, Gareth? It will only be for a few months' time. I can begin your payment now."

"No, at the end you can pay me what you think I've earned." He hesitated. "Or maybe your *husband* can pay me."

"Fine," she said crisply, holding out her hand. "Then we have an agreement?"

He looked down at her hand, but didn't touch it. "Not yet. As a guard, I would be with you at all times. Yet you complicate matters by insisting this be kept private between us. What reason will you give your servants and guests for my presence at your side?"

Gareth couldn't miss the panic in Margery's eyes. She was a desperate woman, and hadn't thought through this new plan. He had a hard time believing that all she was frightened of were suitors pressing their courtship a bit too far. Glancing down her body, he reluctantly thought that he couldn't blame the men.

She sighed and rubbed the bridge of her nose. "Can you come up with a reason, Gareth? Let me know what you feel would be best."

"Very well. I have another suggestion to protect you. Wallace Desmond will become your new captain of the guard."

She stiffened. "I already have a captain."

"A youngster, is he not?" he asked.

"Well—"

"I'm sure he will be honored to train under Desmond."

She hesitated, and he could almost read her thoughts. He could tell she agreed with his assessment, but she didn't like being told what to do. That would have to change.

"Very well, Gareth. I accept the offer—if you're certain Sir Wallace doesn't mind."

"He doesn't mind."

"But please allow me to introduce him to the soldiers tomorrow. Then he and I can discuss his payment with my steward."

"Very well."

She got to her feet and Gareth leaned back on his hands to look up at her. He kept his pose relaxed, casual, though he felt anything but. He told himself this was just another task he was being paid to do. So why did some deep part of him relish looking up at her in the sunlight? He flustered her, perturbed her, and the feeling was not unpleasant.

"Come inside when you like," Margery said. "A juggling troupe arrived today."

"Oh, I'll be inside soon enough. You will no longer be alone much, remember?"

He deliberately reminded her of the consequences of her request. Her face stiffened as she gave him a polite nod and walked away.

Gareth told himself he was beyond the anger that had consumed him for years after Margery's family had dispensed with him. He was at Hawksbury to do a task, then leave. Yet he took such grim pleasure in annoying her.

He sat in the stillness of the early evening and came up with the perfect way to stay near her. She would not like it, but she would learn soon enough that he would rule this business between them.

While the jugglers were performing, Margery bit her lip and stared into the distance. What had she done by inviting Gareth into her life? She could barely get him to speak to her, and now he would be following her about indefinitely, a large, unsettling shadow at her back.

He entered the great hall, and though he was dressed as the plainest of knights, his good looks attracted every eye. But beneath that was a cold man, warped by whatever experiences he'd had.

When he approached the head table she was sitting across from her two suitors, who were desperately trying to win her attention on this last night of their visit.

Gareth sat down beside her, so close her skirts were caught beneath him. Before she could ask him to move, he suddenly slid his hand over hers. Margery gaped at their fingers, then looked up into his face. His hot eyes were rife with intimate promises. A more fainted-hearted woman would surely swoon from his beauty, but all she could do was let her mouth fall open, fishlike.

"Mistress Margery," he said, in a voice low and smooth as honey.

He leaned forward, and she leaned away, wide-eyed.

"I was thinking about your gift room. I hope you will never have cause to relegate my gifts to such a place. They are given in homage to your beauty."

Her two suitors crossed their arms over their chests and glared. At the same moment, they said, "Mistress Margery—"

She held up her hand, never taking her gaze from Gareth, who raised her other hand to his lips and kissed her knuckles. A shock of astonishment surged through her. What was he doing? Had he planned all along to court her, and be paid as a bodyguard at the same time?

Her disappointment grew until she could no longer look into his face. Had she trusted the wrong man?

Margery pulled her hand away, struggling to remember every rumor she'd ever heard. Her brother James had once tried to tell her about Gareth's disgrace and his flight from the country. She hadn't believed James, but now she wished she'd paid more attention.

She looked into Gareth's golden eyes. They were narrowed, and seemed to be studying her intently. Was he looking for weaknesses?

He would find none. He was just one more man in a long parade of suitors she could never marry.

Grief threatened to overwhelm her at the futility of her life. But in these last trying months, she had learned to be strong—or at least to pretend she was. She called on that strength now and met his intensity with a smile.

"How sweet of you to promise gifts, Sir Gareth. But it is most certainly not the way to my heart. You would only be one of many."

The twins glanced away, their smiles bolder. Her two suitors looked baffled, uneasy.

Gareth said, "I promise you, mistress, that you shall not put aside my gifts. They will be humble, yet from my heart."

For the first time since childhood, Margery experienced the blinding power of his smile. But she saw it now for what it was: an imitation of an emotion he could not begin to grasp.

When the jugglers were finished, she had Gareth shown to a bedchamber. A few moments later she said her own good-nights and went to her room, but Gareth's behavior would not leave her mind. She waited for a brief time, pacing before the hearth, then peeked down the corridor. There were no servants in sight.

She tiptoed past Anne's and Cicely's closed doors until she reached the chamber she had assigned Gareth. She put her ear against the wood, heard no sounds, then burst in and leaned back to close the door.

Gareth already had his sword drawn. When he saw her, he slammed it back into the scabbard. "Margery, never do something so foolish again. You will need protection for the rest of your life if you continue to make such thoughtless mistakes." He threw his saddle bag on the bed and leaned over to open it.

"So now it is protection again?" She strode toward him, hands on her hips. "Make up your mind. After all, if you're my suitor, I shall need protection from you!"

He straightened, and she took a step backward. He seemed suddenly as tall and wild as the Viking ancestors he resembled. And she'd come in here alone?

"Protection from me?" he said. "You have already hired me as your guard. Did you think—"

He broke off and studied her for an uncomfortable moment, while she began to think she'd miscalculated.

"I was worried my acting would not be skilled enough." He looked down her body. "I've never had to make an effort to court a woman before."

Acting? A blush of mortification swept from her chest to her forehead. When he'd kissed her fingers, when he'd spoken of her beauty, he'd been *acting*?

"You asked me to come up with something to hide my true purpose here," Gareth said calmly. "I'm going to pretend to be another of your suitors. What better way can I be near you, keeping you from any danger?"

Margery remembered the heat of his gaze,

the touch of his lips on her hand. Of course it was all an act. She donned a grudging smile, and buried the tiny pain that touched her heart. "I did suggest we keep your position a secret, but I never thought of—of this."

"Then you approve?"

She hesitated. "I can think of nothing better." She slowly frowned as she watched him remove garments from his bag. "Gareth, are you planning to court me wearing those clothes?"

He stilled, and the gaze he lifted to her was even colder. She'd made a mistake.

"I work hard for everything I have."

"I know that!" she quickly said. "But you're in disguise now. I could have my brother Reynold send along some clothes. They might be a bit large for you, but James would certainly never part with any garments."

Gareth shook his head. "Sounds like the James I remember."

"Be easy on him. He has changed for the better since his marriage. He just . . . likes his clothes."

He leaned against the bedpost, folding his arms across his chest. "You don't think your brothers would be suspicious as to why you're sending for good quality male garments?"

She winced. "I hadn't thought of that."

"I shall just tell everyone I lost most of my clothes in a storm off the coast."

"You were never very good at telling stories."

"When I chose to, I could be." His voice was suddenly low and gruff, not quite so cold. "The marshall once bribed me with gingerbread to keep you out of the stables so they could get some work done. How else do you think I amused you?"

She didn't remember that. Unexpected tears pricked her eyes. Life was so uncomplicated then. She had spent her days following Gareth around, trying to get his attention.

But everything had changed. He would be following her—and he was angry about it.

"Regardless of how you feel, you still need some new clothes," she said awkwardly as she moved toward the door. "I'll talk to my seamstresses."

"Hold!"

Anger overwhelmed her sadness. "I am not one of your soldiers!"

"One of my soldiers would make sure the corridor was empty if he didn't want to be seen leaving a certain room."

She felt a momentary weakness at her stupidity. She had almost walked out of a man's bedchamber, regardless of who might be watching. Gareth opened the door, looked outside, then closed it again.

" 'Tis clear."

Margery swallowed. "Thank you."

He leaned against the door, too close to her, studying her face with that coolness she hated.

"Perhaps you need a keeper more than a guard."

She controlled the hurt that suffused her. "I'm not paying you for insults. Move away from the door."

After Margery had gone, Gareth told himself that she deserved every cruel remark he had made. She and her family had thrown him away when he was no longer useful, like an enfeebled dog. Even his clothing wasn't fine enough for her.

She was still a spoiled little girl, who had the "terrible" task of picking any man she wanted. If she thought this was such a dreadful problem, she didn't know what life was really like.

But he had sworn an oath to protect her, and he could not turn his back on that. At least now he would be getting paid for it.

Chapter 4

After her argument with Gareth, Margery was too upset to return to the great hall. Her bedchamber usually soothed her; it was decorated with colorful tapestries, cushions, and draperies, things she brought with her wherever she traveled. And though she'd resigned herself to sleeping alone for the rest of her life, tonight she felt especially sad and uncertain. The king's bequest had changed her entire life—and not for the better, as he'd hoped.

But then again, King Henry thought she was a normal young woman, with dreams of the perfect husband to fall in love with. He didn't know that she would never marry.

How could she tell him without exposing all her sins? How could she tell him that she and Peter Fitzwilliam had—

Margery burst into tears. She clutched her fists to her chest, trying to ease the ache that never went away.

How could she have been so foolish? She had been the envy of every woman because of her wonderful family and her wealth. She could have chosen any man who'd pleased her. But she'd chosen Peter Fitzwilliam, who revealed himself to be nothing more than a scoundrel, a slave to his family.

She'd let herself be charmed by his good looks, his easy manner. And then she'd let herself be seduced.

She had a sudden memory of lying naked in a garden, and Peter looking at her body.

Margery shook with humiliation. Oh, they'd exchanged heartfelt vows of love—or so she'd thought. They spent every spare moment together, whispering of betrothal and marriage and children. She had thought her perfect life was just getting better and better.

She'd been a gullible fool. After Peter's talk of a quick betrothal the moment his father was back in London, she'd agreed to meet him in the garden late one night. They were so in love, she'd thought, they didn't need to wait for the formality of a contract. Margery let him take her virginity.

And the shame of it was—she'd enjoyed it! She sank into a chair and rubbed her arms, feeling like she could never get warm again. Tears continued to fall down her cheeks, and she wiped them away with both hands.

Peter had been considerate and gentle, and she'd felt no embarrassment whatsoever. When he'd suggested they meet again, she had gladly sneaked away a week later. After that they couldn't manage to be alone, but she'd thought about Peter every moment of every day, thrilled to be in love with the man she was marrying, when so many of her friends were being forced into loveless marriages. When she realized she wasn't with child, she'd thought her unending luck had continued.

My lord, she'd been so naive. When Peter asked her if she carried his child, she'd been happy to ease his mind by saying no. And then her whole world had tilted, spilling her into the abyss. Peter had told her he couldn't marry a barren woman, that he needed an heir to carry on as earl.

She remembered staring at him, feeling the heat rise to her cheeks at the enormity of what she'd done. Could it be true? She had no mother to ask, no true friends she could confide her sins to.

With a sob, Margery covered her face and leaned over her lap. So she'd let Peter go. A man who'd say such a thing obviously didn't love her, and his betrayal hurt as much as if he'd stabbed her. She'd given him her love, her respect, her trust—her body. And he hadn't wanted any of it, if it meant disappointing his family.

She'd thought briefly of telling her brothers, of *making* Peter marry her after he'd taken her maidenhead. But they'd want to kill him, and her terrible shame would become public knowledge. Everyone would know what a sinful woman she was, and she and Peter would despise each other for the rest of their lives.

So she had picked herself up out of her sorrow, and resolved never to marry. She was luckier than most, with a few manors and a small inheritance at her disposal. She would live well, alone.

But then the king had decided to gift her with more land and wealth, and her own choice of husband. How could she refuse it? She certainly couldn't tell him the truth. So here she was, trying to figure a way out of marriage, something she'd wanted all her life, but now could never have. No man would want another man's leavings. If she lied and married some poor man, she would be found out eventually, and her husband could annul the marriage and reveal her shame to all. And if it were true that she was barren, she couldn't let a man think he could have heirs.

No matter how hard she prayed at Mass or did penance, nothing helped the endless guilt that tore apart her soul. She also had to live with the constant worry that Peter would tell someone what she'd done.

And now she'd hired Gareth, another man she had to circumvent. And she only had two months left to do it, for the king had given her until the beginning of October to choose—or he would choose for her.

* * *

Margery awoke before dawn and lay still in bed, prepared to face another dreaded day— one day less for her to solve her problems.

And now she had Gareth to deal with.

With a groan, she pushed aside the blankets and coverlet, and rose to her feet.

She couldn't deny that it was good to know that he was alive and unharmed. After what he'd done for her when they were children, he was the one man she thought she could trust to help her. Yet he had changed. The wary watchfulness that had always been a part of him in childhood had grown.

She didn't relish the coming days of outwitting him, as she'd been forced to do with so many of her friends and family. Here in this castle, she'd become numb, existing day to day during the brief respite she'd allowed herself. Sometimes she could almost forget the king's decree looming over her.

Why did she feel that Gareth's presence could change all that?

After she'd washed and dressed, Margery left the keep to attend Mass at the peaceful stone chapel tucked in a corner of the inner ward. She walked across the packed earth, absorbing yesterday's warmth beneath her feet, listening to the early morning sounds of roosters crowing and the welcoming bark of a dog.

As she entered the building, she looked up at the cut-glass window high in the wall. In direct sunlight, one could stand beneath it and feel bathed in the magic of colors and the warmth of God's love. But with the gray dawn, the window looked as lifeless as Margery felt. Some mornings, her guilt almost choked her.

At the completion of Mass, she introduced Sir Wallace, the new captain of the guard, to the company of soldiers and knights employed at Hawksbury Castle. Afterward she found Gareth waiting for her. She came to a halt and looked up into his eyes, where there was no emotion, only a perception that made her feel exposed, vulnerable. If he knew what kind of a woman she was, he'd think she deserved her fate.

When everyone had gone past them, Gareth spoke in a low, angry voice. "Apparently I need to make the rules clearer."

"I did not know there were rules." She raised her chin as she walked by him.

He moved to her side.

As people called good morning, Margery smiled at each. "I thought I had hired you to do a service for me," she said quietly to Gareth.

"You hired me to protect you. If you want me to do my task successfully, I need to know where you are at all times. You cannot leave the castle without telling me."

She bit her lip and risked a glance at him. He looked straight ahead, his eyes scanning the inner ward. At least he took his task seriously; she would be well cared for.

"I'm sorry," she murmured. "You are right—
I'm too used to controlling my own fate."

"I thought that was your brothers' task."

Again she heard that edge of bitterness, but
his face showed nothing.

"They trust me. They trust my judgment."
And they were wrong.

"So what are we doing today?" Gareth
asked.

"We?"

"I go where you go."

She sighed. "We are eating. I'm famished."

He nodded and lifted his arm toward her.
She stared at it for a moment in puzzlement.

"You're supposed to take it," he said gruffly.
"I am your suitor, you know."

"Oh, yes. Of course."

After only the briefest hesitation, she slid her
hand beneath his elbow and lightly touched his
arm. He pulled his elbow in and she was firmly
trapped against the heat of his body, intimately
aware of his strength, of the power that lay
dormant inside him, waiting. All at her command.

At the head table he insisted on sitting beside her. Her two suitors, short and dark to
Gareth's golden height, showed their displea-
sure with frowns and whispers to each other.

But Gareth seemed strangely oblivious to
their jealousy. He ate only when she was eating. Otherwise he gazed solely at her, until
Anne and Cicely dissolved into giggles, cov-

ering their mouths and pretending to cough. He finally bestowed his smile on them, and even Margery could see their eyes soften and their expressions grow dreamy. His smiles must be few, to be so potent.

When the meal was over, Margery waved good-bye to her two suitors, surprised at the frowns they directed at her as they rode away. Then she turned and saw Gareth standing just behind her, hands linked behind his back, his expression victorious.

She made a low sound of disgust and tried to stalk past him. He took her arm and pulled her to a halt.

"What is wrong?" he asked, his mouth close to her ear.

"I felt like a child's toy between you and those men." She shook off his hand and stepped away, feeling angry and unsettled.

He lifted an eyebrow. "I was only playing my part."

"Too well. What if they return to slit your throat?"

His smile didn't touch his eyes. "They hardly seem to have that much bravery, even between them."

"Do you want to make enemies of all the men who come to court me?" she demanded, fisting her hands on her hips, heedless of the fact that they stood in the center of the ward. "Then *you'll* need your own guard."

Gareth frowned. "You said you have your choice in husband. But those two—"

"And are you the man who shall make my decisions for me? You are supposed to know my own heart better than I do?"

He didn't reply.

"Just do as I ask," she said, softening her voice as she realized how silent the ward had become, how they were being watched by people who didn't bother to hide their amusement. "Let me choose the path of my life—I know what I'm doing."

After a moment's hesitation, he nodded. "I will stay out of it, unless you put yourself in danger."

"I am not in—"

He narrowed his eyes, and she suddenly remembered being chased by Lord Fogge around the bench.

Gareth was a true reminder of the privacy she'd lost. Every time she looked at him, she thought of the men who would be coming, the men he'd promised to protect her from.

And they were coming sooner than she'd thought. She sent a silent prayer to the heavens that Peter Fitzwilliam would not be one of them.

Margery stifled a shiver of dread. She wanted to mount her horse and ride through the Severn Valley until her problems were far behind her. But her freedom, her choices, were gone, lost in the grass along with her virginity

Why couldn't she keep on pretending that she could solve all her problems and live her life as she wanted? Why couldn't she be left alone?

But there was Gareth, looking too deeply, seeing things he had no right to see. Even Peter had never made her feel that she had no privacy.

Walking beside Margery, Gareth noticed how distracted and pensive she was. She wore her hair like a maiden, with long waves of curls falling forward over her shoulders and breasts, as she kept her head bowed. He quickly looked away.

He didn't understand her. Hawksbury was an impressive castle, and her people already seemed loyal to her. She should be content with such wealth—he certainly would be.

But something else was bothering her, something buried so deeply she showed no one. As long as her girlish secrets didn't interfere with his duties, she was welcome to them. After all, what could be so terrible in her sheltered life?

They stopped before the massive double doors leading into the castle. She gave him a brisk, impersonal smile.

"I have duties to attend to, Sir Gareth," she said.

"I will join you."

"It is but women's work. You would be bored."

"Then I'll have to be bored."

She studied him for a moment, her blue eyes direct and assessing. He felt an uncomfortable urge to squirm like a boy caught following a dairymaid. Though he told himself he was merely doing his duty, he was relieved when she finally led him toward the rear of the inner ward. An extensive series of gardens began as square beds of kitchen herbs and vegetables, and ended in an elaborate, tree-shaded lady's garden, full of blooming flowers, graveled paths, and vine tunnels. Low fencing of entwined hazel branches separated the gardens.

She opened a small gate and entered, waving to her waiting ladies. Gareth stood still, caught by the overwhelming fragrance of roses. He was reminded sharply of woman, of Margery.

He refused to think of her like that. She was just a problem he had to conquer before moving on, back to the solitary life he preferred.

"Sir Gareth?"

Margery stared at him with a bemused expression. Her two ladies, the twins he hadn't bothered to notice much yet, were openly smiling at him as they flanked her.

"Sir Gareth," she continued, "do you have an unusual fear of gardens?"

He bowed his head and gritted his teeth. "No, mistress, I was just enjoying the day."

She turned away and started down a path. He opened the gate and found the twins waiting for him.

"You might need our guidance in such a maze," said one of them.

The young women, both reddish blonds, took his arms to draw him forward.

"Are you wondering how to tell us apart?" the other one asked.

He wasn't, but saw no point in telling her that.

The lady on his left slanted her green-eyed gaze up at him, showing the sparkle of wit and good humor. "I am Lady Anne, Sir Gareth, but I fear you will never be able to tell us apart. Many a good man has tried."

The twin on his right gave a shocked gasp, clearly a more demure, responsible young woman.

"I am Lady Cicely," she said, and gave her sister a scolding look. "Please excuse Anne for her lack of manners, Sir Gareth. I don't think she quite knows how words can be misunderstood."

Lady Anne stuck out her tongue at her sister.

"Ladies, you have given me all I need to know to tell you apart," he said dryly.

A few rows away, Margery, now wearing an apron that covered her from bodice to toes, was kneeling in the dirt, plucking out weeds like any kitchen maid. Gareth guided the giggling twins to a bench in the shade of the lady's garden, then returned to Margery. Damn, it *would* have to be weeding.

He stood over her, deliberately casting his shadow across her body.

She looked up and shaded her eyes. "Yes, Sir Gareth? Wouldn't you rather keep Anne and Cicely amused?"

"You are the lesser of evils," he said, sitting down beside her.

"Should I be flattered by that?" she asked sweetly.

For a moment he almost smiled, but caught himself in time.

She went back to her task.

He tried not to show his distaste as he braced himself with one hand and plucked a weed.

"That's parsley," Margery said, laughter in her voice.

"Oh." He buried the roots, telling himself that the warmth in his face was from the sun, *not* a blush.

"This is harder than it looks. You don't weed much, do you?"

"I buy or am served the food I need. It is not my task to grow it."

"Ah, then farming is beneath you."

Anger flared within him at such hypocrisy from her mouth. "Nothing is beneath me." He gritted his teeth and controlled himself. "Why do you do such menial tasks? Surely your maidservants are competent."

"I can already tell that, by the beautiful care they've taken with the gardens. But I am trying to meet all of the castle folk. I thought that if I joined them in their work, even if only for a few hours, they might grow to accept me sooner."

He looked at her bent head. He told himself there had to be a selfish reason behind all this.

For a time they worked in silence, Gareth following her lead as to which were weeds. The sun beat warmly down on their backs, and the gentle buzz of bees mixed with the murmuring of the twins' voices. His mind drifted lazily, thinking of nothing in particular, and he almost forgot his purposes here.

Then a sour twist of nausea struck him without warning, and Gareth barely resisted the urge to gasp. When he closed his eyes, he didn't see blackness, but a swirling maelstrom of colors trying to form a picture. *Not now; not with Margery so close.* He put a hand to his head, rubbed the bridge of his nose, and tried as always to force the coming vision away.

His head began to ache, and suddenly the colors in his mind coalesced into Margery riding a horse, a man astride behind her. The vision vanished as fast as it came, leaving him with no clue to the man's face, no knowledge of her emotions. He couldn't even tell if she was in danger. Why was he sent such useless visions? A wave of self-loathing almost choked him.

"Gareth?"

He heard Margery's voice as if from far away. He forced himself to look at her, squint-

ing as the sun pulsed through his eyes like his
headache.

"Gareth, are you ill? You've become so pale."

He focused on her worried face. "I am fine.
I thought I'd beheaded another parsley plant."

Margery knew a falsehood when she heard
it. His face had drained of color, the skin about
his eyes was creased in the corners with sudden strain. And his gaze seemed remote, as if
he no longer saw the ground—or her.

Chapter 5

〜⌒⌒⌒

"**G**areth, I have never met a man who would admit to gardening, let alone do so in full view of the entire castle."

For a long moment, she didn't think he'd answer. When he finally spoke, he sounded distant, preoccupied. "I've always preferred to be outdoors."

She gave up. If he couldn't be bothered to make conversation, then neither would she. She felt so alone in the world, so weighted down by her problems and her guilt that her head was spinning in circles. The sun was hot, her eyes ached, and his presence was suddenly too unsettling.

She stood up, and he rose to his feet beside her. She handed the basket of weeds to one of the kitchen maids. The girl bobbled the basket, she was so busy ogling Gareth. When he actually noticed the maid, she almost lost her hold on the basket completely.

Suppressing a groan of frustration, Margery

marched out of the garden, not even bothering to ask if Anne and Cicely wanted to accompany her inside. She felt irrationally angry, miserable, defeated. She would leave the twins in Gareth's capable hands.

But when she glanced over her shoulder, he was there behind her, taking one stride to her two, looking determined—and so handsome he outshone the day. She felt like she'd never know a moment of peace again. She picked up her pace, climbing the steps two at a time into the great hall.

She could tell by the interested expressions of the people they passed that he was still behind her. She entered a corridor, and after the first turn, the sounds of the great hall vanished. She was alone with Gareth, who followed her from one circle of torchlight to the next. He was so close she could hear his breathing.

Suddenly, Margery could take no more. Gareth was a stunning reminder of her problem every time she looked at him. She wanted to don her armor of numbness, to pretend her problems would wait for another day.

She whirled around and planted a hand on his chest.

"You cannot follow me everywhere," she said. "My people will begin to talk—and not in a flattering manner."

He pushed her hand away as if her touch repulsed him.

"I am your guard," he insisted angrily. "I

swore an oath to you—and to your father long ago. I will follow you wherever I deem necessary."

His words and actions hurt like a betrayal. She was just an oath to him, a duty—not a real flesh and blood woman or long-ago friend. She didn't understand what had happened to change him so. Did he not even want to be near her?

Then why was he standing so close, his breath the faintest breeze across her cheek? She was not a short woman, but he was above her, surrounding her. She couldn't make out much of his face in the windowless hall, but his intense gaze held her captive. He was nothing like the men at court, who pranced for her favor.

Why couldn't she look away from those searing eyes? A shot of heat through her middle made her gasp. What was wrong with her?

She stumbled back a step to break this sudden, unwanted connection between them.

"Margery," he said, his voice low, husky, "if I allow you out of my sight, you must promise that you will not leave the castle without telling me."

"Very well," she murmured. "I shall be fine. These are all my people."

"You've known them but a few short months. You cannot afford to trust them."

*   *   *

After seeing Margery to the kitchens, Gareth returned to the great hall, where even summer could not touch the cool dampness. He sat in a chair before the hearth and absently accepted a tankard of ale from one blushing maidservant, then refused an offer of food from another. When they finally left him alone, he surveyed the room, seeing merely a few women cleaning.

He tried to tell himself that he was angry, but what he really felt was—stunned. He could no longer deny that since the moment he'd arrived, he'd felt an undercurrent of attraction to Margery. When she had put her hand on his chest, it was a fire he had to thrust away before he was burned.

There had been other unsuitable women he'd been attracted to. He'd always overcome such a dangerous weakness, and this time would be no exception. He only bedded experienced women who expected nothing from him, not maidens with marriage on their minds.

Another serving maid interrupted Gareth's thoughts, holding a shaking pitcher in her hands.

"More ale, milord?" she asked timidly.

The awe in her eyes as she filled his tankard made him wary, and he told himself it was only his face which caused her reaction. He didn't know how much longer his anonymity would last, especially when he was not hiding his name. He could only hope the story of War-field's Wizard had not spread from the southern coast of England. Then every girl here would flee from him, and men would fear him.

But why was he having visions at all? Before he'd found Margery, he'd often gone months feeling normal, with no clue of the future. Now in a span of weeks, he'd felt and seen too many things that made no sense.

He could tell Margery was in danger, but what could he make of the vision today? His frustration and anger mounted.

As another maidservant began to make her approach, Gareth quickly left the hall. There was only one place to go when he felt his emotions ready to erupt.

The tiltyard took up half of one side of the inner ward. Dust rose in hazy clouds as the packed earth was trampled by horses and men. Troops of soldiers practiced archery and sword-fighting, or took turns riding low over their mounts, trying to jab the quintain with their lance. Overall, he thought they showed much promise, especially with someone as skilled as Wallace Desmond to guide them.

Desmond himself sauntered over a few minutes later. He was coated in sweat and dust, but looked quite pleased with himself. He waved at the dairymaids who'd gathered to gawk and giggle.

Gareth linked his hands behind his back, finding his frown hard to keep. " 'Tis a good thing I don't feel any guilt for making you take this position."

"Well, you should feel guilty," Desmond said. "While you have a private chamber, I'm sleeping in the barracks."

A young man wearing an overlarge plated brigantine ran toward them. "Excuse me, Sir Wallace, but we could use your help with the archers."

"In a moment, lad." Desmond watched the man bow and walk away. "*That* was the captain of the guard just yesterday."

" 'Tis rather amazing their mistress hasn't been hurt before now."

"Did you know a man tried to capture her and her ladies in the woods just a month ago?"

Gareth felt his stomach clench with anger—at Margery, he told himself. "She never told me."

"Probably because before the man could do more than struggle with her, she kicked him between the legs and they escaped."

Desmond grinned, but Gareth saw nothing amusing. "Are the defenses secure now?"

"Yes. The gatehouse is never unguarded. But has she told you her troubles yet?"

"Some, but not all."

"And . . ." Desmond leaned forward.

"Her problems are her own, and not to be bandied about the tiltyard."

The smile left Desmond's face. "You think I would tell a woman's secrets to the world?"

Gareth said nothing.

"I know I'm not your friend," Desmond said coldly. "But I'm the only man here you can trust. How can I help her if I don't know what I'm looking for?"

Gareth stared hard into Desmond's eyes. He hadn't trusted a soul in so many years that he was unsure who was an enemy and who was not. But Desmond had no stake in Margery's troubles, and had been faithful—so far.

Gareth leaned against a fence, and motioned Desmond nearer. "The king recently gifted her with wealth and the power to choose her own husband. Since then various men have been trying to compromise her. Her brothers are away with the king, and she's been dealing with this all alone."

"So are we here to play midwife to a marriage?" Desmond asked in disbelief.

"No. She's hired me as her personal guard. But she doesn't want anyone to know she's become desperate. To stay near her, I'm pretending to be another of her suitors."

Desmond grinned. "So when I saw you earlier in the garden on your hands and knees . . ."

"I was acting as a suitor," Gareth said uncomfortably.

"Have *you* ever courted a woman?"

Why had he ever felt it was necessary to confide in Desmond? The man was a fool. "Is it so inconceivable?"

"But women usually crawl into your lap. I

never quite understood why they would want to warm up that cold demeanor of yours, when they could have sunny, cheerful me."

Gareth clenched his fists. "Wait here while I find a sword."

Desmond shot him an amused glance. "You look . . . aggravated."

"Only from lack of training."

"I don't think so."

Desmond was waiting, sword drawn, when Gareth returned from the armory carrying a blunt sword. Gareth immediately attacked. With a grunt, Desmond parried the weapon aside and stepped back.

"You're not one to waste words," Desmond said. He thrust forward.

Gareth stepped aside. "Not when my meaning is clear. You, on the other hand, talk too much."

Gareth let himself merge with the fury of emotions he never showed the world. Anger, frustration, bitterness, all poured down his arm to power his sword. He drove Desmond back across the tiltyard.

It took almost all his concentration to keep from wounding his opponent, yet he still noticed the soldiers and knights stepping back, wary looks on their faces. No one would bother him at Hawksbury now, for fear of igniting this consuming wrath that threatened the edge of his control.

Sweat ran in rivulets down his face and

chest. He jumped to avoid Desmond's swipe at his knees, then turned—and saw Margery.

She stood at the top of a flight of stairs near a side entrance to the castle, frozen as if she'd been watching them for quite some time.

She must be horrified. Good, let her fear him; let her never risk touching him again. He straightened and faced her, proud of his sweat and his skill and the fear he inspired.

But she didn't run. She stared at him for a moment longer, her face unreadable. Then she walked down the stairs, carrying something in her apron. She came out from the shadow of the castle and lifted her face to the sun, which shimmered around her in a golden haze. Her skirt swayed with the movement of her feet, raising small clouds of dust that sparkled about the ground. She made clucking sounds with her tongue, and soon dozens of squawking hens clustered around her. She scattered handfuls of grain as she walked, and the chickens pecked in her wake.

Gareth had seen countless noblewomen in their finest garments, giving parties and hunts for others of their kind. He had no wish to be a part of such a world. But watching Margery do a servant's humblest task shook everything he had known women to be. He couldn't begin to understand her.

"Gareth!"

He turned to Desmond.

"I've called your name three times. No matter what she is doing, you cannot keep your gaze off Mistress Margery."

"My duty is to protect her," he said stiffly.

Desmond groaned. "Saints above, save me from foolish men. I think you feel something for her."

"In case you forgot, I'm also supposed to be her suitor," Gareth said with a scowl. "A suitor would stare."

"A suitor would also give her flowers."

"What?" Gareth asked defensively.

"A suitor would give her flowers, unless he had more money than he knew what to do with. Then he'd buy her jewelry." Desmond wiggled his eyebrows. "Women like jewelry—and flowers."

Gareth opened his mouth to tell him what he thought of his unwanted advice, but . . . it was a good suggestion. "I'll keep that in mind."

He lifted his sword and resumed the attack.

Though her back was turned, Margery felt the clash of their weapons reverberate through her spine. She scattered more grain and told herself to ignore the masculine contest being waged behind her. Women never felt a need to discover who was strongest, who was quickest.

But men were different.

She peeked over her shoulder and saw Gareth and Sir Wallace straining against each other, their swords meeting above their heads.

Sir Wallace finally stumbled backward, laughing at his own failure.

Gareth didn't laugh, but raised his sword for more. Any other man she knew would have been happy for the victory, would have waited for his opponent to recover.

But in Gareth, she sensed an elemental need to win, to prove something. He was the focus of all eyes, as in command of the tiltyard as if he were the captain of the guard, not Sir Wallace.

She forgot her chores, forgot that her people were watching her, and simply stood holding an apron full of grain and staring at Gareth Beaumont.

Chapter 6

That afternoon, Margery received a missive announcing the arrival the next morning of her London suitors. A dark cloud enveloped her as she supervised the household preparations for her guests. She felt as if she was still a little girl, alone and defenseless because her brothers had to foster elsewhere. Then, as well as now, she was well guarded, but that did not stop her from feeling vulnerable.

During the evening meal, she surrounded herself with her ladies and seated Gareth as far from herself as she could. She talked incessantly to the twins, but whenever there was a lull in the conversation, her mind returned to the scene in the dark corridor that morning. She relived that moment when they hadn't spoken, when their breath had mingled, when she'd touched him. Had she imagined the look in his eyes, the shared awareness of each other?

She felt a shiver of astonishment move through her, and knew she was being ridiculous. He had pushed her away, and rightly so. She was a woman no man would ever want, let alone marry.

Shame crept up on her unannounced. Was she such a wanton that she imagined feelings for a man who openly despised her and her family?

Though she shouldn't, she looked down the table at Gareth, and found him watching her. His eyes glittered above his serious mouth. Then he slowly smiled, and it was amused and devilish. Her whole body heated with a furious blush.

He was acting—oh, of course, he was acting. He was here only to complete a task, and be paid for it. She raised her chin, giving him a cool smile, then turned away as if his regard was worth nothing to her.

Instead of retreating to her solar after supper, Margery and the twins sat before the fire in the hall. She was enjoying the relative quiet of the household with only one guest—Gareth—in attendance. She kept Anne and Cicely on either side of her, and if they noticed her awkwardness, they did not mention it. One strummed a lute while the other sang in a soft, pretty voice.

Margery's embroidery rested in her lap, untouched, as she drifted through memories of her brother James singing to her. She wanted to think about earlier times, when life had seemed so full of promise. But four years of her childhood involved Gareth, his reluctant friendship, his rescue of her.

This evening, she had thought she'd managed to keep him away by surrounding herself with her friends, but he was in her mind—unsettling her feelings, making her remember hoop games and archery and trying to make a serious boy smile.

Gareth pulled up a chair directly opposite her, startling her. With the twins, they were almost a cozy foursome. Every time she looked from one twin to the other, there he was in the center, watching her, his long legs stretched out, booted feet almost touching hers. His hose were threadbare, his plain blue tunic tattered at the hem. His white shirt had seen too many days. She had never in her life been wooed by a man so obviously lacking in money.

And she wasn't now, she reminded herself. Gareth was a soldier she had hired, nothing more. She moved her feet away. He shifted his feet near again, like a childish game—or a suitor trying to get her attention.

She didn't know why she was so tense; she knew his actions meant nothing. She should practice controlling her anger, for she knew tomorrow would begin a real courtship, when those wild young men came from London. Then she would be thankful for Gareth and his protection.

Cicely continued to strum the lute, but Anne stopped singing.

She gave Margery a conspiratorial smile, then said, "Sir Gareth, have you come to Hawksbury Castle to better acquaint yourself with Mistress Margery?"

He linked his hands across his stomach. "Yes, my lady," he said, his deep voice deferential.

Margery's heart sped up with unexpected worry. She and Gareth had never discussed what story they would tell the world. He could create any wild, outlandish tale, and she could not say him wrong.

"So you have met before?" Anne continued.

"We knew one another as children, when I fostered at Wellespring Castle."

"As children," Anne repeated, glancing from Margery to Cicely, her eyes gleaming with wicked amusement.

He nodded. "I was a few years older, and in my youthful foolishness, thought myself quite beyond the childish games she wanted to play with me."

The twins giggled, while Margery's gaze was frozen on him. She had never thought he would be capable of banter.

"She followed me everywhere," he said, glancing at her. "I confess that I often made certain she could not find me."

Margery wanted to jump to her feet and defend herself, to swear that he was making up lies. But a deep part of her wondered if it was true. Had she been so annoying? Surely that couldn't be the only reason he was bitter toward her and her family.

Then Gareth leaned forward and took her hands in his. Though she tried to pull away, he gripped them harder, uncomfortably so. Was this just another contest he needed to win?

"Mistress Margery, I have learned the error of my ways."

She opened her mouth, but nothing came out. His skin was warm, rough, and callused from hard work. It heated her palms, and the warmth spread up her arms to tingle through her breasts. When those golden eyes captured hers, she had a hard time disbelieving anything he said.

Cicely stopped strumming the lute to openly watch this new entertainment.

Anne said, "Sir Gareth, if you fostered with Margery's family, why have you not visited her before? Did you think she was still a child?"

His gaze dropped down her body. Margery thought, *Please let him not feel my foolish trembling*.

"No, not a child," he said, his eyes returning once more to search her face. "I have lived in Europe for the last four years. I met many women, but always, in the back of my mind, I wondered about my childhood friend."

She heard the subtle sarcasm meant only for her ears. He hadn't thought of her at all. "According to you, I was more of a childhood tormentor."

Everyone laughed, and she forced her own smile.

"But that does not mean I didn't admire your spirit."

Gareth finally released her hands and she quickly sat back. She felt the prickle of perspiration on her upper lip, and she desperately wished to wipe it—and any trace of her reaction to him—away. How humiliating to be so affected by a man who stayed with her only out of duty. She fervently wished that she hadn't thrown away her innocence, that she didn't know where such feelings could lead.

"But why return now?" Cicely asked, setting the lute aside.

Margery could see what they were doing. The twins wanted to know if he returned merely because he'd heard about the king's bequest. She held her breath, as if she, too, needed to hear the answer.

"I grew restless in France. Battles and tournaments held little allure, so it was time to find my place in life, to look for a good English girl to marry."

She felt herself blush again. Lies, all lies. As if he would ever trust anyone.

"Please, ladies, do not think I considered myself worthy of Mistress Margery." Gareth leaned forward in his chair, pitching his voice lower and looking deeply into her eyes. "But I knew I had to see you again."

Margery thought that even Anne sighed.

Though it was all an illusion, part of her clung to his words. She wished that a man *would* want her just for herself—not her money or status or property.

But then, Peter hadn't wanted any of that, either. He had wanted to conquer her body, to make a fool of her. Even in the spirit of make-believe, she couldn't let another man think he was seducing her so easily.

"Then how did you find me, Sir Gareth?" she asked, rather amazed at her own cool voice.

He raised one eyebrow, then sat back. "I went to London first and asked about you at court."

She thought she detected the first hint of wariness in his voice, and warmed to this game they played with the truth. "And what did they tell you?"

"That you had come here, to one of your new holdings."

"And what else?"

He looked away, and seemed almost to squirm in his chair. Was this another act? Why did she sense a deep mystery about him?

"Mistress Margery, I—"

"The truth, Sir Gareth." She wanted to laugh aloud at that.

"I heard that you are free to choose a husband."

He suddenly dropped forward on his knees, practically in her lap. Cicely and Anne shrieked and started to giggle. He took her hands, pressing his lips against her knuckles.

"Mistress Margery," he whispered, lifting his head to look into her face, so close she could feel the warmth of his body, "I freely admit I rejoiced on hearing that you are looking for a husband. Can you blame me? I am looking for a wife. I knew what kind of girl you were, and I thought I would see what kind of woman you had become." He looked down her body, then back up. "A magnificent woman."

"And very rich," she said, her cynical smile unforced.

Gareth stiffened, searching her eyes. She pulled her hands from his, then watched as he got to his feet. He towered above her, and the twins no longer giggled as they, too, looked up at him in awe.

"You believe the worst of me?" he asked softly.

"I do not know what to believe."

"Even after everything that happened when we were children?"

"Men change." She knew that from experience. Men lied, too.

He took a step backward, and his chair almost toppled to the floor. "I shall prove to you that my intentions are honorable. What would you have me do, mistress?"

"Sir Gareth, only time will tell if you are honorable."

There was an uncomfortable silence. Gareth stood between the three women, a big man who seemed too uncivilized for lutes and singing and embroidery. When she looked up at him, she saw bonfires in the wilderness, the howl of wild animals kept at bay, the protection and warmth of a man's body through the night.

Anne cleared her throat. "Margery, would you like to play a game with me?"

She shook away such dangerous, forbidden dreams, and quickly agreed. A contest was just the thing to distract her. Anne brought out the Tables board and playing pieces, and began to set them up at the head table.

Gareth remained still, looking down on Margery, who stared at the fire, not at him. He reluctantly admired her quick wit and intelligent responses. To his surprise, he had almost enjoyed saying just enough of the truth to make her uneasy. He couldn't remember the last time he had had such a conversation with a woman.

Or the last time he had become so easily lost in a woman's eyes. When she had stared up at him, he'd felt . . . strange, remote, as if there was more beneath the surface of their shared glance.

He told himself he had simply missed the company of gentlewomen for too long.

Margery stood up without warning. Her

shoulder brushed his chest; her skirts surrounded his legs. He caught her elbow, and noticed that the twins' backs were turned.

"I taught you this game," he whispered.

She was silent. He tried not to breathe, so as
not to smell the scent of roses that was a part
of her.

"Do you remember?"

"Did we play before a hearth?" she asked,
and he could hear the hesitation in her voice.
She slowly turned to look up at him.

"We lay on our stomachs."

She shook her head. "I did not remember
that."

She pulled her arm away and Gareth let her
go, watching as she seated herself at the table.
After a moment's indecision, he moved to
stand behind Lady Anne. The head table was
on a raised dais, which put the Tables board at
Gareth's chest, and the women's heads equal
with his own.

Margery began the game. For a few minutes
they played in silence, and Gareth watched her
slender fingers roll the dice. He should leave
the women alone, but he was amused by Margery's concentration. With lucky rolls of the
dice, her skill should let her win.

She seemed to win at anything she attempted, just like her entire family. His humor
faded, replaced by anger—anything was better
than the memory of the hollow emptiness in

his soul when he'd ridden away from her family home so long ago.

Gareth stepped up and slid onto the bench beside Lady Anne. When she was about to make a move, he said, "No, not that piece."

All three women looked at him and he shrugged.

Margery puffed out her lower lip in a pout and glanced up at him with storm-cloud blue eyes. "Why, Sir Gareth, you're not going to help me?"

"You do not need my help."

He could see why she got her way, even with her brothers. He wanted to tell her that her problems couldn't be solved with a flutter of her eyelashes—but he'd settle for watching her soundly defeated at Tables.

He boldly studied her, and not always her face. He told himself he merely wished to fluster her, but more than once his eyes lingered on the shadowy indentation between her breasts, and his thoughts were not only of anger.

He whispered suggestions in Lady Anne's ear, and soon Margery was floundering. They'd attracted a vocal audience of soldiers and knights, who were actively betting.

"Anne, you've blocked me," Margery said pleasantly, but she was almost glaring at Gareth.

There was laughter all around them, Desmond the loudest of all.

"Gareth," he called, "Don't make me lose a day's wage on Mistress Margery."

"You should have bet on Lady Anne." Gareth smiled. "I may not yet have convinced Mistress Margery of my worthiness as her suitor, but even she cannot doubt my skills."

As everyone laughed, Margery's gaze was locked with his in a contest of wills older than any table game. Couldn't she see that her wiles were no match for his?

Yet she soon beat Anne at Tables, and the knights led her away, showering her with admiring congratulations. Gareth put the game away, and tried not to let his frustration show.

Later in his bedchamber, Gareth set a candleholder on the table and moved to the windows. The room was dark, shadowy, with only the single candle for light. He'd asked the maids to leave his fireplace cold, since the summer nights were warm enough.

He opened the shutters and pulled back the glass window. He'd been at Hawksbury Castle for only two days, and already he was growing used to the luxury of glass in every window. Life here was making him soft.

Outside, the landscape was illuminated by a half moon, and he could see the faint traces of the descending hillsides and wooded glens between squares of farm fields. In the southeast, the Cotswold hills jutted toward the stars.

Margery lingered on his mind. He wasn't

quite sure why he felt the need to defeat her, and why he was so disappointed that it hadn't happened. She was just a woman he was being paid to help; just an ancient oath he had sworn to a dead man.

He heard a sudden muffled clatter in the hall and he froze, listening. It wasn't repeated.

He crossed his room and opened the door to find the corridor dark, silent, empty. He walked toward Margery's bedchamber, three rooms down from his, put his ear against the door, and listened. He heard the faintest movement inside.

Could someone be with her?

Just before he touched the door latch, he heard the sound of booted feet echoing through the hall. He swore softly. It must be the patrol he'd had Desmond assign.

As two men rounded the corner, Gareth nodded to them and stepped into the garderobe. Perhaps they'd think he just didn't like to use a chamberpot.

The moment they passed, he burst into Margery's room.

Chapter 7

Margery felt sluggish, weary, as she changed into her nightclothes. She lit candles on the bed tables and mantel, hoping the cheery light would help. The fire crackled its warmth as she sank down amid the cushions scattered on the carpet.

Her head ached in dull waves. Tomorrow all her noble young visitors would arrive. Only six months ago, before her infatuation with Peter, she would have been thrilled to be the object of so much attention, to have her choice of husband. Now all she felt was discouraged. She would have to be polite yet keep her distance, wondering which of the men would be desperate enough to try to force her hand in marriage. She felt as if she had long since lost any control over her own fate. She had to come up with a solution.

The door was suddenly flung open, and Margery came up on her knees in shock to see Gareth Beaumont wielding a dagger, an angry scowl distorting his face. He slammed the door shut and gazed about the chamber. With a gasp, she scrambled to her feet, pulling her dressing gown tighter.

"Gareth, what—"

"I heard something in the hall," he said, moving farther into the room. "Did someone come in here?"

"No."

He checked behind the draperies and under the bed. He obviously didn't think her word was enough. When he approached her near the fireplace, she folded her arms below her chest and glared at him.

"Did you think I was hiding someone?" she demanded.

He slid the dagger back into his belt. "I could not be certain you were answering of your own free will."

She relented with a sigh, but continued to eye him warily. "I suppose I can understand that. Thank you for your diligence."

She waited for him to leave, but instead he studied the room, especially the cushions heaped before the fire.

"Your bedchamber is . . . frilly," he finally said.

She didn't take it as a compliment. "And you've never been in a woman's chamber before?"

He arched a brow. "I didn't say that."

"Oh, of course not." She raised both hands. "How dare I encroach upon your manliness?"

Gareth scowled. "By the saints, what are you talking about?"

"Nothing understandable, obviously." She slumped into a chair before the fire. "Never mind. A good evening to you."

He didn't leave. They were alone in her bed-chamber, in the silence of the night. She should force him out the door—but she didn't. She had behaved like this before, and it had brought her nothing but trouble, yet once again she couldn't stop herself. She sat with her eyes half-closed and let herself feel the dangerous thrill of not knowing what he would do next.

He sat down in the chair beside her, and Margery held her breath. She noticed the width of his legs, the muscles that sloped and curved. As he stared into the fire, she studied his lips and the curve of his cheek. His blond hair fell forward, and she felt the urge to tuck it back.

Gareth felt like a fool. There had been no intruder, no reason for him to burst in on Margery. There was nothing he wanted to say to her. So why had he sat down?

It could only be his physical attraction to her—and that angered him all the more. Yes, she was beautiful, with long dark hair that tumbled about her shoulders. She looked smaller, frailer in her thin nightclothes.

But all this blossoming femininity hid a spoiled, selfish heart. She and her family expected the world to bow to their demands. They used people for their own ends, just like Margery now used her beauty to keep his attention. She must know what she looked like sitting there in the firelit shadows, soft and sleepy.

He heard her sigh. She pulled her legs up beneath her and propped her chin on her hand. It had been a long time since he'd been alone with a woman. And she wore so little. The bed suddenly seemed large and conspicuous, and it was a struggle not to glance at it.

This line of thought had to stop. He tried to remember his first night away from Wellespring Castle, the cold rain that had soaked his garments and ruined his food, how desolate he'd felt. But it was all so long ago. He was a man now, and thoughts of Margery called to him.

"So . . ." she said in too bright a voice. "When you're not working, what do you do with yourself?"

"Do?" he said thickly. "I train."

"But 'tis the same as working. Have you no interests that don't include . . ." she hesitated, "hurting people?"

He glared at her. "That is how I survive, and that is what *you* hired me for. I do not have time for poetry or painting pictures. Without my sword-fighting skills, I would have been dead long ago. But I imagine a woman can't understand that."

She gripped the chair arms, and her eyes flashed angrily at him. "Some women can. My sister by marriage is an excellent swords-woman."

His eyes widened. "I do not believe you."

"So now I'm a liar, besides a silly fool?" she demanded.

Surely she couldn't expect him to trust her, and he knew she was already lying to him about something in her past. "All right then, which brother is she married to?"

"James."

"That pompous—"

"Gareth!"

"From what I remember of him, I thought his wife would be a meek noblewoman with no thoughts of her own."

For a brief moment, he saw amusement in her eyes. "He thought he wanted that, too. But King Henry gave him Isabel, who's almost as tall as James, and fights just as well."

He remembered the last time he'd seen her brother, barely an adult, looking down at Gareth with all the arrogance of an earl who thought his bloodlines made him a better man. Bolton had judged him unworthy of friendship or loyalty.

His bitterness, always so near the surface, flamed to life.

"And your other brothers?" He wanted to look in Margery's eyes and think revenge not sexual release.

She smiled sadly. "Edmund died a few years ago. He took sick after an injury."

"I am sorry for your loss." Edmund had been frail, and destined for the priesthood. They had little in common, but Edmund had taught him to read.

And since Edmund hadn't protested when they sent Gareth away, he must have known and approved.

"Reynold is married, too," she said, "though at first he took Edmund's place in the monastery."

"However did he meet a woman?"

"She was imprisoned there. He rescued her and they fell in love."

"So all of your brothers are at peace," he said. His voice was careful, as if the anger might erupt at any moment.

"It took a long time, but yes, they're happy."

She smiled at him, ignorant of the savagery that lurked in his soul, panting and straining like a leashed beast.

They were all so happy, the Bolton and Welles families. Her brothers had found women who loved them, women they trusted, and Margery would soon choose her own husband.

The last decent threads of his life had begun to unravel when her family had thrown him out. He turned slowly to look on her, his neck moving stiffly, as if it would shatter with the eruption of his rage.

As he gazed upon her lovely face, suddenly everything became clear. Margery was the answer to his retribution.

She *owed* him.

For payment, he would take her to wife.

Her dowry and lands could keep him from starving, and give him back the respectability his family had long since lost. She was looking for a husband—who better than he? She would be protected, and he would have the use of her body and her money. What else was marriage about—except begetting heirs, something he would have no problem beginning immediately.

They were alone in her bedchamber, with the bed turned down. He could take her maidenhead right now, and they'd be married in the morning. There would be nothing her brothers could do when they returned.

But . . . if he took his time, made Margery care for him and choose him of her own free will, how much sweeter would be his revenge on her brothers.

For the first time, Gareth let himself truly admire her beauty. It would soon be only his. Perhaps he should begin his slow seduction tonight: just a touch of her cheek, a longing stare into her eyes. That was all he'd ever needed before.

Margery met his gaze, and her smile slowly died.

He rose to his full height, then stepped before her, letting his knees brush hers.

There was a sharp knock on the door, and they both flinched.

Chapter 8

As the knock sounded again, Margery jumped to her feet, wondering frantically where Gareth could hide. To be discovered like this, to ruin both their lives with her sins—she couldn't bear it.

"Just one moment!" she called, her hands on his lower back as she pushed him toward the window.

She motioned to the draperies and he stepped behind them. She glimpsed the dark amusement in his face as she arranged the folds of fabric to fall around him, making sure his feet were covered. After walking quickly to the door, she took a deep breath and opened it.

Anne stood in the dark corridor, her hair loose, a robe and blanket around her shoulders. She gave Margery a frown and looked toward the bed. "Were you asleep? I did not mean to awaken you."

"I wasn't asleep yet," she said, then gave a wide yawn. "Can I help you with something?"

Nodding, Anne walked in. Margery's shoulders slumped as she closed the door in resignation and watched the girl curl up in the chair Gareth had recently vacated.

"Anne, I am actually quite tired. Could this wait until morning?" Margery was certain she could hear Gareth breathing. Did the draperies rise and fall with his chest?

"I promise this will take but a moment."

Anne proceeded to talk about one of the young men who'd be arriving on the morrow. Margery painted a smile on her face and worriedly watched the draperies over Anne's shoulder.

It suddenly occurred to her that Gareth could take advantage of this situation. He was a poor knight; just by stepping into the room again, he would have the most eligible heiress in England, and all the reward that went with it. She found herself holding her breath with anxiety, her gaze darting constantly to the windows.

Gareth's face was covered in fabric, and he inhaled his own warm breath, trying not to feel light-headed. He longed to turn his head, but didn't dare move. Perspiration dripped down his temples.

All he had to do was step out from the draperies—or better yet, pretend to sneeze. It would seem an accident, and Margery would never have to know that it had really been deliberate.

But she would be humiliated, and might never forgive him for taking away her choice. And it wouldn't allow him the ultimate revenge against her brothers.

No, there was still time. *He* would be her choice for husband.

"Margery!" Lady Anne said. "You are so tired your eyes are glazed."

"Forgive me." Margery didn't sound nervous so much as distracted. "What was the last thing you said?"

"If Lord George should not take your fancy, could you guide him my way? And make sure 'tis I, not Cicely."

"Anne, you are the daughter of an earl, and could have any young man in England. I am sure Lord George will be quite taken with you."

"You are a dear, Margery. I must say, that new man following you about is interesting."

"Sir Gareth?"

Margery's voice sounded a bit faint, and Gareth's interest intensified.

"He is blindingly handsome, wouldn't you say?"

"I'm not sure 'blindingly' is the right—"

"Oh, you know what I mean," Lady Anne interrupted. " 'Tis a shame he is only a knight. My father expects at least an earl from me. But you have your choice—what freedom."

"Sometimes I wish I had let my brothers choose for me long ago," Margery said.

Gareth heard the sad wistfulness in her voice, and wondered again what secrets were hidden in her past.

"I'll let you sleep," Lady Anne said. "Perhaps Sir Gareth's pursuit is tiring you."

"I think not."

Once he heard them move toward the door, he slowly turned his head to take a deep breath.

"Have a good night, Margery," Lady Anne said.

Gareth waited a few moments after he heard the door close, then stepped from behind the draperies. Margery was slumped with her back against the door, her face pensive. She looked up, and they stared at each other across the room.

"My coming to your room put you in needless danger," he said.

"Danger?"

"If she had discovered me—"

Margery raised a hand. "But she did not. And you were only trying to keep me safe."

He knew he should find something light to say, some way to endear himself to her. But nothing in his experience had prepared him for trying to make a woman like him. Usually women just wanted something from him; he wanted something from them. It was simple.

He cleared his throat. "So I'm not blindingly handsome?"

Her eyes widened and she laughed, covering her mouth quickly. "Anne is young. I could not encourage her in such pursuit."

"Then I *am* blindingly handsome?"

"Just go," she said, pointing to the door behind her, her lips twitching with a smile.

He leaned against the door to listen for footsteps, but instead noticed how close she stood beside him. She had translucent skin draped in thin fabric, hinting at curves he knew he would soon explore. Now that he'd decided to marry her, he could hardly keep his gaze on her face.

"Gareth, you must leave," she whispered.

"Not until the guards pass by."

"How do you know they will?"

"Because I planned the route myself."

She said nothing else, and he forced his attention to the corridor. The guards should pass Margery's bedchamber every hour. For a few minutes he remained still, listening through the wood, trying not to feel her gaze on his back. She finally moved away from him.

A while later, Gareth glanced over and found her curled in one of the hearth chairs. She was asleep, her head cocked at an awkward angle, her arms hanging limply. He went to her bed and pulled aside the coverlet and blankets. The sheets seemed to beckon him with the promise of warmth and satisfaction. Clenching his jaw, he went to stand above Mar-

gery, bracing himself for the feel of her body
in his arms, for her head tucked beneath his
chin. Now that he had given himself permission to think of her sexually, he had a difficult
time doing anything else.

He slid one arm behind her back, and the
other beneath her knees, lifting her against
him. With a little sigh, she nuzzled her cheek
against his chest, as if she trusted him. She was
a fool. Someday she would learn to trust no
one but herself.

He lowered her into the bed and pulled up
the blankets. She rolled to her side, head pillowed in her hand, her forehead creased in the
smallest of frowns. What worries followed her
into sleep?

As Margery dressed at dawn, she thought
about the previous night instead of her problems. She remembered sitting down, watching
Gareth listen for the guards.

She had awakened in bed, alone. He must
have carried her there, and she didn't remember it. She was surprised he hadn't just left her.

God, she was a fool thinking about him—a
man who obviously trusted no one, not even a
family he had spent years with. He was only
here for the money. He would go back to his
life, and she would be someone's sister or aunt.
Never a wife, never a mother. The sooner she
put aside her fantasies of a normal life, the
sooner she could escape the king's sentence—

his prison sentence. That's all marriage was for her.

And the would-be jailers arrived today.

Gareth held the sword high over his head, his muscles on fire, sweat streaming from his brow. He brought the weapon down hard and Desmond met it with his own sword, parrying it and staggering to one side.

Gareth stepped back, bringing the sword up in readiness.

Gasping for breath, Desmond bent over, hands braced on his knees. "No more!" he said, raising one hand. "What the hell . . . has gotten into you?"

Gareth slowly straightened, feeling his heart pound, welcoming the exhaustion that appeased his body and took his thoughts away from Margery. "We have not trained much recently. I felt the need for it."

"You mean *you* have not trained. I have done nothing but."

Desmond set down his sword and reached for a drinking horn hung from a nearby post. He swallowed some and offered it to Gareth, who took a sip, then lifted his eyebrows in surprise.

"Water?"

Desmond shrugged. "I need my wits about me today when Mistress Margery's next suitors arrive."

Gareth tensed. "Who is arriving today?"

"You have not heard?" Desmond said, his stare playfully disapproving. "Your talents are slipping, Sir Gareth."

"Just tell me."

"A whole contingent of young swains are due from London."

"How many?" Gareth asked, feeling his anger at Margery grow. How could she not tell him something so vitally important to her safety?

Desmond shrugged. "A half dozen, a dozen—who knows how many will take up the challenge of the wealthy Mistress Margery?"

Gareth turned to watch a baggage train emerge from the gatehouse. "Could they already be arriving?"

"Probably just the servants. I imagine their lordships are pillaging through the countryside about now."

"You're one of those 'lordships.' "

Desmond sighed. "A coincidence of birth. These youngsters are far above me at court, as they'll happily remind me." He picked up his sword. "We'd best get back to it, then. Mustn't let the pups show us up."

"They'll most likely remember me, even though I've been gone a few years," Gareth said, hoping they only remembered his fierceness in battle.

"Do not worry so. You defeated either them or their brothers or their fathers. I'm sure your reputation will scare at least a few of them away."

They spent another couple of hours exhausting each other and every knight and soldier on the tiltyard. Gareth kept a close watch on the gatehouse, and occasionally sent a page inside the castle to see how Margery was busying herself. She was overseeing the cleaning and the cooking, and airing out bedchambers.

Just before the noon meal, the inner ward came alive with the shouts of young men on horseback racing through the gatehouse. In a pack they galloped about, yelling and raising clouds of dust, and in general making a nuisance of themselves.

Gareth stood beside Desmond and crossed his arms over his chest. "They're barely old enough for whiskers," he said with some satisfaction.

He felt Desmond's amused regard.

"Now, Gareth, Mistress Margery is a wealthy young lady. Of course any marriageable man—"

"Boy."

"—man would want to woo her. You're here to protect her from the unscrupulous ones. She is paying you for that."

The young noblemen galloped by the henhouse, frightening the flock and sending a little serving girl running in terror.

Margery descended the steps from the great hall, her ladies behind her. She wore the vivid green of springtime, and she'd adorned her long, dark curls with flowers. He realized she'd used the daisies he'd left beside her plate that morning, which gave him some satisfaction. Desmond had been right about the flowers.

He walked toward her as the young men dismounted, handing off their reins to waiting servants. Soon a cluster of men gathered below Margery, who remained a few steps above them, smiling.

Gareth, sweaty and filthy, stood beside the elegantly clothed young men in their silks and velvets. They doffed hats and caps as they each presented Margery with a gift.

She smiled and laughed and blushed as she handed the gifts to her ladies, obviously basking in the adoration of all these wealthy men.

He would make sure none of them suited her.

Margery knew her face was going to betray her at any moment. Couldn't they all see how forced her smile was, how ill-at-ease she felt? She was a fraud, a sinner, not an innocent maid. She wanted to shout her faults to the world, to send these men away so she could weep in lonely peace.

Their eager faces blended together before her stinging eyes. They handed her gifts and sang her praises, until their reaching hands and garbled voices threatened to overwhelm her.

Just as Margery thought she would run

screaming from them all, she saw Gareth standing alone at the back of the crowd.

He was an island of maturity amid a sea of boyish faces. Surrounded by men garbed in clothing more ostentatious than her own, Gareth wore only a sleeveless leather jerkin and carried a sword as if it were a part of his powerful arm. The sweat of hard work glistened on his body, and his stunning face was stubbled in golden whiskers. She wanted to gape in awe at him, not pretend to smile at the rising tide of suitors. She wanted to touch the flowers in her hair, knowing he'd given them to her.

She was such a fool. She didn't know *how* she wanted to be treated. Shallow noblemen worshipped and fought over her for her money, while Gareth treated her as distantly as if he were only a servant.

Margery had had enough. She'd done nothing but agonize over being unable to offer her virginity to a man, but did they deserve her worry? These men treated her as a piece of property, as a font of wealth for the lucky man who won her. None of them cared for her personally.

Suddenly the answer to her problem seemed clear, and Margery's heart lifted. Why should she worry that she wasn't a virgin? She highly doubted that her husband would come to their marriage bed untouched by a woman. Why should she behave any differently?

The first time she had lain with Peter Fitzwilliam, there had been some discomfort. She could pretend that she felt the same thing on her wedding night. And if there had to be blood on the sheets, she would find a way to deal with that, too.

Her conscience gave a faint twinge, but she ignored it. It was true she had not conceived a child with Peter, but it was God's will if she ever did. Surely every married couple took such a chance. Why should she make herself an outcast, when none of her suitors were even worthy of her respect?

For the first time in months, Margery felt as if she could take a deep breath. The great weight of despair that had compressed her lungs was gone. She still had to find the perfect man to marry, but at least she had a plan.

Of course, love would not be a consideration. She had fallen in love once, and it had brought her nothing but heartache. No man deserved to have that much control over her. She would pick a man for the attributes she could most use, but love would not be one of them.

If that made her a cold woman, so be it.

Chapter 9

F inally the greetings were done, and Margery announced that dinner would soon be served. Her suitors followed each other into the great hall of Hawksbury Castle, laughing and gesturing as they kissed her hands. Five had gone past her, leaving the last man, Lord George Wharton, still beside his horse.

He looked about and saw Gareth nearby. In a clipped, superior tone, he said, "You, man, take my horse to the stables. Heaven knows where my squire has disappeared to."

She held her breath as Gareth's eyes darkened to the yellow of the skies before the fiercest storm. He rammed his sword into the scabbard at his waist.

She saw the exact moment Lord George gave a start of recognition. He backed away and almost tripped. What did he know about Gareth?

"Sir Gareth!" Margery said quickly. "You will of course be joining us at dinner."

"Certainly, mistress," Gareth answered. She

watched the storm recede from his eyes as he looked up at her. "But please do not wait for me. I have to wash and change."

"We will wait, Sir Gareth. I'll have hot water sent up to your bedchamber."

Lord George almost raced past her, not meeting her eyes. She told herself Gareth's reputation only made him an even better protector. But still, she could not hide her curiosity.

The meal itself was a disaster. Margery tried to keep six bickering men from elbowing one another aside to sit near her. Anne and Cicely were constantly whispering into her ears, telling her which man was a duke's younger son, and which was but a simple knight.

Margery was alone in a room full of people who seemed desperate to see her married, but none of their opinions mattered. She felt stronger, better, than she had in weeks. No longer would she trudge through each day, waiting passively for a fate decreed by the king. She would find a husband on her own terms.

After the awkward meal was over, she spent the afternoon embroidering, introducing herself to some of the men, reacquainting herself with others. The men played cards and gambled at dice. They seemed to have every intention of uselessly whiling the day away. *Her* husband would definitely have to be busy—no idle amusement for him. That only encouraged a man to think he should be waited on.

Yet she had to think of Anne and Cicely, too, both of whom would soon be looking for husbands. They were basking in the attentions of so many men. Anne played cards, and even shy Cicely carried on an occasional gentle conversation.

Margery would use such afternoons to further study her suitors. She had to give thought to exactly what kind of man she was looking for.

She smiled absently at Sir Humphrey Townsend, the boldest of them all, who was recounting another of his deeds in service to King Henry. Her gaze often strayed to Gareth, who sat at his own table, a book opened before him. He didn't gamble with the other men; in fact, he ignored them. She had promised to have the seamstresses make him new clothing, but she had yet to do so. It made her feel ungrateful, considering all that he was doing for her.

Sir Humphrey suddenly said, "And who is that poor fellow, the one who's made such bold use of your library, mistress?"

Margery felt startled, uneasy. "Do you mean Sir Gareth? He is here for the same reasons you are, sir. I gave him permission to use my library."

Gareth lifted his head and looked at them, and it was as if his golden eyes had become ice.

Sir Humphrey's voice grew even louder. "Mistress Margery, what is his full name?"

Something was wrong. Some wariness that she didn't understand moved through the room. Everyone was looking at Gareth, who closed his book and sat back, arms folded across his chest. He gazed at Sir Humphrey calmly, yet danger simmered beneath the surface, like a pot about to boil. Sir Humphrey must be a fool not to see it.

"He is Sir Gareth Beaumont," she said.

Looks passed between the knight and his companions, and their frowns made her even more nervous. She didn't know what was happening, what knowledge had been loosed through her great hall.

"Gareth Beaumont," Sir Humphrey said in a loud voice. "Why, Mistress Margery, do you know what kind of man dares to court you?"

Gareth studied Sir Humphrey coldly. "I have nothing to hide. Say what you will."

Margery set down her embroidery frame and tried not to panic at the animosity between the two knights. "Any good man is welcome in my castle."

"Even ones who carry with them a curse?" Sir Humphrey said with a smirk.

Her various suitors looked either triumphant or uneasy. Her brother James had used that same word in connection with Gareth. Why had she put off asking Gareth what it meant?

"What superstition is this, Sir Humphrey?" she said coolly. "Do you enjoy judging another man so unfairly?"

Sir Humphrey shook his head. His long, lank hair swayed. "I am only concerned for your safety, mistress. You do not know—"

"For a man so concerned with my safety, you seem gleeful."

The knight paled for a moment before he smiled. "Did you not ask Sir Gareth about his family?"

"He and I are just renewing our acquaintance," she said, forcing herself not to look at Gareth. "Am I questioning you about your ancestors?"

"Mayhap you should, mistress. I thought for certain your brothers would have told you about the Beaumont Curse."

Margery took a deep breath, and this time couldn't stop herself from glancing at Gareth. His face expressionless, he studied the other knight from under lowered brows.

"Sir Humphrey, I do not indulge in idle rumors," she said with winter frost in her voice.

"This is no rumor, mistress, but fact. Have you not heard how Sir Gareth's parents and grandparents died?"

Had Gareth lied about his parents dying in a fire? Well, she would not let cruel rumors be spoken in her presence. He could explain his past in his own time—in private.

"Mistress Margery," Gareth said, raising those golden eyes to look at her.

She did not wish for him to play into the hands of this petty knight who took such pleasure in other people's sorrows. But she was as frozen as everyone else in the hall, waiting for the words Gareth would say.

" 'Tis no secret that my parents died in a fire when I was but a child," he said.

"Who started the fire?" Sir Humphrey asked.

"We never knew."

"A witness said your father drank heavily that day. Perhaps—"

"My father drank heavily every day," Gareth interrupted coldly. "As do many of you. Are you claiming someone saw him start the fire?"

In that emotionless voice, Margery imagined a world of suffering. So this was the curse— rumors about a sad death? She could barely swallow past the lump in her throat.

But Sir Humphrey seemed unaffected. "You do not think such a death is worthy of suspicion, considering the way your grandmothers died?"

Margery saw Gareth's knuckles whiten where they grasped his tankard, but his face betrayed little. She couldn't imagine being the focus of so much condemnation.

He rose to his feet, looking powerful, remote, as if his past had never touched him. The room was hushed, save for the crackling of the fire and the distant sounds of servants' laughing voices. Margery felt raised bumps along her arms.

"My great-grandfather killed my great-grandmother," Gareth said flatly. "My grandfather blamed himself for my grandmother's death. None of it touches me. If you wish to make more of it, I can meet you at the tiltyard."

Sir Humphrey surged to his feet, but two of his friends grabbed his arms. Gareth waited, wearing a curve to his lips that wasn't really a smile.

Sir Humphrey's voice was furious as he strained against his friends' restraints. "You have no control over your fate, Beaumont. We're destined for good marriages"—he shot a triumphant glance at Margery—"wealth and honor. You are destined only for madness."

There was a collective hiss, as if just that word made Gareth a man to be shunned.

Gareth inclined his head. "If I am destined only for madness, it is truly amazing how many of your friends and family I have defeated at tournaments. Would you like to join their ranks? I will test my destiny against yours any date you choose."

Sir Humphrey guffawed, as if the challenge were worthless. But Margery saw the wariness he tried to conceal.

Gareth seemed ruthless, cold, a man who feared no one. But before it all he had been a child, and he'd been hurting, while she'd been spoiled and unthinking. She didn't remember even asking about his family, or how he felt about it. She hadn't a clue to anyone's problems but her own, and that selfishness now haunted her.

Gareth sat down and opened the book. Margery picked up her embroidery, but she couldn't stop herself from studying him, and wondering.

"Mistress Margery?" Lord George Wharton said.

She looked up into his aristocratic face, with its thin nose and arrogant eyes. She was unable to forget how frightened he'd been of Gareth. "Yes, Lord George?"

"My father the duke tells me that you have but two months left to announce your choice in husband. Is this so?"

At Lord George's pointed reference to his noble father, the room erupted in snickers and laughter. Even his younger brother, Lord Shaw, rolled his eyes.

Margery no longer dreaded making the announcement of her husband. Now that she had a plan, surely she could find the perfect man—she just hadn't decided yet exactly what kind of man she would need.

She glanced at Gareth, who watched her with narrowed eyes. Hadn't she told him that the king wouldn't wait forever for her to choose a husband? Had she been so embarrassed as she revealed all her problems to him, that this final humiliation had been forgotten?

"I have until the first day in October to name my husband," she answered Lord George, smiling as graciously as possible.

"And do you have a man in mind as of yet?"

Every pair of male eyes inspected her body as if they planned to buy her. She sat up straighter. Let them look—she would do the purchasing. "No, my lord. Do not tell me that is why you gracious gentlemen came to visit me."

Laughter traveled through the room.

"We came to celebrate your twentieth birthday," Lord George said. "The queen regretted that you would not be with her, and she wanted to make sure we gave you a party befitting her close friend. She is even sending her own minstrels."

A birthday party in her honor, where she would be doing much of the work. She didn't know who was more ignorant at times—the queen or men as a whole.

Margery couldn't stand to be with her suitors for another moment—and they'd only just arrived. She called her ladies together to retire briefly before supper. She could feel Gareth watching her leave, as if he actually touched her, but she refused to look at him. He would only want to accompany her, and she didn't want a man just now.

Once in her solar, Margery stood at the large glass window and looked out over the flatlands of the Severn Valley. Anne and Cicely stood beside her.

"Margery?" Anne finally said.

"Hmm?"

"What is wrong? Surely it must be wonderful to have so many men seeking your hand."

"It would seem so," she said, turning to smile at her friend. "But I must keep in mind that these men are looking for a suitable match to bring prestige and wealth to their families—which does not necessarily have much to do with me. Sometimes I feel like I am just an additional benefit—me and any child I would bear."

"Oh, no," Cicely said, touching Margery's arm. "You must not think that way."

"I'm trying not to." Margery smiled briskly. "That is why I brought you two with me. I need to plan my strategy."

"Strategy?" Anne echoed. "It sounds like you're marching off to war."

"I am, and 'tis time for a battle plan. I need to know exactly what kind of man I am looking for."

"Oh, that should be easy," Anne said, clapping her hands together. "Handsome and kind, well-spoken, strong—"

Margery interrupted. "I only agree with two of those. Of course I want a man who will be kind, and strong enough to take care of our family. But appearance and manner of speaking are not so important."

Cicely looked crestfallen.

"Ladies, we will be married to one man for all of our lives. Handsomeness won't last forever. I've been thinking of what I would like in a man. First, he shall be a nobleman."

"Oh, of course," Anne agreed

Cicely nodded.

"But only because I wish him to *stay* at court for much of the year."

Anne seemed puzzled for a moment before she smiled. "Ah, the prestige."

"No. I am simply used to running my own household and I do not want any interference. Besides, a husband needs to keep busy. I will tolerate no gambling or excessive drinking."

Cicely looked bewildered as she took a seat in a cushioned chair.

Margery pushed on. "He must be intelligent, but not too strong-willed. A husband should be content with a good life and a happy family, not roaming the countryside looking to battle."

"But Margery," Anne said tentatively, "what about love?"

She stared at their innocent faces, then turned her back to look out the window. She hated to disillusion them. "I made that mistake once before," she said softly. "From now on, it will not be my first consideration."

She would *never* fall in love again. With Peter Fitzwilliam, she had lost all control of herself and lived only to be with him. He'd had all the power in their relationship, and it had almost destroyed her.

She would have remained a lonely spinster— until she had finally come to her senses and realized that most men were no better than Peter. So now she would negotiate her own marriage. She would be a good wife, and never give her husband cause to regret his choice. But it would really be *her* choice.

Gareth stood outside the solar, his back against the wall, disgusted by Margery's words. Her cold-blooded plan only proved to him that he had been right all along. She was a woman who thought she could control every aspect of her life—and his, too. She hadn't even told him about this group of visiting suitors, or the king's insistence that she choose a husband by a certain date.

And for a husband, she wanted a weak-willed eunuch, a man who would dance attendance on her every word. The few times a month she'd let a husband bed her, she'd probably insist on being on top.

Margery's entire life had taught her that she could have anything she wanted—but not this time.

During supper, Gareth watched Margery pick at her food. As she spoke with the suitors arrayed across from her, her face was as animated as always, but there was a tension in her eyes.

His anger was still so strong that he wanted to drag her outside and demand to know why she had lied to him. How could she expect him to be an effective guard if he didn't know everything that was happening to her?

She stared into the distance, a pensive look on her face, while Gareth struggled to ignore his body's reaction to her. The servants began to clear away the last course. During the confusion of people leaving the table, Margery slipped away from her guests and down a side corridor. Had she already agreed to meet the first of her suitors privately?

Gareth followed her.

She led him outside into the fading sunlight of early evening, and disappeared into the chapel. He stepped behind a mound of hay near the stables to wait. No one else entered; what could she be doing?

The sun had set behind the curtain wall before she emerged again. She walked slowly, her head down, her hands clasped loosely before her. He stepped into view.

Margery stopped in obvious surprise, her lips parted, her eyes wary. "Gareth, is something wrong? What are you doing here?"

"Following you." He realized suddenly that he could say nothing to her about her behavior, no matter how she angered him. He had to win her favor.

She sighed and looked away. "I do not need your protection this night. I was just feeling overwhelmed by having so many guests."

"And you go to a chapel instead of the peace of your own bedchamber?"

She shrugged and began to walk again. He kept pace beside her, as the hard earth gave way to the gravel paths of the garden. They entered the gate to the lady's garden, and overhead apple and pear trees closed out the pale pink sky.

"Believe me, Gareth, I am grateful that these boys show an interest in me."

"Boys?" he repeated.

She smiled and shook her head. "Men. Forgive me. 'Tis just that they seem like boys fighting over a new toy."

"An accurate description." He took a deep breath and tried to sound relaxed. "I did not know of the king's request that you choose a husband soon."

Since a shrug was her only answer, her lies and their discovery must mean little to her. He wanted to shake out whatever truths she was still holding back. From her behavior, there had to be more.

Margery turned away from him and sat down on a small bench in the middle of tall stalks of columbines. She started to move her skirts aside, but he'd never fit there. Feeling awkward and annoyed, he lowered himself to sit at her feet.

"Gareth, I can make room for you. 'Tis too damp on the ground."

He ignored her words as he rested one elbow on the bench, his hand dangling close to her silk skirt. She bent toward him and he looked into the deep shadow between her breasts. His anger subsided into a distant grumble that was suddenly easier to ignore.

He couldn't even remember what they were talking about. Margery's perfume surrounded him, and he wanted nothing more than to taste her, to lose himself in the feel of her.

Chapter 10

Margery sat up straighter, her head above his, her face shadowed. "Forgive me for not telling you about the rest of the king's proclamation."

Gareth took a deep breath and looked down at his hand, grazed by her skirts. Then he lied, to further his plan for revenge. "There is nothing to forgive. It is a strange thing King Henry has done."

"He only wanted to help," she said, sighing. "He thought it would make me happy. I'm sure the king believed that making me choose by October would give me a husband sooner. But also," she added with a touch of sadness, "he could not afford to allow my lands to languish too long unsettled."

Gareth let his fingertips brush the cool silk of her dress. By the saints, even her skirt aroused him. "But instead, the king made you a target."

She nodded, biting her lip and looking down into her lap. He almost felt sorry for her.

"Then it is my duty to protect you."

"I do not like being your duty."

Margery said the words so softly that Gareth almost missed them.

He said, "I do not mean to sound as if my time here is a chore I must get through. It is a chance to renew our friendship, to remember some of the better moments in my life."

"You seem to have had few."

He heard sympathy in her voice, and it made his gut clench. He wanted to tell her that all his pain was because of her family, but even that was not the full truth. His own family curse threaded through every decision he'd ever made.

"Gareth, Sir Humphrey's cruelty cannot be borne. I'll make him leave, I'll—"

"You cannot punish a man for speaking the truth. There are things you don't know about me. Yes, my grandfathers killed their wives, one way or another. And my father—" His breath caught. He was too close to the truths in his life, and it was none of her business. "I do not know how that fire started. But I should never have left them. I knew he was drinking too much."

He was appalled and angry, as the words he hadn't meant to say spilled out of him. He usually held his emotions in such tight restraint, buried deep inside him. The weak words oozing from him like a slow blood loss, sickened him.

He hated her pity. He would rather have her afraid of him, even despise him.

Margery felt sorrow wash through her, overwhelming her caution. "Gareth, you were but eight years old! You were burdened with knowledge no child should have, and could have done nothing for your parents but be a good son to them. And you saved my life, which your parents would be proud of."

The garden was almost dark now. Gareth was a study in shadows before her, his hair still gleaming. Slowly he looked up into her face. He seemed to examine her every feature. She shivered when his gaze dropped to her chest.

This wasn't right. She felt again that shot of languid heat surge through her. Forbidden thoughts clawed at the edges of her mind. She felt wild, unrestrained, something she'd vowed to never let happen again.

This was Gareth, her personal guard. If he had been one of her suitors, she would have made him leave. He fit none of her requirements of the proper husband.

But still, she felt an intense, almost painful pleasure at having him so near to her. She wanted to lean into him. She had felt excitement and anticipation with Peter, but nothing compared to this overwhelming need to touch Gareth, to comfort him.

The proper side of her shouted *no* . . . but the

wickedness that had stolen into her these last few months slyly urged her on.

She let her trembling fingers thread into the soft hair above his ear.

She heard Gareth take a quick breath as his gaze rose to hers. Deep in those cold eyes she saw an awakening, answering heat.

He whispered her name in a hoarse voice.

Unable to stop herself, Margery slid her fingers through his hair again.

He came up onto his knees and gripped her arms. "You don't mean to do this."

But she did. Her wicked body yearned to be held against him, to feel the pleasure of his lips on hers. Their chests were separated by mere inches, their mouths by but a breath. If she slid forward, she could feel his body against hers.

Gareth needed her.

But was comfort enough? Was she just inventing any excuse to lose herself in the arms of a dangerously attractive man, to forget the empty marriage she would soon choose?

Tears stung Margery's eyes, and she pressed her hands against his chest. "Release me."

With only the barest hesitation, he did as she requested, sitting back on his heels to look at her. He must wonder what kind of woman she was.

He suddenly grimaced and brought both hands up to his head.

"Gareth?" she whispered, reaching out, but not trusting herself to touch him.

He shook his head. "I'm fine." His voice sounded weak. "My head aches, 'tis all."

After a moment, he put a hand on the bench beside her as if to steady himself. This couldn't be just an aching head.

"Perhaps the healer—" Margery began, but he interrupted.

"Do not worry yourself. I had too much to drink."

She knew that was a lie. Was he trying to pretend that what had almost happened between them was because of ale?

"Let us go in," she said.

They walked back inside, then stood awkwardly in a torchlit corridor. Margery clasped her hands together and met his gaze. "I cannot leave my guests without bidding them goodnight."

Gareth nodded. She thought his face looked pinched with strain.

"I shall not return to the great hall with you," he said. "It would look . . ."

She gave a hasty nod. "Thank you."

"A good night to you, Margery," he murmured.

When his gaze dropped to her lips, she felt a blush sweep across her face. She took a step back. "Good night, Gareth."

She knew he watched her until she reached the entrance to the hall. It made her feel safe and uncomfortable at the same time. After a few pleasantries with her suitors she escaped to her bedchamber, where she prayed for an end to this wildness inside her.

Gareth was the first person in the chapel before dawn. He'd searched his bags for that stone Margery had given him so long ago, but he still couldn't find it. It would be the perfect sentimental gift to woo her.

Things had gone surprisingly well in the garden last night. She was not unaffected by his presence, regardless of the revelation of part of the Beaumont Curse. She'd stood up to Townsend with more courage than he'd seen in many a man. Soon he'd be the only man she'd think of when she considered marriage. The prospect of bedding her certainly held no distaste for him.

But then he'd had another vision in front of her, reminding him of how little he really controlled. If this kept up, his headache excuse would no longer suffice. The same image had appeared as before—Margery seated on a horse before a shadowed man. Why couldn't he sense her emotions? Who was this man?

Margery arrived soon after, looking shocked to see him in the chapel. He wondered if she, too, had been thinking about their evening in the garden. He'd have to subtly remind her about it all day. He himself needed no other reminder than the smell of her perfume as she neared him. What it did to his insides was best not dwelt on in church.

She gave him a strained smile as she knelt beside him. Her suitors stumbled in one at a time, and it was obvious from their bleary faces that they'd drunk and gambled the night away.

After Mass, they went into the great hall to break their fast. Gareth watched Margery's face when she noticed the rose beside her plate, saw the half smile that touched her lips as she raised her gaze to his. Desmond was right, he grudgingly admitted again. Flowers helped.

He tried not to smile as she convinced all her young suitors that she'd keep busy while they spent the morning training at the tiltyard. He followed them outside, determined to show them all that if prowess mattered to Margery, then he had them beat. And maybe someone would think twice before trying to harm her.

But Gareth never had a chance that day to spar with any of her six suitors. He heard the words "Beaumont Curse" more than once, and felt many a disapproving eye on his back. He would be patient, because sooner or later one of them would want to test himself against his deadly reputation.

He had to admit that Humphrey Townsend had good reason to boast. His skills were exceptional, and even Desmond had a difficult time fighting him.

Before the noon meal, Margery and her ladies came outside, making themselves comfortable in the shade. Margery watched the men with a critical eye. Lord Seabrook held his shield too low. Sir Chester, never far from the influence of the Wharton brothers, rushed through his fight and almost was injured because of his carelessness.

She found fault with all six of her suitors, and told herself she was being too demanding. She could expect perfection from no man.

Her gaze occasionally sought Gareth. His back was to her, and he wore a plated brigantine to protect his chest. He wielded a blunt sword against one of her soldiers with a strength and skill that almost overwhelmed her, and made her feel glad to be a woman. He ducked a sword slash and whirled around, ready to fight—until he saw her. He stumbled to a halt and gave her the most devilish of grins.

My, he was good at courting her.

Though she kept trying to forget it, their evening in the garden rushed back to her. She remembered his hands gripping her arms, their bodies straining together but not quite touching. She had thankfully stopped herself from kissing him.

She told herself that her lapse in judgment was because he made her feel safe for the first time in months.

But of course she felt safe—she was paying him for that.

She wondered what would have happened if Gareth had not left Wellespring Castle all those years ago. The little girl inside her still remembered feeling betrayed when she had finally realized her friend would never return.

But there was no going back in time, wondering how things could have been different. She couldn't wish away her recent mistakes, either.

Margery watched the lists as mounted men began to gallop at the quintain, wielding blunted lances. More than one suitor had the whirling arm swing around and knock him to the ground. She kept a tally in her head.

When it was Gareth's turn, she shifted on her bench. He glowed under the sun, and the muscles of his arm rippled as he jousted with the quintain and galloped away unscathed.

"I wonder who you could be watching," a voice whispered in her ear.

Margery gave a start, then glanced casually at Cicely. "All of the men are very talented, are they not?"

"I quite agree." The young woman smiled demurely as she held her headdress in place against the breeze.

With a nod to her steward, Margery signaled the beginnings of the outdoor meal she'd planned. Trestle tables and benches were brought outside, and courses of food were laid out for the hungry men and all of her people.

Gareth found a place at a table away from her, and she watched the maidservants take special care that he was pleased. The women didn't seem at all concerned with this curse the men whispered about.

Sir Humphrey set down his plate opposite her and took a seat, blocking her view of Gareth. She gave the knight a strained smile as he expounded on his various training methods. She wanted to tell him she'd grown up with three brothers, but she held her tongue and pretended he was just fascinating. He was already off her list of possible husbands.

The knight's condescension on the subject of archery proved to be his undoing at the end of the meal. She smiled her prettiest.

"Sir Humphrey, I well understand a bow. It was my weapon of choice when I hunted with my brothers. But alas, I've been at court recently, and have not had the chance to practice."

Sir Humphrey's back straightened with ill-concealed self-importance. "I would be happy to assist you. I am quite skilled, you know."

"Really?" She dropped her napkin on the table as she stood. "Then let us practice now."

Sir Humphrey remained seated and gave her a patronizing smile. "Now, now, mistress, I'm sure you'd rather wait for a more private moment. I wouldn't want you to feel inferior to me in any way."

Margery barely controlled her temper. Inferior to him, indeed!

Gareth stood up. "I could use some practice with the bow."

She tried not to take pleasure at the thought of testing herself against him. "Why, Sir Gareth, I can't believe you are not proficient at every aspect of war."

"As a lad, I used to fish when I should have been using my bow."

She smiled as she remembered their afternoon fishing, so long ago. "I could give you some instruction at that, too."

Sir Humphrey scowled. "He is merely trying to win your attention, mistress."

"And aren't you?" she asked sweetly.

He gave a stiff bow and went back to his friends, who had already risen to come watch the competition.

Margery put her hands on her hips and glanced about, wondering if the bows were stored in the armory. Sure enough, Sir Wallace came out of that building, carrying two unstrung bows and a quiver of arrows, which he handed to Gareth.

Gareth stood beside her and strung the bows. He murmured, "Mistress, I hope you don't intend to abuse your poor guard."

"You'll only get what you deserve," she said, shivering at the husky tone of his voice. Her smile died as she gazed at him with narrowed eyes. He was behaving differently, no longer quite the cold, remote stranger he had been just a few days ago. He was almost . . . playful. It made her suspicious.

But perhaps she was *too* suspicious lately;

perhaps the last few months of her life had made her cynical. Surely he was finally relaxing into the friendship they had once shared.

Gareth watched Margery stroll away from him, the bow dangling from her hand. She looked over her shoulder, and her blue eyes glinted with mischief. The summer breeze ruffled her hair, and the sun pinkened her cheeks.

"As the challenger, you may go first, Sir Gareth."

He nodded and positioned himself across the tiltyard from the wooden targets, which rested against mounds of straw. They were shaped crudely like men, with a circle drawn over the man's heart. Gareth drew his arrow back.

Before he could release it, Margery walked behind him. "Are you sure you don't need my help? Your right elbow is low."

He realized she meant to distract him. Just like the rest of her family, she always had to win. Well, she might be skilled at Tables, but he would not let her win at games of war.

Yet she was so close to his back, if she took a deep enough breath, he'd feel her breasts. Sweat broke out on his brow. He refused to let himself be affected by her nearness. He was the one controlling this seduction, not her. But damn if he wasn't grateful he was wearing a longer tunic this day.

He blocked her from his mind and let fly his arrow. It just missed the heart, and there was a smattering of applause—from the women, he was certain.

Gareth lowered his arms and deliberately brushed his elbow against Margery's chest. She stepped away quickly. He raised his eyebrows in innocence, and she gave him a frown.

Then she lifted her bow. Just as she pulled back the string, he dropped to one knee in her line of sight and gazed at her with worshipful eyes. Actually, he was admiring the way her gown molded to her breasts as she aimed.

She glanced at him, and a little frown line appeared between her eyes. As she pulled back the string he let out a loud, lovesick sigh, and she jerked as the arrow was released. Though she hit the target, it was nowhere near the heart. With her back to the crowd, she glared at him.

"Mistress Margery," he said, "your form is just wondrous."

There was reluctant laughter from their audience.

"My arrow barely hit the target," she said dryly.

"I had not even noticed, mistress. Allow me to shoot again."

As he aimed, he felt her moving around behind him, and wondered more about what she was doing than where his arrow should go. Just as he concentrated and took serious aim, she appeared to his right, holding a strawberry tart to her lips. Her pink tongue licked at a stray crumb.

His arrow landed farther from the target heart, but not as far as hers.

She swallowed the last of the tart, then licked two of her fingers in a saucy manner before taking her bow from Desmond.

Chapter 11

Margery felt a wave of excitement which she could no longer ignore. How had an archery competition turned into something so . . . personal? Her heart was beating loudly in her ears, and her body seemed to vibrate with its own music whenever Gareth stepped near. Though she was suspicious of his motives, she couldn't deny that she felt more alive than she had in months.

As she took aim, she suddenly heard his voice close behind her.

"A little higher, Margery."

A shudder moved through her, centered low in her stomach. "Shh!"

"Such fire in your eyes."

Her arrow landed just outside the circle that represented the heart. She barely resisted the urge to stomp her foot in frustration. Even his voice affected her!

She moved briskly behind him. "Your turn, Sir Gareth. Shall I help you align your shot?"

Again she stood at his back. She ran her hand down his right arm to lift his elbow higher, feeling pleasure in touching him. As if encouraging him, she rested her hand on his shoulder. She was close enough to see sweat trickle down his temple, and she took satisfaction from it.

Then he let fly the arrow, and it hit one side of the heart. Margery wanted to groan. It would all come down to her last shot.

She picked up her bow and stepped into position. She fitted the arrow in place, pulling the string back toward her cheek. There was nothing stopping her from making a perfect shot, of which she knew she was capable. But a sudden movement at her left made her glance that way.

Gareth was smiling at her. His eyes seemed to glow, as if he knew her every secret, and none of it mattered.

It was all feigned. She *knew* it was. She crushed the warmth that lit her from the inside. He was only a guard who remained merely because she would be paying him.

Margery's arrow hit straw.

By God, he'd won. With a glower she could barely hide, she watched him make his way back to her side, then stand close enough that their sleeves brushed.

He pointedly looked at the target. "I don't see your arrow," he said in an amused voice.

"A fly bit me."

He chuckled. "Is that your excuse?"

"No excuses."

As Gareth went to the table and took a slice of cake from the giggling twins, Margery saw Sir Humphrey giving Gareth a venomous stare.

A chill moved through her, darkening the day and her confidence. Gareth's presence was supposed to keep her safe, not endanger him.

She was distracted by a rider on horseback emerging from the gatehouse. Shielding her eyes from the sunlight, she felt her stomach clench when she recognized the colors the man was wearing. He was a servant of Viscount Peter Fitzwilliam: the one man who knew all her shameful secrets. With just a well-placed word, Peter could guarantee that she was never again accepted by her friends at court, that her brothers would be disappointed and dishonored by her. She didn't need this, just when she'd finally decided on a course for her life. Her hands started trembling, and she clutched them together.

The servant dismounted before her and gave a little bow. He held out a folded piece of parchment, sealed with the wax symbol of the earldom of Kent.

"From Lord Fitzwilliam," the man said, his high-pitched voice a startling contrast to his wide, stocky body.

Unnerved, Margery let him put the letter into her hands. The man turned around and remounted his horse.

Her eyes widened. "Come, sir, surely you would like a meal for your effort. And does not the letter require a reply?"

"No time, mistress. Lord Fitzwilliam did not ask me to wait for your answer. Good day." He wheeled the horse about and trotted toward the gatehouse.

Feeling stunned, she looked down at the missive. She should retire to her bedchamber and read in private, but waiting even another moment would make her dread escalate sharply. She ripped open the wax seal. She had once thought the familiar handwriting boldly enthusiastic; now it just looked arrogant.

Peter was with the king in the north, and sent greetings from her brothers. Just knowing that Reynold and James were spending time with him made her dinner sour in her stomach. Nowhere did he mention the things they'd done together, but she thought she could feel it behind every sentence. He didn't beg her forgiveness—not that she would have given it.

She continued reading in mounting disbelief as Peter inquired blandly about her health. He wrote as if they were casual acquaintances, not two people who had lain together, who had almost married.

Then her hands shook as she discovered the true purpose of the letter. Now that the pretender to the throne had been defeated at Stoke, Reynold and James were coming to visit her on their journey home, and Peter thought he might travel with them.

She should be happy that her brothers were safe, that they had sent her warm greetings through Peter. She wanted to look forward to their visit. But how could she, knowing that Peter might be there? What possible reason could he have to come, unless he meant to expose her?

Gareth sat at the table, watching Margery frown over the letter. At first he ignored the low conversation among her suitors, until he realized that they were discussing the delivery of the letter.

"I tell you," said Townsend, "he wore Fitzwilliam's livery."

The Earl of Chadwick, who so far had proved himself a decent, quiet man—and a threat to Gareth's courtship—shook his head. "It cannot be. He and Mistress Margery are no longer speaking."

Gareth leaned forward for another bite of cake, trying not to be obvious as he strained to listen.

"It was rumored they would definitely marry," said Lord Seabrook tentatively.

The Wharton brothers exchanged glances. The eldest, Lord George, said, "Fitzwilliam himself told me he was no longer pursuing her—and he was damned mysterious about why."

Gareth looked once more at Margery, who

stared at the gatehouse, the letter crumpled in her hand. With all his plans, he had never considered that she had had a serious suitor, that she'd come close to marrying.

But what could have happened that made her look so forlorn on reading Fitzwilliam's letter? And why, suddenly, did he care about Margery's sorrow? Surely it was because Fitzwilliam was a threat to his own seduction of her. He didn't need a rival who had the advantage of a prior relationship.

Margery spent the afternoon spinning thread with her ladies and maidservants in her solar. She put Peter's letter from her mind as best she could. After all, she had been living with the threat of him for months now. She refused to let him affect her plans for marrying the perfect husband. Instead, she listened to the castle gossip about her suitors and how each treated his servants.

Twice, Gareth passed by the open doorway, but he never came in. He distracted her, made her wonder about this curse and his more relaxed behavior.

Just before supper, she sent a page to find out where Gareth had been keeping himself for the afternoon. The boy, without even the first fuzz of manhood on his chin, stammered as he told her that Gareth was in the library.

Margery nodded and dismissed him, looking speculatively down the corridor toward the room. Not very far away after all. As she neared the room, she heard the sound of women's voices, and found Anne and Cicely sitting across the table from Gareth. When they looked up and saw her, their gazes slid away with guilty haste.

The library was darkly paneled, hung with portraits and landscapes. One wall contained shelves of rare bound books. There was a table and comfortable chairs, even a desk where her steward sometimes worked on the castle ledgers.

Gareth seemed to make the room his own, books spread out before him, his manner confident. Margery hated the momentary doubts that gnawed at her, that made her wonder if he had another motive besides her protection. She'd never had thoughts like this before Peter had destroyed her trust.

"Mistress Margery," Gareth said, leaning back in his chair. "I was just having an interesting conversation with your two ladies."

"Pertaining to what?" she asked.

Both Anne and Cicely got to their feet.

"You can have my chair, Margery," Cicely said, taking hold of her sister's arm. "We have much to accomplish before supper."

"And what could that be?" Margery asked.

They didn't answer as they disappeared down the corridor.

She rested her hands on the table and leaned

forward. "Sir Gareth, may I ask why you are working your wiles on my ladies?"

"My wiles?" he repeated. "I have no motives—other than information."

"What kind of information would that be?" she asked, sitting down opposite him at the table.

"About you, of course."

She kept a smile on her face as a shiver of apprehension worked its way up her back.

"Your ladies told me about how the three of you were attacked in the glen before I arrived."

"It was nothing," she said, lowering her gaze to hide her relief.

"Nothing? It was so 'nothing' that you had to struggle to escape. No, no, wait," he said, lifting a hand. "I think Anne said it better. Her exact words were, 'Margery kicked him *there.*' "

She was unable to decide if he was amused or angry. "It worked."

"How did you learn to do that?"

"My brothers."

"Did you tell them how well it had succeeded?"

She didn't answer.

"Of course not. You did not even tell your brothers the kind of trouble you're in, did you?"

"I could not," she said. "You don't know what it's like to be a woman, Gareth, and to finally be given a taste of freedom. Do you think I wanted to be locked up in some remote castle for my protection? Besides, my brothers are with the army."

"But now you have me," he said in a low voice. He remained silent for a moment, his stare skeptical. "Why do you sometimes go to the chapel twice a day?" he asked suddenly.

Her face heated. "I—"

"I think 'tis all related. The attacks, and this thing you pray for."

"I pray for the protection of my people, and for mercy from God."

"Mercy for them—or for you?"

Gareth watched Margery's face turn a sickly white. He gripped the arms of his chair and remained still, waiting for a grain of truth. He felt as if he uncovered another of her lies every day.

There was more going on in Hawksbury Castle than her decision about a husband. Peter Fitzwilliam's letter had something to do with it, but it would be awkward to ask her about a man she'd almost married. He didn't want her to think he could possibly be jealous.

"We are all sinners," she said in a low voice. "Even you."

The blueness of her accusing eyes pierced him like an arrow, but he felt no guilt in his attempt to marry Margery. His revenge was justified. Still, he was uncomfortable. Did she suspect something?

"I make no pretensions to sainthood," he

said. "I am farther from heaven than most. But my ability to protect you is hampered if you do not tell me the truth."

She sighed. "Gareth, the only truth is that I didn't want you to worry about me more than you already do. I feel smothered sometimes— by you, by Sir Wallace, and especially by these men who feel they have every right to come to my home to inspect me like a new purchase."

"Let me help you make the decision. I know something of each of these men by now."

She shoved back her chair and began to pace. "The choice of my husband was first my father's, then my brothers', then the king's—and now you want it as well? Am I not intelligent enough to make my own decisions?"

"You know that is not what I mean," he said. "But I can see these men in a way they won't show you. On the tiltyard, they reveal themselves to anyone who pays attention to the signs. Humphrey Townsend—"

"—is a greedy braggart," she finished angrily. She stood above him, hands on her hips. "And my woman's heart senses even more— that you put yourself in danger by crossing him."

"Crossing him?" Gareth echoed, leaning back in his chair to study her. She was worried about him? This must be a good sign.

"Mayhap you were too busy trying to win with your bow this afternoon, but I saw Sir

Humphrey's face when you defeated me. Don't you see that now you stand in his way?"

"That's where I should be." He came to his feet in anger. "Between you and other men. I am your shield, Margery," he said, catching hold of her upper arms, "not the other way around. I know what I am doing."

Her head dropped back, and he saw that the anger had drained from her face. "But I don't want you hurt in this mess," she whispered.

He gave her a little shake. "What mess? Does it have something to do with the letter you received today?"

She let out a strangled gasp, then pressed her lips together.

Gareth searched her face, thinking she was too stubborn. "I overheard the men say it was from Peter Fitzwilliam."

"He was sending greetings from my brothers," she said in an emotionless voice. "That is all."

He wanted to ask what kind of a man Fitzwilliam was, why she'd almost married him. But a tear fell from her eye and ran down her cheek, and he suddenly felt an overwhelming need to protect her from whatever she feared. She would soon be his wife, he told himself. Nothing would harm her. He drew her against his chest and put his arms around her.

Her dark curls seemed to wrap themselves around his arms. The merest thought of another man near her made him primitive with anger. He alone would win her.

Her hands slid up his back, and in a heart-beat, his anger and possessiveness blazed into unexpected passion. Her breasts were pressed against his chest, her breath fanned his neck, their thighs brushed together. She suddenly looked up at him, eyes wide, lips parted. He could see her moist tongue, could imagine the feel of it rasping against his skin. He pressed his lips to her temple. She gave a soft gasp and arched against him. He wanted to grasp her hips and pull her even harder against him.

He waited an endless moment, his lips just above hers, both of them breathing raggedly. He needed to plunder her mouth, to lose him-self in the mystery that was Margery.

But it was too soon. A hurried kiss was not in the careful plan he had created to win her to wife.

She broke from his arms, stumbling back un-til she bumped into the table. "Forgive me," she whispered, tears etching her cheeks. "It is cruel of me to use you for my own comfort."

"Margery, 'tis my fault." He reached out a hand.

"No, no, Gareth, it isn't you, never think that. 'Tis all me. Now do you see why I pray?"

She ran from the room. Gareth felt satisfied that she turned to him for comfort, but frus-

trated that he still hadn't discovered her secrets.

A shadow suddenly darkened the doorway,
and he looked up. Wallace Desmond stood
there, his face serious and cold.

Chapter 12

Gareth waited in resignation for Desmond to speak.

Desmond stepped into the room and closed the door. He eyed the books on the table, then Gareth. "I didn't know an embrace was one of the duties of a personal guard."

"This is none of your concern, Desmond," he said in a low voice.

"Then I'll make it my concern. What is going on?"

Gareth refused to answer. He walked past Desmond, but the man caught his arm.

"You have become close to Margery, Beaumont," Desmond said, his narrowed blue eyes determined. "This is not a crime. But I don't like secrets being kept from me—or her."

Gareth gritted his teeth until his jaw ached. To trust Desmond with the truth went against everything he'd experienced in a life full of betrayals. Yet the man had not betrayed him so far, and he could have made trouble for Gareth if he wanted to.

"I have decided I want to marry her," he said stiffly.

Desmond released his arm, then rolled his eyes. "Then just ask her! Why do you keep this to yourself?"

"Besides the danger to Margery, there is something she's not telling me, some secret I can't trust," Gareth said slowly, trying to rein in his temper. "How can I announce my changed intentions, and have her include me with all the other men she distrusts? Hell, I'm landless and close to poverty—two attributes that make me unsuitable to a lady." He was powerless to stop the words pouring from him. "She and her family sent me away when I was a child because I wasn't the right sort of 'friend' for her. She needs to learn to trust me again. Then I know she'll want to marry me."

Gareth took a deep breath and looked into Desmond's astonished eyes. He wouldn't blame the man if he ran out laughing, if he told the entire castle about Gareth's need to marry into a family that had rejected him.

Desmond gave him a crooked smile. "I've never seen this side of you. Did it make you feel better to confide in me?"

"No."

Desmond laughed. "I swear it helps. You talk about Margery not trusting you, but you can't trust anyone, can you?"

Gareth closed his eyes and forced down his impatient anger. Someday Desmond would learn that a man could only trust himself. "Are you going to stand in my way? Margery is looking for a husband, and you cannot be unaware of her charms."

Desmond shook his head. "Have no fear, Gareth. I would not go against a friend. But be careful; it is a dangerous game to ask a woman to trust you while you lie to her."

Gareth opened his mouth, then closed it angrily. Desmond was heir to a barony and a decent inheritance. How could he possibly understand what it felt like to be desperate, to know that one family had stolen his only chance at happiness?

After a sleepless night, Margery was angry at herself. Over and over she replayed her actions with Gareth. How had an argument led to being held in his arms? Yes, he had begun the embrace, but she had let herself sink against his body as if starved for a man's attention.

None of this was part of her plan! Gareth was certainly not the perfect man for her. He could be kind when he wanted to, but contentment would never be one of his virtues. He was strong-willed—and he was dangerous. She could not control her feelings when she looked into those golden eyes. She would find a man who didn't make her feel wild, reckless;

a man whom she wouldn't mind lying to.

She imagined Gareth's face when she told him her sins, told him she couldn't bear children. She felt ill just imagining the contempt and disgust he would try to hide.

So why did she keep allowing him to touch her? She could still feel his thighs against hers, his chest a solid wall of strength.

Margery reminded herself that she had employed him for his strength and skill. Of course she admired those qualities—but from now on, she had better admire them from a distance.

When Gareth faced Desmond at the tiltyard the next morning, he wondered what to expect. Would the man now feel free to intrude on Gareth's private concerns, to discuss his pursuit of Margery as if he were entitled?

The day was hot and damp, and he needed to battle out his frustrations, not talk about Margery. His training partner merely grinned, hefted his sword, and began the attack. Gareth wanted peaceful silence, but Desmond could easily talk and fight at the same time. Gareth sighed as he listened to Desmond discuss the castle defenses, Margery's suitors, anything that seemed to surface in his cluttered mind between grunts of exertion. Gareth attacked harder and harder, but still Desmond had enough wind to prattle on.

He suddenly realized that Desmond had mentioned Margery's plans for the day.

"What?" Gareth said, ducking away as the sword arced past his head.

Desmond laughed. "I knew you were not listening."

"If I listened to everything you said, my mind would explode." Gareth parried away Desmond's sword. "Did you say that Margery wants to eat a meal in the glen?" He crashed his sword down toward Desmond's head, and watched him use his shield to parry it. "You just want to get rid of me so you don't have to fight."

Desmond gasped for breath and slashed with his own blunt sword. "Not . . . true. Remember, I train . . . all day, while you . . . pick flowers."

Gareth drove him back, until Desmond came up flat against the curtain wall. He heard a whistle of wind only a moment before he had time to knock Desmond's sword aside.

"You're good," Gareth said, stumbling toward Desmond's right.

Desmond crouched and held his sword before him. "You are too easily distracted these days."

Desmond was right, and it was all because of Margery. Gareth straightened and let his sword dangle. He looked toward the castle, wondering what she was doing. They hadn't spoken since the previous afternoon. He'd pushed too hard about her secrets, even though he knew she didn't yet trust him. In penance, he'd left flowers by her plate again this morn.

Desmond came up beside him and put a hand on his shoulder. "My friend, I've been thinking."

"Instead of talking?" Gareth asked dryly. "I am amazed."

Desmond laughed. "Why do you not declare yourself her true suitor? I think she would welcome it, and you would not have to lie anymore."

Gareth shook his head. "We discussed this yesterday. Nothing has changed."

"I heard what they've been saying about this family curse of yours. Why didn't you tell me before? It explains why you came to France, why you're lying to Margery. If I don't hold your ancestors' deeds against you, she won't."

"You don't have to marry me," Gareth said coldly. "Nor do you have to convince your brothers to accept me with all my poverty." He shrugged Desmond's hand off his shoulder and forced a smile. "I have an outing to prepare for."

Late in the morning the servants set off for the glen, driving carts loaded with provisions, even pavilions in case of rainfall. Gareth, mounted on his stallion, looked up at the bright sky and hazy sun. Perfect courting weather.

Squires dressed in the colors of their lords

stood ready with the horses. Margery and her ladies and suitors descended from the great hall in a boisterous group. Gareth watched them take up their reins, saw who bothered to thank his servant. Already he knew how well each man fought. Now he just had to talk to them. Surely he could find a good· reason for Margery to dismiss every one of these men as unsuitable.

He settled on Rutherford Norton, the Earl of Chadwick, as his first target. The man seemed quiet and easygoing, which perfectly matched Margery's definition of a husband. Perhaps he hated court politics, and would never leave Margery's side. Then she'd be burdened with Chadwick every day of her life.

By the time they reached the clearing Margery had chosen, Gareth could hardly stay awake in the saddle. Lord Chadwick cared mostly about farming and chess. All he needed was a brood mare to continue his line—and he *loved* court politics. Gareth would have to keep Margery away from this "ideal" man.

During their conversation, Gareth had brought up Fitzwilliam. Lord Chadwick said he and all his friends were late to court Margery, because they thought it inevitable that she would be betrothed to the heir to the earldom of Kent. Chadwick had confided that earlier in the year Margery and Fitzwilliam had seemed on good terms, but something went wrong in their relationship, opening the door for Chadwick and his friends.

Gareth remembered her frightened face when she'd looked at Fitzwilliam's letter. Whatever had happened, he didn't think the worst was over. But how to get her to confide in him?

Margery pulled her horse to a stop, closed her eyes, and just breathed deeply of the summer breeze and the scents of wildflowers. The gelding moved restlessly beneath her, and she patted its neck as she opened her eyes.

She could now see the reason for the animal's distress—suitors were rushing at her from all sides, their hands lifted, all wanting to help her dismount. She sighed, tempted to kick her horse into a gallop and escape to ride blissfully alone. But no, there were still so many men she had to converse with. She allowed Lord George to help her to the ground.

Soon she and her ladies were seated on blankets, the men sprawled out all around them in the grass. She ate her meat pie and sipped her wine and tried not to notice how Gareth sat apart from everyone, how little anyone except she or the twins spoke to him. She could not believe that grown men gave any credence to a superstitious curse.

What must it be like to be shunned, not for anything he'd done, but because of his lineage? Should her sins become public, she, too, would be shunned. But she would never be able to handle it with the arrogant self-assurance Gareth did.

She watched the breeze lifting his blond hair, his solid body clothed in that plain brown tunic. My lord, she'd forgotten all about his wardrobe again. He deserved a new garment for this birthday party the queen had planned for her.

Margery turned her attention back to the men around her. She chose the government as her topic of conversation, and listened closely to each of her suitors. Many of them said they would prefer to be home with their wives instead of at court. Surely they were saying what they thought she wanted to hear, so she kept asking questions, hoping at least one man might slip and tell the truth. Finally Lord George, the duke's son, admitted he had a fondness for London.

As she continued to chip away at her suitors' politics, she kept watch on Anne, who walked the edge of the clearing with Lord Shaw. For a brief while she couldn't see Gareth, but then he reappeared through the trees. He spread marigolds at her feet with a bow.

"Mistress Margery," he said, "I searched far and wide to find flowers to match your beauty, but as you can see, I did not succeed."

She made an attempt at a cool smile. "So you have been my secret gardener these last few days?"

He bowed. Behind him, she saw men rolling

their eyes or shaking their heads. She knew they must secretly wish they had come up with such a romantic gesture.

Romance was not something she would care for in her perfect husband. That would require too much of his attention—and might involve love.

She had thought Peter romantic until she realized it was all physical; that he wanted only her body, not her heart and mind and soul.

"Mistress Margery!" called Sir Chester, a man who did his best to hover near the duke's two sons. "I believe we should play a game."

She was grateful for the distraction. "Very well, Sir Chester, what do you suggest?"

"A game of chase, mistress, like a fox hunt. Only you could be the prize."

Everyone laughed as Margery nodded her head. "I hope you mean that a moment of my company would be the prize."

The knight reddened. "Oh, of c-course. I did not mean to imply—"

She lifted a hand. "I understand, Sir Chester. I feel quite youthful today, so a child's game suits me. My ladies and I will await you gentlemen among the trees. Do promise to give us a suitable start."

Sir Humphrey got to his feet. "And how shall we catch you, mistress?" he asked, his lips twisted in a sly smile.

"How?" she repeated, wishing he didn't make her feel so uncomfortable.

"If we see you, do we win?"

"That seems a bit too easy." She opened her purse, then pulled forth a lace scarf and tucked it into her belt. "The one who has this, wins."

Margery saw Gareth frown as all the men roared their approval. Did even a game of chase seem too dangerous to him?

"But I cannot promise which lady will have the token," she said quickly.

That did not appease Gareth. "Mistress Margery, perhaps your servants could roam the outer trees of the glen, to alert us to any strangers."

She gave her approval, but when her guests returned to court, they would most likely talk. What would King Henry think if his noblemen reported that Margery lived in fear of an attack? All choices would be taken from her, and she'd be brought back to court.

She rose to her feet, motioned the servants to scatter, then led Anne and Cicely toward the edge of the clearing.

She turned back to the men, who were already waiting to follow. "Give us some moments alone, my lords," she said, smiling sweetly as she lifted the scarf from her belt. "I wonder which of us will have this?"

With a final wave, they walked deeper into the woods, until the sun only crossed the path in dappled shades. When they were no longer in sight of the men, they picked up their skirts and began to run.

Margery laughed with a sudden breathless excitement. "Ladies, which of you would like the scarf?"

"You keep it!" Anne said, already veering away on her own. "They'll expect you to pass it off."

"Very well!" Margery called, climbing up an embankment and into a dense growth of trees. "Enjoy yourselves!"

Soon she was alone but for the sounds of her own breathing and the chattering of squirrels. She ran faster, determined to be the last one caught.

Soon enough she heard the men laughing and calling to one another. Heedless of her gown, she crouched on her knees in the densest copse of trees and felt a rush of excitement when she was passed by. Moments later she finally felt safe enough to stand.

As she leaned around a tree to spy on her opponents, she felt a presence at her back. Before she could even take a breath, she was caught about the waist, and a hand covered her mouth.

" 'Tis me," the voice whispered.

Margery recognized Gareth and sagged in his grip. He removed his hand from her mouth, but didn't let her go.

"Gareth—"

"Shh! Sir Humphrey stalks you," he whispered.

She listened to the occasional crack of a twig

and the rustle of long grass. But her sense of hearing was soon overwhelmed by her sense of touch. She tried mightily not to feel his hips against her backside, not to notice that his arm rested just beneath her breasts—but her heart began a mad thump. She couldn't allow this to happen again.

"Is he gone?" she whispered.

Gareth removed his arm from around her waist. "I think we have successfully eluded him," he murmured, and his breath stirred her hair.

She turned in the closeness of the trees and looked up at him. He gave her a slow smile as his gaze dropped below her face.

Margery stiffened. "And what are you looking at, Sir Gareth?"

"The token in your belt," he answered, then glanced back to her face. "Should I be looking at something else?"

She felt a blush sweep her cheeks, and she couldn't find words to answer. She was being a foolish girl.

"Does this mean I won?" He leaned against a tree and crossed his arms over his chest.

She glowered at him as she handed over the scarf.

His voice softened. "Do you remember when last we played this game of chase?"

"I remember chasing you about the court-yard many times. I even won a few."

He gave her a lazy grin, the one that always shocked her with its rarity.

"Oh, I imagine you think you *let* me win," Margery said.

He arched a golden eyebrow. "I was a few years older."

"But I had intelligence."

He chuckled and she quickly covered his mouth with her hand.

"Sir Humphrey could still be about!" she whispered.

They froze, listening. She had leaned one arm against his chest, and her hand on his lips felt so warm, bathed in his breath. She looked up into his face. His humor had fled, leaving that spark of intoxicating danger in his eyes. What was it about him that called to her, that drew her toward emotions she'd vowed to deny?

She yanked her hand away and stumbled back a step. She looked about and saw no one but the two of them in the dense greenery of trees.

Gareth moved beside her as they began to walk. "The last time we played chase was in the forest outside Wellespring Castle."

She sighed. "I remember being terribly frightened, but feeling safe, too. It has not been easy for me to think on those moments with you, because I still feel guilty that my father was dying at the same time."

He hesitated before he said, "I understand."

They came upon a brook meandering between rocks, glittering wherever the sun touched it through the shadow of trees. There were pools and rippling shallows, and the sounds of water falling. It was so very soothing to her frayed nerves.

She smiled at Gareth, and saw a blur of pink moving on the edges of their little clearing. Keeping her expression as normal as possible, she said, "What other games did we play in the forest?"

Before he could answer, the pink blur became shy Cicely, running with all her might. She snatched the token out of Gareth's hand, and as he reached for her, Margery mischievously pushed him into the brook. But at the last second he gripped Margery's wrist, and with a shriek she fell on top of him.

Chapter 13

G areth's backside hit the stone bed of the brook, and Margery came down on top of him. The water splashed over them on its way down to the Severn River. He held her there, letting her feel the way their legs entwined and their hips met—letting his own arousal awaken his senses.

Margery's hair slapped across his face in a sodden mass, getting into his mouth and tickling his nose. Grinning, he heaved her to one side, and she rolled facefirst into the water. She came up on her hands and knees, gasping and spitting.

Gareth started to laugh. Seldom-used muscles in his throat and chest soon ached with the effort, but he couldn't help himself. The normally pristine, regal, perfect Margery Welles was a muddy disaster.

He vaguely saw Lady Cicely waving the scarf in triumph, then the duke's two sons emerged from the undergrowth to chase her into the trees.

Gareth struggled to his feet, his tunic streaming water. He turned to help Margery, but she pushed his hand away and crawled ashore, her dripping skirts clinging to her legs.

"I hope you realize," she said, gasping as she flopped onto her back in the grass, "that a gentleman would not laugh."

"I have never claimed to be a gentleman." He tried to speak solemnly, but the corners of his lips kept twitching uncontrollably.

He sat down beside her and started wringing the water from his sleeves, seeing from her expression that she was trying hard not to laugh herself. He didn't think it wise just yet to inform her that her face was smeared in mud, and that a fern leaf was caught in her hair.

Margery sniffed and wiped her arm across her face. "You could have *pretended* to be a gentleman and not pulled me in after you." When she saw the mud on her sleeve, she moaned.

"You could have been a lady and not pushed me."

She shrugged and closed her eyes, leaning back on her hands until the sun shone on her face. "I was simply shocked that Cicely—not Anne!—had thrown herself so completely into the game, and I wanted to help her."

Gareth dropped back on his elbows, gazing at Margery's wet, clinging gown. The pale yellow fabric molded to every curve, from her

hardened nipples down to the indentation between her thighs. The impulse to cover her
body with his was suddenly overwhelming.

He came up on one hand and leaned over
her. All he had to do was remove a piece of
her clothing—almost any piece—and let themselves be discovered. The game would be over
and she'd be his, married as soon as the banns
could be read. She desired him; he knew it.
What would she do if he licked the moisture
from her skin?

She frowned. "Gareth, what are you doing?"

Yet he didn't have her trust. He needed her
to choose him as her husband, to stand against
her brothers.

"Forgive me, mistress. I sometimes forget I
am a paid servant."

"Do not say that," she murmured, looking
up at him so earnestly. "We are also friends."

"Even after what happened yesterday?"

She remained silent, and Gareth waited,
searching her face.

"I was as much at fault as you," she finally
whispered. "You were only trying to comfort
me. I was distraught and overwhelmed at
having too many choices for husband."

"I think it is more than that. What pain do
you hide, Margery?"

He lightly brushed her hair from her cheek.
She stared almost wildly at him as her eyes
filled with tears.

"Tell me," he whispered. He cupped her face

in one hand, wiping a tear away with his thumb. She closed her eyes and bit her trembling lip, and more tears escaped. He looked down into her beautiful face, so full of sorrow, and something painful lurched inside his chest.

Then familiar anger bubbled back to life inside him, and he was relieved. He could trust nothing Margery said or did. Maybe this behavior was just her way to soften a man.

She rolled away from him and rose unsteadily to her feet. "We should return and see who won." She plucked at her skirts. "My, this is heavy."

Gareth got to his feet and caught up with her.

When they finally reached the clearing where everyone else had already gathered, Margery moved farther away from him. Conversations stopped and every gaze fastened on them.

"I'm all right," she said. "I fell in the water, and Sir Gareth rescued me."

She put on a good performance, marching across the clearing with abused dignity. Her suitors surrounded her, asking what they could do.

Lady Cicely finally approached him, her smile tentative, a blanket in her hands. "Sir Gareth, please accept my apologies. In my haste to win, I did not think of the consequences to you."

He wrapped the blanket about his shoulders.

"No lasting consequences, Lady Cicely. Did you win?"

"Lord Shaw caught me and the token," she admitted, a faint blush staining her freckled cheeks.

His gaze returned to Margery, and he was distracted again, wondering how Peter Fitzwilliam was connected to her secrets.

At Mass the next morning, Margery immediately noticed that Gareth was missing. She was almost through eating her morning meal when he finally entered the great hall. He was again wearing that leather jerkin he trained in, but this time he had done without the shirt. His muscled arms were tan from the sun. Though his hands seemed best suited to holding weapons, now they held wildflowers of all colors. The blossoms dropped from his arms, trailing across the hall behind him.

Margery sat back in surprise as he strewed her table with flowers. They fell into her goblet, across her plate, and into her lap.

"Did I not see these near the clearing where we ate yesterday?" she asked, feeling flustered and touched, and trying not to show it.

"Yes, mistress," Gareth said. "I had to have them for you. I must confess, I couldn't quite remember where I had seen them, so I had to search. Forgive me for being late."

She was well aware of the grumbling of her

suitors, some in amusement, some in disdain. "Thank you for your gift," she said softly.

He sat down at the end of the head table, and she watched as three giggling maidservants converged on him at once, offering food.

Before the meal was through, she managed to whisper a message to one of the servants, asking Gareth to join her in the sewing rooms. It was time to follow through on her promise.

When Gareth finally arrived, Margery looked up from the work table where she was cutting out garments. There were many tables, spread with the different fabrics needed for every kind of servant, from soldiers to serving maids to kitchen boys.

Her seamstresses stopped working to stare at Gareth, and Margery tried to pretend that it was not admiration but shock at having a knight invade their domain.

"Ethel," Margery called to the woman in charge, "Sir Gareth lost his trunks on the crossing from France, and I offered to provide him with a few new items of clothing. Would you measure him to begin?"

Ethel was a woman of middle-age, graying, stoop-shouldered from cutting and sewing fabric all day. Her manner was brisk as she circled Gareth.

"Aye, mistress, we can help the lad. Go on about yer duties."

"I'd like to help pick out the colors and—"

Ethel gave her a disapproving frown. " 'Tisn't

right that a lady be with a man discussin' such
a subject. Go on with ye, now."

Margery thought Gareth gave her a rather
irritated look as two more women circled and
studied him. She could only shrug and back
out into the corridor. Since no one else was
about, she lingered, peeking in as the women
held up cut pieces of fabric for size. He would
look handsome no matter what his garment.

A hand suddenly covered her mouth. Margery gave a muffled scream, but already the
man was dragging her backward. She tried to
dislodge his arm, even caught her heels in the
floorboards. Panic overwhelmed her and she
flailed helplessly.

They didn't go far. He dragged her into the
garderobe and shut the door. Only then was
she turned around to face Sir Humphrey
Townsend. He grinned at her.

"What is the meaning of this?" she demanded, backing up against the wall.

The knight shrugged. "I don't mean to hurt
you, Mistress Margery. I never get a moment
of your time, and Beaumont always does. How
does he manage that, I wonder?"

"This isn't an abduction?" she asked in
shock.

"Of course not. I just needed some time to
convince you that I am the perfect husband."

She didn't know whether to laugh or hit him.
"Do you think it is romantic to bring me into
the *garderobe*? The smell alone—" She broke off,

red-faced, trying to look anywhere but at the two holes near the far wall.

Sir Humphrey glanced around and had the decency to seem embarrassed. "I guess this was not the best location."

"No, it most certainly was not. And the *manner* in which you brought me here—" She took a deep breath, controlling herself, knowing that she shouldn't anger him.

Sir Humphrey stepped nearer. He wasn't very tall, but he was broad and muscular. He gave her a cajoling smile. "Now, Margery, can you not see how much passion I feel for you?"

As he slid his hand along her arm, Margery pressed so close to the wall she could feel the indentations of the mortar. Her panic was returning. Was this his clumsy attempt to compromise her? Clumsy or not, it could actually work.

Just as the knight took another step closer, and she was thinking of making a dash for freedom, the door slammed open.

Gareth stood there, hands on his hips, looking as cold and dangerous as ever. Margery sagged with relief, then worried that there would be immediate bloodshed. She didn't want anyone hurt.

"Townsend," Gareth said, "did you wish to speak with me? I saw you lingering outside the sewing room."

Sir Humphrey's face was mottled with red

and white splotches. "Beaumont, leave now while you can."

"Leave? I cannot do that." Gareth turned to Margery. "Mistress, Ethel would like to speak to you. It seems I am hopeless about the colors to choose for the garments. Remember to let me know the price."

"Of course. I'll go now," she said quickly. She didn't even look at Sir Humphrey as she escaped. She knew she should run as far away as she could, but she was curious to see how Gareth handled the situation. She had never thought he would be the kind of man who could moderate his reaction, manipulate a situation to his own advantage. She was still impressed that he was able to play the suitor while being her guard. She hid in a doorway, out of their sight.

"Beaumont, you should not have interfered," Sir Humphrey said in a sneering voice. "I was only doing what we all are trying to do—especially you, in your poverty."

She expected Gareth to defend himself, but he simply laughed. "At least I am doing it more subtly, Townsend. In your ignorance, you frighten Margery and leave the way open for me."

Margery was beginning to wish she hadn't stayed. Gareth's voice sounded so different, so amused and cold at the same time. She told herself it was all part of his act; if he'd wanted her money in truth, he could have compromised her a half dozen times by now. But he wouldn't do such a thing.

"You will regret this, Beaumont," Sir Humphrey said.

Gareth's voice grew softer, deadlier. "Will I? You obviously still wish to test your skills on me. Are you asking to name a time?"

Without hesitating, the knight said, "I am. But I'd understand if you thought you weren't up to the . . . challenge."

Margery couldn't believe what was happening. Gareth had been controlling the situation, but then a line had been crossed, one visible only to men. She held her breath, thinking how foolhardy men could be.

"I am quite ready for you," Gareth said. "I shall be at the tiltyard, an hour past dawn tomorrow."

Chills danced along Margery's arms as she fled down the hall.

Gareth spent the rest of the morning training at the tiltyard. There were dozens of men in groups at the quintain, the archery targets, and the jousting lists. They perspired in the sun, groaned as they exerted themselves.

Everything made sense in a man's world. But inside the castle, where women manipulated lives, Gareth was adrift. He had tried to handle Margery's dilemma this morn in a civilized fashion, but he still ended up challenging

Townsend. Deep inside him, he knew he'd disappointed her.

Why did he care? She had hired him to guard her, and he'd kept her safe. He would never be the kind of man she wanted, but he was the kind of man she desired. That was all that mattered. His plans were succeeding—she depended on him more each day.

As Gareth worked with the bow, he knew Humphrey Townsend watched him constantly, even tried to intimidate him by beating up on poor Lord Chadwick, whose skills as an earl were better than his skills on the field.

Gareth ignored Townsend. Now that a time was set, he didn't care what the man did. But he still felt distracted, uneasy, and he wasn't sure why.

He had performed his duty well; Margery had been unhurt. So why did he wonder what she was thinking and feeling? She must have been frightened by Townsend's attack, yet she'd gone on with her day's business as if it hadn't happened. Even now, she was meeting with one of the village bailiffs about the coming harvest. She was a woman who did what was necessary. At least that was something to admire.

That night, Margery was determined to retire early to her bedchamber. Throughout supper she had avoided looking at Sir Humphrey, because just the sight of his sly, knowing gaze made her shudder. It was as if he knew something of her secrets. Was it so easy to tell what kind of a woman she was?

Sir Humphrey and Gareth would meet in the morning, perhaps injure each other grievously. It was all she could think about. She told herself that she was worried about her guard being injured, but deep inside, she knew it was more than that. She had begun to count on Gareth, which she knew was ridiculous. When she chose her husband, Gareth would go back to his own life.

It would be better that way. He made her feel reckless, needy, whenever he touched her, and she had promised herself she would never experience those emotions again. She would live a sedate, proper life.

But the danger in his golden eyes called to her. He would gladly pit his strength against an enemy, even if he died in the attempt. Or maybe his arrogance was so great, he didn't think anyone was capable of defeating him. He was too confident, too self-assured—all the qualities that made her wary.

She said good night to Anne and Cicely, who both gave her concerned looks. She glanced toward the hearth and saw Gareth pacing, his hands clasped behind his back. His big body moved with the usual easy assurance, but he wore an intent frown. He took a step toward her, but she shook her head. If they talked about his duel with Sir Humphrey, Gareth would know that she was concerned for him. She wouldn't give him that kind of power over her.

The great double doors to the inner ward were suddenly thrown open. "Mistress Margery!" cried a soldier as he skidded to a stop. "The queen's minstrels have come. I can hear them singin' outside the gates. Should I let 'em in?"

Margery forced a smile as Anne and Cicely led her outside. The night was still warm; the stars glistened in the dark sky high above the torchlit battlements. A hush settled over the ward, and she could suddenly hear many voices raised in song.

As the gates were opened for the minstrels, the others rushed forward to greet their visitors while she remained in the darker shadows near the keep.

A man stepped near her, and the torchlight glittered in his blond hair. Gareth.

"Are you all right?" he asked impassively.

"I'm fine," she said with a strained smile. What else was there to say? She struggled not to feel thrilled at being alone with him in the shadows, where a person could stumble on them any time. Yet she didn't move away.

"I assume you heard about my challenge to Sir Humphrey."

"I wish you had not put yourself in danger on my account," she said softly.

"Danger?"

The arrogance in his voice made her smile.

"He is no danger to me. I've studied his methods: he is hotheaded and overconfident. It will defeat him in the end."

She hugged her arms against the chill and leaned back against the wall to look up at him. "And you are not overconfident?"

His teeth flashed in a smile. "Not overly. Just certain I will defeat him."

Chapter 14

Well past midnight, Gareth lay awake in bed, staring blankly at the ceiling. He had been feeling restless, closed in by too many people, full of the tension of pretending to be something he wasn't.

He was so eager for tomorrow's contest that he couldn't sleep. He wished he were fighting one of Margery's brothers, so he could let his fury and bitterness guide his sword. When Margery chose *him* over them, they would know that all their manipulations had been futile.

The dark cloud of his visions nagged at Gareth. He still hadn't discovered the meaning of Margery riding with a shadowy man. But it would come to him. He had no doubt he could keep her safe.

Ladies Anne and Cicely walked on either side of Margery as she left the chapel. The day was depressingly gray and overcast; the clouds seemed as heavy as her heart. She hated having men fight over her. *Her* husband would be tactful, a man who could let slights go.

"Margery," Cicely said, "please change your mind. You do not need to watch these men fight."

"Hawksbury is my castle. I must be involved in everything that happens here." She glanced sternly from one twin to the other. "And if I'm not at the tiltyard, one of them might kill the other."

"No, surely . . ." Cicely began.

Margery felt a momentary stab of dread. How could she watch Gareth be attacked and not wince with every blow? What if he wasn't as skilled as he thought?

The tiltyard usually rang with the clash of metal, and the cheerful shouts of the soldiers and knights. But this morning it was eerily quiet, as if the gloom and the impending battle preyed on every mind. Men stood in small groups, talking in low voices. The wind picked up, raising swirls of dust. There was no sign of Gareth or Sir Humphrey.

Sir Wallace strode toward them, a grim expression on his face. "Mistress Margery, you should not be here."

"I want to be here." She kept her voice calm, reasonable.

"This is like a squabble between two boys. I am sure they'll just—"

"Two boys with swords, who hate each

other. Sir Wallace, ask some of the pages to fetch benches for my ladies and me. We are not leaving."

He clamped his mouth shut and turned away.

As benches were being placed for them and more spectators gathered, Gareth finally entered the field. He didn't wear full armor, just a plated brigantine to protect his chest and back. He wore a shield on his left arm.

If he saw her, he gave no sign.

Sir Humphrey arrived next wearing no armor at all, as if Gareth could not lay a sword on him. He boasted and he strutted and he laughed with his friends. Gareth waited alone in the center of the tiltyard, his face calm, watchful. His focus seemed totally on Sir Humphrey, and Margery shivered at his intensity.

He wouldn't kill Sir Humphrey—would he? Fighting over her was bad enough, but no matter what the romantic songs said, the thought of men dying for her repulsed Margery.

Sir Wallace strode into the center of the tiltyard to stand near Gareth, and Sir Humphrey left his cheering friends. The three men talked together, but the wind carried their words away. Was Sir Wallace going over the rules? *Were* there rules? When he offered both combatants blunted swords, she relaxed the smallest bit.

Sir Wallace put a hand on the shoulder of each man, smiled, and said loudly, "For our spectators, who might not be aware of the true nature of this contest, this is a training exercise only, not a fight to the death."

Margery heard some scattered boos and hisses, but when she frowned toward the crowd, they settled down.

"Sir Humphrey, you will need protection," Sir Wallace said.

The knight grumbled, but allowed himself to be strapped into a brigantine.

"When one man has had enough," Sir Wallace continued, "he will raise his arm in signal that he is finished—unless he has passed out."

The crowd roared with laughter.

"There will be no rest periods. Any questions?"

Gareth and Sir Humphrey just stared at each other with equal confidence. When Sir Wallace stepped back, both men brought up their swords and crouched, circling each other. Gareth had the advantage of height, but Sir Humphrey had the massive chest of a bear.

The sudden shouting of the crowd behind her almost made Margery flinch. She composed herself and studied the combatants. Both men held their swords with obvious experience. Sir Humphrey was the first to strike a blow, which Gareth parried aside easily.

They fought evenly for a while, trying to tire each other out. Margery grew so relaxed that she began to study Gareth instead of the battle. He had well-muscled arms, which seemed powerful enough to stop any blow of Sir Humphrey's.

She began to feel rather warm, though the day was overcast. She shouldn't stare at Gareth—although he did move with considerable grace for a man. But when she watched how skilled he was with his body, she couldn't help but wonder—

She bit down hard on her lip to stop her wicked thoughts. Her face felt hot; her palms were damp. She had promised herself that she would forget her experience with a man. Then why was it constantly on her mind when she looked at Gareth? And it wasn't Peter she was thinking of.

Out of the corner of her eye, she checked to see if the twins noticed her odd behavior. Cicely was watching the contest with her eyes partially shielded by her hand, while Anne only stared, her face grim.

With a grunt of triumph, Sir Humphrey whirled aside, then brought the flat of his sword down hard on Gareth's left arm, just above his shield. Margery winced as if the sting were her own. She could only imagine the raised welt he would have. She wrapped her hand around the purse hung from her belt, and clutched the crystal stone hidden inside as if it could protect him.

Gareth barely felt the blow. He ducked as Townsend's sword whistled past his face, then whirled and hit Townsend's back. Though the man gave a hiss of pain, he fought without slowing. Their swords met and caught at the hilt, bringing them close.

Townsend grinned. "Even this blunt sword can cut your pretty face, Beaumont."

Gareth pushed him away, then began a flurry of blows that left the other knight faltering and gasping for breath. Their swords clashed and slid together, bringing them face to face again. When Gareth would have broken away, Townsend held him still.

"Poor Beaumont," Townsend hissed in a soft voice. "Win or lose, I'll soon be lifting Margery's skirts."

Gareth tried to tell himself that Townsend's boast meant nothing, but it was as if his sanity fled at the thought of Margery with someone else. With a burst of power, he thrust Townsend away. Before the other man could recover, Gareth hit him across the head with his shield. Townsend fell hard and lay still.

The tiltyard was utterly silent—even the birds didn't sing. Feeling powerful and alone, more like himself, Gareth raised his head and looked at the silent crowd. If he had to fight them all to prove he belonged here, so be it. He gripped his sword tightly and awaited their condemnation.

Margery rose to her feet. "Well done, Sir Gareth," she said. "My dear guests, shall we break our fast?"

She and her ladies turned and walked away.

The men gave him angry looks, but began to exchange coins at a furious pace so that they could keep up with Margery. Gareth let his sword dangle as he stared down at Townsend's slumbering body.

Desmond came up beside him with a bucket of water, wearing a satisfied grin. "That was a good display of swordsmanship you put on."

Gareth shrugged. "I try to educate where I can."

"Was that an actual joke?" Desmond asked in feigned astonishment.

"Just the truth."

"What did he say to you before the final blow?"

"Something crude about his intentions toward Margery."

"Ahh." Desmond nodded. "Maybe you'd better leave before I revive him."

"Why?" Gareth asked. "If he wishes to continue fighting, I shall gladly oblige him. And we won't use these childish weapons."

"Mistress Margery doesn't need you to kill each other. Go eat with her while I clean up your mess."

Inside the great hall, Margery tried not to watch the door as she waited for Gareth to come in. Some of her suitors refused to speak to each other, others debated the battle heatedly. They all but ignored her, and she was grateful.

It gave her a chance to see which of her suitors was particularly strong-willed. Certainly that man would go to the bottom of her list—the list that was getting shorter every day. Lord Shaw Wharton, one of the duke's sons, was particularly mild-mannered. Though he bickered with his brother, he didn't force his own opinion on others. His height was not much more than her own, but his face was acceptable.

She inwardly berated herself, remembering that she had told the twins that a man's appearance was unimportant.

Why was it so difficult to find a decent husband?

Soon enough Gareth came in. He seated himself at the end of the head table, leaned over his trencher, and began to eat as if he'd been fasting in a monastery. If he noticed the noblemen giving him uneasy glances, he didn't show it.

Margery sighed, glad that he wasn't hurt. She hoped Sir Humphrey recovered just as easily. Maybe the knight would leave, solving one of her problems.

Her other problems would not go away. She wished she could eagerly anticipate her brothers' visit, but even that was denied her. Peter Fitzwilliam might be with them. How could she face her former lover in full view of her brothers, who would know immediately that something was wrong? Just the thought of the deceptions she would have to employ made her stomach twist with nausea.

So, she must have a man in mind before she saw Peter and her brothers.

When Gareth finally turned to look at her, Margery saw that a purplish bruise colored his face. She would see to that—later. First she would do what she had sworn she wouldn't: use Gareth's knowledge of her suitors. She needed a husband, soon. She walked toward him, then slid onto the bench beside him, noticing that they were at least a half a table length from anyone else.

As she leaned near, Gareth paused with his spoon partway into his mouth, eyeing her. Slowly, he took a mouthful, then waited.

Margery licked her lips nervously, gave him a smile, then looked over her shoulder once more. No one was paying them any attention.

"Gareth, remember when I told you I did not need your help to find a husband?"

He narrowed his eyes and nodded.

"I admit I was wrong."

"Then this isn't about my battle with Sir Humphrey?" he asked.

"No—though, of course, you should never have let the situation deteriorate into a sword fight."

"I am certain your husband will never let such a thing happen."

"Never." She heard his sarcasm, but she ignored it. "The husband I choose will not want to fight. There are better ways to handle disagreements." She gave him a quick look. "You know I mean no offense to your methods."

He smiled the slow smile that made her insides weak. "I take no offense. I do what I must to keep you safe. Now tell me what else I can do for you."

Just looking into his face made all thoughts leave her head. She watched the movement of his jaw as he ate, the concentration in the depths of his eyes when he looked at her.

"Margery?" he prompted.

"Oh, yes," she said, flustered. By the saints, what was wrong with her? "I need to ask you about Lord Shaw Wharton. He is the son of a duke, so I assume he would be at court often."

Gareth chewed the lumps in his porridge, his gaze thoughtful. "He lets his elder brothers handle the family business at court. He rarely goes at all."

"Oh." Margery felt the first stirrings of dismay—and the length of his thigh against hers. She couldn't move without being obvious, so she remained still. What was she thinking about? Oh, yes, Lord Shaw. "But I've seen him at court so often."

"He's searching for a wife, someone who loves the country life as much as he does."

"He said that?" This was looking worse and worse.

Gareth's arm brushed against hers as he

wiped his mouth with a napkin. "Yes. He also needs a woman to raise his son."

"Son? He's been married already? But he seems so young."

"No, never married." He folded his arms and rested his elbows on the table. He turned to look at her, and their shoulders touched.

Margery stared into his eyes, so unusual in color, so intense. It took a moment before his words sank in. "Never married? That means the boy is—"

"The boy cannot help his father's mistake."

"Of course not! But Lord Shaw certainly had no problem creating his own mistakes."

She felt a sudden rise of anger within her. No one thought anything of Lord Shaw having a bastard. They probably patted him on the back for "doing right" by the child. But what about the mother? Was anyone patting her back?

No, the poor girl would probably live in disgrace for the rest of her life, while Lord Shaw was toasted for his way with women. The same thing would have happened if Margery had conceived a child. Even now, if she married Lord Shaw, she'd be expected to raise any illegitimate child he brought home.

She shook with fury at life's unfairness, where women were scorned for what men did openly. Probably every man in the hall had bedded a woman. She had bedded a man—and what did it get her? Despair, self-loathing, guilt. She would wager that Lord Shaw experienced none of these emotions, nor did her brothers, who had not always been the family men they were now.

Margery was finished with guilt.

She suddenly pushed to her feet. The bench tipped back, and Gareth caught the table to keep from falling. Startled, she looked down into his battered face.

"Gareth, you must have other bruises and injuries."

He stood up. "This is nothing."

"You should go rest. I'll come up with salve for your wounds."

He hesitated, then nodded. He was right to wonder about her motives, she thought. She didn't understand them herself.

After Gareth finished eating and left, Margery sent a maidservant for a tray of linens and salves. She hugged herself and stood alone, still feeling shocked at her revelation.

A burst of angry voices at the head table made her turn around. The Earl of Chadwick, one of the quietest men she'd ever met, was on his feet, pointing a finger at Lord Seabrook. There were shouts of agreement from both sides of the table. When she approached, they all subsided into a guilty silence. Lord Chadwick's face reddened.

"Gentlemen," she said, "what disagreement harms your friendship?"

Lord Chadwick cleared his throat. "Mistress

Margery, our actual argument is not so important as the fact that we're all beginning to argue in excess."

"I do not understand."

"I fear the strain of competing for your attention has proved too much, as was evidenced by the fight this morn." Some men grumbled, but Lord Chadwick's look silenced them. "Rather than allow our friendships to die, we've agreed to return to London after your birthday celebration. You can think in peace on your choice for husband."

How patronizing of them! Margery's anger rose up her throat. She was sick of men altogether.

"Gentlemen, I do not know what to say." She forced a smile. "It has been difficult to choose a husband with such a multitude of worthy men."

She thought they began to seem resigned rather than angry, and that was a good sign.

"Mistress Margery," Lord George said, "will you be attending Lord Cabot's annual tournament next month?"

"Of course. I will enjoy seeing each of you there."

Avery Cabot was married to Sarah, a dear friend of hers. They had grown up on neighboring estates, and had spent time together in London. Margery's brother James had once courted Sarah before she fell in love with Avery. It was expected that Margery would journey to their home.

But the tournament would be an ordeal; every knight would have heard of the king's proclamation. She should look on this tournament as a good thing, though, since she had less than two months left to make a decision. There would be even more suitors to whom she could apply her standards.

Yet at this moment, the thought of looking at more groveling men simply made her ill.

Margery stood before Gareth's door, balancing a tray in one hand, with linens draped over her arm. She had chosen to come alone, and could not play the coward now. She knocked briskly.

Gareth opened the door, wearing just a shirt dangling loosely over his hose, and she walked past him. He stood in the doorway for a moment, watching as she set the tray on the bed table.

When she turned back to face him, he deliberately closed the door, his face expressionless. The sound set off a little echo inside her.

"Margery, are you my healer this day?" he asked, walking slowly toward her.

"I am competent. You will not die under my ministrations."

He studied her silently, then one corner of his mouth turned up in a half smile. "What do you want me to do?"

She wet her lips. "Take off your shirt and let me see your injuries."

He never broke eye contact as he unlaced his shirt and reached for the hem. A wild, reckless need to see him unclothed made her breath come too fast. Though there was no fire, the room felt overly warm.

He lifted his shirt over his head, then tossed it. She watched its flight until it landed on the bed. She stared at the bed a moment too long before looking back at Gareth.

Once, Margery had thought he looked like the statue of an angel, but she was wrong. He had the sculpted muscles and physical beauty of a statue, but he was clearly a man: a man with golden eyes that saw through her pretenses to the wildness underneath. If she walked to him, he would take her in his arms.

Then she noticed blood and purple bruises marring the perfection of his skin.

"Gareth!"

His name was barely a whisper on her lips as she saw what damage a blunted sword could do. Bruises dotted his skin, some the exact width of a sword. Red welts oozed trickles of blood.

He stared at her lips. "They look much worse than they feel. An ordinary day's training can give a man these meager injuries."

"I've lived beside soldiers my entire life, Gareth, and these are not ordinary injuries. Sit down on this stool, please."

Margery tried to be objective; she had washed and treated many wounds. But the thought of touching Gareth's bare skin made her feel all hot inside, especially between her thighs.

He wasn't helping much. He sat down, bringing him to her eye level. He didn't even blink as he stared at her, his eyes molten.

Though it was difficult, she broke their shared gaze and wrung a cloth in the basin of steaming water on her tray. Then she walked around him and stopped at his back. His head turned. She wanted to rest her cheek against his skin, to press her mouth to Gareth's. Her fingers itched to reach over his shoulder and trail through the scattered hair on his chest.

Using soft strokes, she washed his back, pausing often to rinse the cloth. She felt flushed, and so boneless she could collapse against him at any moment. She dipped the cloth again and moved around to his front.

She didn't look into his face—she couldn't. His gaze was like a physical thing. She stood between his knees to wash his wounds, and touched him as she'd only touched one other man. But even that had never affected her like this. She was breathless with longing, with the excitement of doing the forbidden.

Somehow she had to distract herself.

Chapter 15

Margery said, "My suitors have decided to return to London after the celebration."

Gareth listened to her voice, husky, low, arousing. Never had he let a woman affect him so. Though she was only tending his wounds, a shudder moved through him as if she were making love to him.

He stared in surprised fascination at her hands. She took a fresh cloth and dipped one edge in wine. Her free hand rested on his shoulder as she dabbed the welt on his arm. He was light-headed from the smell of roses, and the danger of her secrets seemed far away.

"Why did the noblemen decide to leave?" he finally asked. He knew he had the upper hand, yet his voice sounded dazed.

"I think your battle this morning brought to light a division among themselves. They found it amusing to court me as a group, but never considered how competition could divide them."

"They've been divided? It hasn't seemed that way to me."

Her eyes glistened with angry satisfaction as she dried him off with a towel. "Gareth, they've become so quarrelsome that some were backing you this morn."

"Hard to believe," he murmured. His gaze followed the tumble of her hair down to her breasts. If he reached out now, he knew she'd let him touch her. He could barely resist dragging her to the floor beneath him. He wanted to pull her clothes off and lick her body as if it were the sweetest marzipan candy.

"I've promised that I would see them all again at Avery Cabot's annual tournament. Have you attended before?" She reached into a glass jar until her fingers were coated in something gray, like old grease.

"Until they refused to invite me. What is that?" he asked, grabbing her wrist before she could touch him.

"A salve to protect your wounds," she said in a bewildered, dreamy voice.

He watched her eyes drop down his body. "I won't need it," he said. "Besides, it will get all over the bed."

What would she do if he led her there now? Once again, they were alone in a bedchamber. Her blushes were lovely.

"I have bandages," she said. "And why did the Cabots refuse to invite you?"

He took a cloth and began to wipe the salve off her hands. "I kept winning. Rather than treat me as a competitor, they were frightened of me."

"Does this happen often?"

"It happens enough." He tossed the towel on the tray and she pulled back her hand. He looked into her eyes. "It is difficult to earn money to eat when no one will let you do what you're best at."

Margery backed away from him. He gripped his hands together to keep from pulling her against his chest. He could almost taste victory and revenge—and he could almost taste the sweet saltiness of her skin against his tongue.

"I should go," she said awkwardly, turning to straighten up the tray.

"But my legs are grievously wounded, mistress."

She looked over her shoulder with skeptical amusement. "Then I shall leave the tray for you. Bring it down when you're through."

Gareth shook his head. "But I am not as skilled as you."

"You'll learn." She opened the door, looked both ways, and disappeared into the corridor.

The next evening, Gareth blocked Desmond's way out of the stables. "Margery's birthday celebration is tomorrow. I need you to teach me how to dance."

Desmond shot him a surprised look. "You know as much about dancing as I do." He lit two small lanterns, throwing hazy shadows over the sleeping horses and mounds of straw.

"That cannot be true, for that means you know nothing. A baron's son, not trained in dancing?"

"A knight, not trained in dancing? When you were fostered, did you not learn with your lord's daughters?"

"No." Everyone had been afraid to touch him, let alone dance—the cowards.

Desmond swore softly and looked around. "What if the grooms come, or worse yet, a soldier?"

Gareth smiled. "Surely you are not worried about being seen dancing with me?"

"Is there not a place more . . . private?"

"Being discovered someplace private would be worse, do you not think?"

"Oh, very well," Desmond said with a growl. "You know, I am already quite tired of your smile. Just a week ago, I would have sworn you were incapable of one."

Gareth shrugged as he leaned back against a stall.

"Let us do this quickly. Really, 'tis nothing difficult—just occasional patterns of steps, and lots of dancing in big circles."

"Show me."

They were tromping about in the straw when they heard a woman's giggle. Margery leaned in the doorway, holding back her laughter with a hand over her mouth.

"Sir Gareth, I grew worried when you disappeared from the hall," she said. "I asked a squire where you'd gone, but ... maybe ... you didn't want to be found." She erupted into peals of laughter, letting the door post hold her up.

Desmond's face was red. Gareth had a suspicion that so was his own.

"Then you teach him!" Desmond said, stomping out into the night.

Margery wiped tears from the corners of her eyes with her fingers. "Teach you what?"

Gareth linked his hands behind his back, and struggled not to let his embarrassment become anger. He hated feeling ridiculous. "How to dance."

"The last place you fostered was negligent in your training," she said, moving forward into the stables.

They were alone. His body forgot anger and remembered the smoky heat of desire, and her hands touching his bare skin. She was a dark, seductive shadow, illuminated with glimmers of lantern light. All he could think about was throwing a blanket over a pile of hay, pulling her down on top of him, and—

"Gareth?" she said, coming close. "Did you hear me?"

He cleared his throat. "What?"

"Why did you never learn to dance?"

He shrugged. "You know of the curse. Not many wanted to touch me."

"But surely the women—" She broke off, searching his face.

Margery wondered what woman could resist him. She would have given anything in her foolish youth to dance with him.

Well, she was a grown woman now, with a woman's needs. Why shouldn't she enjoy herself? She wanted to touch him, to surround herself with the danger he represented. This was Gareth, who from boyhood to manhood had always protected her—but could he protect himself against this wildness that rose up inside her?

She reached for his hand and saw his narrowed eyes focus on where they touched. His hand was warm, callused from hard work, and so much larger than her own. She wanted to feel it against her skin.

"Let me teach you to dance," she said, pulling him away from the wall to where the lanterns spilled their meager light. "The dances we do in the country are much simpler than those at court."

Gareth said nothing as she took his shoulders to position him opposite her. It was as if a fire raged between them, drawing them ever nearer to something forbidden.

"We step toward each other, then back," she said.

He stared at her body, following her movements. Awareness of his smoldering gaze burst to life within her.

"Step forward again," she whispered, and this time she let her body brush against his.

His eyes closed and she saw him shudder as he stepped away.

"Again."

Before the dance even brought them together, Gareth pulled her hard against him, turning around to press her to the wall. Her body heated with new, dangerous sensations as they stared at each other, poised on the threshold of something so explosive, it would change their relationship forever.

She could stop this now.

Instead, she put her hands on either side of his face. His skin burned her palms, his rough whiskers scraped her. She wanted the passion of his mouth covering hers. She moistened her lips, puckered them, waiting—

With a groan, Gareth lifted her clear off the floor and ground his body into hers. The hot onslaught of his lips slanted over hers. She gasped as a lightning burst of desire moved through her, chasing all thoughts from her mind. His tongue licked along her lips, then between them. She surrendered her mouth gladly, sucking his tongue, tasting his mouth in return.

The feel of his body completed her, made all her problems and worries disappear with the passion she finally released. She gripped his hair, holding him close.

"Margery," he whispered hoarsely, his mouth trailing across her jaw and down her neck.

"Gareth." His name was a groan of desire, of need. She parted her legs, wanting to feel all of him. He caught her knees up around his waist and rubbed his erection against her. He held her hard against the wall, his face buried between her neck and shoulder.

Every movement of his body against hers made Margery shudder. She linked her legs around his hips, swept beyond the shock of his aggressive passion into a world where there was only their ragged breathing, their barely suppressed groans. She had known another man and thought there was nothing that could surprise her. But her stark need of Gareth made her feel primitive, alive, as if there were no constraints, no civilization.

His hands slid beneath her thighs, working slow erotic circles on her bare flesh with the tips of his fingers, ever closer to where they strained to be joined.

He kissed her again, and she groaned as his hands left her thighs and caressed her waist. He lifted his head and watched her. His thumbs suddenly brushed her nipples and she gave a shocked gasp, staring into his eyes, begging him without words to continue.

Margery's sanity returned when a horse neighed in a nearby stall—and regret swept through her. Anyone could find them. Her longing for danger and excitement didn't mean she wanted to be discovered. She brought her legs down and slid along his body to stand shakily on the ground. Yet still she clutched his arms and held him close.

"Gareth." She breathed his name.

He leaned down to kiss her.

She turned her head away. "Not here, not now." She felt his lips nibbling her ear, and she moaned.

"Then let us go somewhere more private," he whispered.

"No, I—"

This was nothing she had planned, nothing she'd meant to happen. She wasn't sure what *should* happen between them.

Her feelings suddenly overwhelmed and frightened her. She broke from his embrace and ran.

Gareth stood on the battlements overlooking the dark countryside. It was deep night, and except for the sounds of the patrols, everything was still. He had run the circle of the battlements until exhaustion cramped his legs and threatened to send him falling into the ward below. Yet nothing helped. What was wrong with him? Margery was just another woman. Because of her, he'd been forced to squire in a castle where their idea of protection against his "wizardry" was to lock him up each night, and release him to labor by day.

But when his eyes closed, Gareth didn't remember the dark, bare rooms of his youth. Instead he saw her face, head tilted back, lips parted in passion. Her response had been more than he'd ever imagined. With her in his arms, nothing else had existed but his need for her. He forgot everything she'd done, everything she was. He'd almost lost control—surely he hadn't been himself.

But he had endangered his own plans. Though he longed to seduce Margery, he didn't want the entire world to know and think her shameless. He didn't want a marriage begun in anger.

She had more passion than he'd ever seen in a woman—but it only made him more suspicious. What had happened with Peter Fitzwilliam, and why did it haunt her so?

Margery couldn't sleep. As she sat in a chair before the hearth, she clutched the crystal stone Gareth had given her.

It was long past midnight. The only sounds she heard were the hourly marching of the guards past her door: the shuffle of their boots, the murmur of their voices.

She opened her palm and looked at the

stone. It glittered like Gareth's eyes, she thought, shivering. She'd squeezed it so hard she'd left indentations in her flesh. They would eventually go away, but her memories of him never would. Their lives were linked in so many ways. She felt bound to him, to this fascination and passion she felt for him.

Never in her life had she been kissed like that, like she was the only food for a starving man. She had reveled in the power of feeling desirable. He was a solitary, dangerous, fierce knight, and she'd held him in her arms and made him shudder.

For an insane moment, Margery wondered what it would be like to have a husband like Gareth, uncontrollable, mysterious. A man like him would do as he pleased, even if it meant breaking her heart.

She had vowed never again to put herself under the spell of a man who could hurt her— but damned if she wasn't going to be as wild as a man while she still could. She deserved it.

Chapter 16

The day of her birthday celebration, Margery was busy with the butler and cellarer, and overseeing the village maids who arrived to bake the pastries. She went to the tiltyard often, where extra pits had been dug to roast oxen. Once or twice she felt Gareth staring at her, but she didn't look his way. She was afraid her face would reveal her excitement, the forbidden recklessness taking over her body. It all seemed new to her, and she didn't want to scrutinize it just yet.

That night, hundreds of candles illuminated the hall. The scents of heavy perfume and larks' tongue pie floated through the air. The lords and ladies were dressed in embroidered brocades and velvets, colorful silken gowns sewn with shining pearls and beads.

Margery caught her breath at how Gareth's new blue doublet made his hair and eyes look even more golden. His new white shirt was pulled through the many slits in his sleeves, in the best court fashion.

Though the noblemen ignored him, he didn't want for company. The serving maids hovered nearby, offering food and drink just to see him smile. Margery couldn't blame them, for whenever he turned that rare smile on her, it was like the sun coming out after a long season of storms.

When the dancing started she joined hands with one suitor after another, circling the floor until her head spun. She brushed shoulders once with Gareth, and awareness tingled through her. But before their gazes could meet, he was already swept away by his partner. Though he didn't know the dances, that didn't stop every woman, from villager to lady, from asking him to dance.

Later, she felt his gaze on her as she danced with yet another suitor. Gareth stood alone, watching her through the crowd. In her mind she relived the feeling of his mouth sliding down her neck, of his hands touching intimate places on her body. She felt warm and flustered and thrilled that he stared at her.

Why couldn't she spend a few minutes dancing in his arms before the entire castle? Everyone thought he was her suitor. She stopped dancing with Lord Seabrook, claiming thirst. He brought her a goblet of wine and tried to start a conversation, but his words faded away as Gareth approached her and bowed over her hand.

She wasn't prepared for the shock of putting her hand in his. A spark of excitement and longing shot between them. His smile vanished for a moment, and his gaze was greedy on her mouth.

Then he changed back into her adoring suitor again. "Mistress Margery, please do me the great honor of dancing with me." He sounded no different, as if he still worshipped her from afar.

She followed him out into the center of the hall, where sweetened rushes were stirred by their feet. They bowed to each other and performed the simple steps of the dance, which other partners had obviously taught him that evening.

When they held hands and swung in circles, Gareth leaned toward her. "You ran away last night," he said in a low voice. "Are you angry with me?"

She smiled. "Should I be?"

"So you kiss men like that every day?"

Though his expression was pleasant, his eyes studied her with a skepticism that angered her. Did even Gareth think only women had to be perfect?

"No, I don't," she said sharply.

"Margery—"

"I'm not ready to talk about it yet."

They were separated by the dance. As they

were reunited, he softly said, "Should I ask for your forgiveness?"

"There's nothing to forgive," she whispered, relenting. "It was . . . mutual."

They were parted again, and Gareth searched for Margery in the circle of dancers. He thought for certain she would feel guilty and ashamed of what they'd shared, that he'd have to woo her more. Instead, there was an unusual intensity about her that confused him.

They came together, linking hands and following a line of dancers. At the end of the dance, he lifted her high and spun her before setting her back on her feet, leaving her flushed and wide-eyed. But she soon left him for her next suitor.

Later in the evening, he watched her open her birthday gifts. She would be his wife; she deserved the only heirlooms of his family, so he gave her a simple chain that was his mother's. She looked at it the same as she looked at all the others—with politeness. He knew she was only treating him as a pretend suitor, but a deep part of him longed for recognition. It was difficult to be patient and let other men ogle what he already considered his.

A voice suddenly boomed out. "Is that plain thing from Beaumont?" Humphrey Townsend asked.

Gareth had not seen Townsend for the entire day. He was amazed that the man had finally confronted him—in public, of course; Gareth had made an enemy of the knight.

"He owes you more than a cheap trinket," Townsend continued, "for exposing you to the curse of his family."

Gareth saw Margery's eyes go cold. "Sir Humphrey, how could one dance expose me to such foolish superstition? I danced more with you, and my aching toes prove it."

Townsend's face whitened. "One dance could lead to more with a Beaumont," he said in a controlled, furious voice. "After all, I'm sure his mother and grandmother thought they knew better, too. But they ended up trapped in marriage and dead."

Gareth's rationality fled as he looked into Townsend's smirking face. The man had slandered his ancestors—and tried to compromise Margery. A cold rage settled in his mind. They would meet again, and this time the swords would be sharp. Gareth didn't need a vision to tell him that.

A violent headache suddenly stabbed between his eyes. As if called forth by the thought, a vision swirled across his sight, and he did his best to keep his expression normal. He vaguely saw Margery step between him and Townsend, heard her voice as if from far away. *Not now, not now*, he chanted silently—but trying to force away a vision only made his headache worse.

He thought Margery was trying to talk to

him. He shook his head and frowned, hoping that she would understand. Of Townsend's words, he heard nothing. The mist before his eyes had taken on color and shape, sharpening again into the image of Margery before a shadowed man on a horse. This time, the vision was clearer. Beneath a cloudy night sky, he could see the Severn Valley stretching out behind the riders, the Cotswolds in the distance. He sensed urgency, but nothing else.

Gareth suddenly felt hands on his arms, shaking him; the vision dissolved in a swirl of mist. He blinked and shook his head, only to see Desmond's worried face before him.

"Gareth?"

He could hear again. People nearby were staring at him, Desmond and Margery with concern, Townsend with triumph.

He gave them all a strained smile. "Forgive me, Mistress Margery. I am not feeling well. I must have eaten something that did not agree with me."

She studied him. "Are you sure I do not need to send for the physician?"

"I'm fine."

"Perhaps you should retire for the evening."

And let a hall full of servants and guests and strangers have easy access to Margery? "I shall sit until I feel better. Go enjoy yourself, mistress."

She was finally persuaded to continue dancing, but the last glance she gave him was more

puzzled than worried. One more public display of his visions, and she would demand an-
swers he couldn't give.

Never had Gareth felt more helpless and
weak. His vision had hit him so strongly, he'd
been unable to see or hear.

What if the strength and increasing fre-
quency of the visions was a warning? Perhaps
whatever danger Margery faced was approaching. She would be safer married to him, when
she would be at his side, night and day.

Their shared kiss burned in his mind—and
other parts of his body. Wiping his perspiring
forehead, he kept his gaze locked on Margery,
who whirled about the room with one man after another. Her green skirts swayed, revealing
her ankles and feet. Men touched her slim
waist or her hand.

It should be him.

Maybe it was time to step up his plans for
seduction. She was certainly receptive, and
there couldn't be many more days before her
brothers arrived.

The celebration went on well into the early
morning. Gareth made sure Margery saw him
drinking often, so he could blame the ale for
making him stumble into her bed.

After everyone had gone to sleep, he waited
a long, frustrating hour. His mind was haunted
by memories of her breathless moans, of the
way her body had shuddered against his. Finally he sneaked into her bedchamber.

A low fire in the hearth lit the room with a soft, shadowy light. Margery lay in bed asleep, and didn't stir as he approached. Her dark lashes rested on her cheeks, her full lips slightly parted with her breathing. Her curls spread out in a sensual disarray across her pillow.

Desire thundered through his body, almost overpowering him, but he refused to bed her as if he were an overly eager boy. He unlaced his doublet, pulled it over his head, and threw it across a small table. As he hurriedly loosened his shirt, her neat handwriting on parchment caught his attention.

It was an unfinished letter to her brothers, James and Reynold. Seeing their names was like immersing himself in a winter river.

He stumbled back. He'd lost sight of his revenge, caring more for getting between Margery's thighs than for what this family owed him. He could not allow his nearness to his goal to make him forget so many years of pain.

He was letting the visions affect his life too much. Margery was in no immediate danger, as long as she obeyed him.

He began to wonder if the vision had a different meaning. Perhaps it was not a warning, but a prediction of a good future.

Could the man on the horse be—himself?

He walked back to her bed and stood over her as he donned his doublet. Though she was covered to her waist by a thin blanket, her white nightclothes fell in shadowy folds across her breasts. With a little sigh, she turned her head away from him.

Gareth smoothed his fingers through her curls. He had forgotten that the visions didn't always foretell doom. Sometimes they told him useless information, like where his mother's knitting needles had gone. Maybe this time his knowledge could be helpful. Perhaps he had let his natural suspicion cloud his judgment where the visions were concerned.

For a moment, he felt an unfamiliar twinge of conscience, which he was determined to ignore. He might be using Margery for revenge, but the rewards to her would be sufficient. She would have his protection and his loyalty, which was more than she had ever given him.

Silently, Gareth returned to his own chamber.

By midday, the noblemen were on their way to London, followed by their baggage carts, their servants, and their squires. Margery returned to an almost empty great hall, and the relief of solitude was nearly overwhelming.

Not that she was really alone. She smiled at the servants dismantling the trestle tables from the last meal. A maidservant hummed as she swept out the old rushes.

For just a moment, Margery pretended that the last few months had not happened, that she

was a carefree girl with the promise of the rest
of her life to look forward to.

Then she saw Gareth sitting in a chair before
the fire, legs spread, a tankard of ale in his fist
resting on one knee.

In her mind, she saw again his pale face
when he'd taken ill, the way his eyes had
glazed over, frightening her. She didn't believe
a simple illness was the cause, especially not
when he looked so . . . healthy.

She should not meet his gaze, but she found
herself caught in his penetrating stare, embarrassed, yet aware of the secret things they had
done to each other. He made her feel self-
conscious and sensual and endangered all at
the same time. She walked toward him slowly.

He looked up into her face. "So, the London
suitors are gone."

"Yes. Your duties should prove lighter."

"I think not," he said with a shake of his
head. "Unless you are locked in a room alone
with me, there is always a danger."

And there wasn't danger when she was
alone with him? 'Tis what attracted them to
each other, she was certain. She must be blushing furiously.

Gareth smiled, which only added to her discomfort. Did he know everything she was
thinking? Did he know that even now she
couldn't forget the way his body had rubbed
against hers, the wild thrill she'd felt with his
tongue in her mouth? She wanted to experi-

ence it all again, for a secret memory to cherish long after he was gone and she was married.

But there was still so much to do, to restock and resettle the household now that their guests had departed. Within the week her brothers would be arriving. Her brief respite from entertaining would be spent supervising the cleaning.

Suddenly, it was all too much. Margery had been trapped in this castle for weeks now, and she needed to get away.

But not alone.

She looked down at Gareth, who sipped his ale and waited patiently for her to speak. She gave him a slow smile, and he raised one eyebrow.

"Wait here," she said, then walked quickly back toward the kitchens. Soon she returned, carrying a basket brimming with food. "Follow me."

She headed toward the double doors leading to the inner ward, and he caught up with her as they crossed the packed earth courtyard.

"Where are we going?" he asked.

"The stables. Do you think you can fit all this food in a saddle pack?" She swung the basket toward him and he caught it against his chest.

"Of course, but—"

"Do not ask questions. I don't know where we're headed or what we're going to do, but I have to get away from here."

Chapter 17

Gareth rode beside Margery beneath the gatehouse, but the moment her horse left the tunnel, she kicked into a gallop and raced away, laughing. He should be annoyed, but he understood her need for freedom after a week of pretenses.

He rode hard until he nearly caught up with her, then decided he preferred the view better from behind. Her blue skirts flared off the horse's back like a cape. He could see her dark hair streaming in the wind, the ruffle of her white smock, her stockinged legs. She looked over her shoulder at him, then laughed with a carefreeness he had never seen in her.

How did she put aside her problems and enjoy a simple ride in the countryside? Nothing was solved by running away, yet she seemed to exist only in the moment. This was a fantasy, but he suddenly wanted to join her in it, to pretend that there was no past or present, no secrets. Just the two of them.

But that was foolishness. She was giving him the perfect opportunity to further his revenge. He had her alone for as long as he liked. If only it would rain, trapping them in an abandoned shelter, the two of them alone in the dripping darkness . . .

"Gareth!"

He realized she was outdistancing him as he daydreamed. She saluted him as her horse entered the dappled greenery of the glen where they'd first seen each other. He leaned over the horse's neck and galloped harder, the wind ruffling his clothes and hair.

He caught up to her just past the last trees, then surged ahead down the slowly winding hillside roads of the Cotswolds. The Severn Valley spread out before them, with the river sparkling in the sunlight as it twisted and turned upon itself. Sheep by the thousands grazed the green pastures, separated by low stone fences and the occasional cluster of trees.

"Gareth!"

He turned his head and saw that Margery had veered off the road, and was now following a narrow line of trees and piles of stones. With a pull on the reins, he brought his stallion up on its hind legs. He turned and headed back up the hillside.

The path disappeared over the crest of a hill. When Gareth reached the top, he looked down into a small wooded valley with a stream running down to join the Severn. Margery was just entering a copse of trees.

He followed and trotted up next to her on the bank of the stream, then slid to the ground. He reached up to help her dismount, but she fell in a breathless heap into his arms. It was as if she trusted him, and he felt stunned, even humbled, in a strange way.

"I won!" she cried, throwing her arms wide and dropping her head back.

He gripped her waist before she fell. "Only because you changed the rules."

Her head came up and she gave him a saucy smile. "They were my rules to change." She lingered a moment, one hand resting on his chest. Though he didn't quite understand it, this reckless, amusing side of Margery appealed to him. Anything she did appealed to him.

He covered her hand with his and grinned at her. Somehow over the last few days, his smiles had become less forced. He could feel the beating of his own heart and thought it was pumping a bit too fast. It must be the exertion of their horse race.

Her eyes narrowed with amusement. "You have changed since you arrived just over a sennight ago."

To distract her, he slid his fingers beneath a wayward curl on her forehead, and followed it with the tip of his finger down her cheek. He tucked it safely behind her ear. He studied her reaction: the soft parting of her lips, the lowering of her eyelids.

"We spent a few days learning to know each other again," he murmured, leaning down to press a gentle kiss to her cheek.

Margery broke from his embrace, not meeting his eyes. "Gareth, I'm hungry."

"You brought enough food for both the horses and us," he said, but inside he wondered if this was another ploy, leading him on, then pulling back.

"Not that kind of food—freshly caught food." She backed away and he stepped nearer. "I haven't fished in ages. Do you still carry string and hooks?"

"Always." He let her keep her distance for the moment.

Soon they were seated side by side, their backs against two tree trunks, their bare legs dangling over the embankment into the cool, gurgling water below. They each held a stick with string attached. They fished in silence, Margery obviously intent and competitive, Gareth because he watched her, wondering at her motives for this private trip.

Soon enough, he began to think of ways he could accidentally touch her. He was just about to rub his foot along her leg when she spoke.

"Gareth, can I ask you something personal?" she said in a low voice.

He tensed. "I don't promise an answer."

"Understood." She tugged on her string,

then turned to look at him. "What is the real Beaumont Curse? How did your grandmothers die?"

Gareth's heart gave a painful squeeze. No one ever asked for something as simple as the truth; they either wanted to jeer at him or to fear him. But not Margery. She wanted an honest answer from a man who never told the truth about his past unless forced into it.

If he told part of the curse, she might trust that he was telling the truth—but she might also run in fear for her life.

"Many years ago," he began, surprised that his voice sounded hoarse, as if this foolish history still affected him, "after victory in a wild, vicious battle, my grandfather's father raped a young woman. The girl's mother was a famous healer, and some even called her a witch. She cursed the Beaumont men to despair and savagery."

Margery gazed intently at him, a frown of concentration on her forehead. "Despair and savagery?" she repeated.

"I give you her words. In his guilt, my great-grandfather believed her, and slowly went mad. He killed my great-grandmother. Their own child, my grandfather, caused the death of his wife in a fall down the stairs. Though people saw the accident and claimed he was innocent, he blamed himself until the grief made him lose his mind."

She touched his arm and whispered, "Oh, Gareth."

He shook off her hand. "I'm not through. You wanted to hear this." He held back the words that pushed for release, about the strange visions that haunted the men in his family, driving them all insane. For a wild moment he wanted to confide everything in her, no matter what she'd done, no matter the lies she was telling.

But Gareth was not one of his ancestors. He let no emotion control him; refused even to worry about what the visions meant for his future.

"Tell me the rest," she murmured. This time her hand rested on his thigh. "It sounds like you've never told anyone."

"You know the rest. My parents died in a fire."

"It must be difficult when people know your history," she began softly. "Does everyone react like my suitors?"

"Most, but it matters not." The unfairness of his life lashed through him, and he wanted to hurt her like she'd hurt him. "Now it is my turn to ask a question. Who is Peter Fitzwilliam?"

Margery felt dizzy, as if the world suddenly had dropped from beneath her feet. When she tried to move her hand from Gareth's thigh, he caught it and held it tight. He looked so deeply into her eyes that she had to turn away.

"Look at me," he said, cupping her cheek and turning her head back. "Who is he? Why do you look like this, like someone died?"

She gave a bitter laugh and pushed his hands away. "He's not dead."

"But you wish he was."

"No, never," she said too quickly.

She fisted her hands. She could tell Gareth some of her story, but not all—she owed him no more than that. She just had to make him believe her.

"Peter courted me, and told me he wanted to marry me." She spoke through a tight, aching throat. "Then he changed his mind."

She blinked back tears and watched Gareth's face. His eyes were narrowed as he studied her. He wasn't a fool; he could probably tell she was holding back something.

"You loved him," he said. It wasn't a question.

She shrugged, then looked away as a tear slid down her cheek. "Yes," she whispered. "Once. But not anymore."

"He sent you a missive."

She glanced at him quickly. "How did you know that?"

"The day Fitzwilliam's servant came, your suitors recognized the color of his livery."

"They were talking about me?" she demanded, feeling anger take away her pain.

"Of course," Gareth said. "You are the prize they all seek."

"Then you had heard something about Peter already," she said warily.

"Not much; only that he was once your suitor." He reached up and rubbed the back of his hand against her wet cheek. "But I saw your face as you read the letter. I was concerned."

"Do not be. Peter was only sending greetings from my brothers, and mentioning that he might come with them when they visit."

His hand slid down to her neck, and he cupped it gently. "How do you feel about that?"

Margery was very aware of their privacy, of his large hand rubbing her neck. The sunlight through the trees flickered light and dark across his face. "Let him come. He will see that my feelings for him are gone."

She came up on her knees, the fishing pole tumbling from her lap, water dripping from her legs. She didn't want to talk about Peter anymore. She put her hands on Gareth's face, and heard his quick intake of breath just before she gave him a swift kiss. "Your lips have haunted me," she whispered.

He caught her arms and pulled her across his lap, her head near his shoulder. Their open mouths came together with an urgency that consumed her, as his tongue explored her lips.

"Sweet Margery," he murmured, nuzzling her throat.

She stroked her hands through his hair, silently urging him on, letting the wildness in her soul take flight. Nothing mattered when Gareth held her. Their past and their mistrust vanished with the need they shared.

His hand slid up from her rib cage to cup her breast. She moaned against his mouth as he stroked her through her gown. She felt afire, restless, aching for more. He smelled wonderful, like the outdoors, not like a court dandy.

He lifted his head and watched her face as he continued to caress her breasts. She gazed at him through half-closed eyes, waiting, wanting. He reached beneath her and loosened the laces at her back. When she made no protest, but sighed and arched her back, his hands stilled.

"You would let me do this," he began, his voice husky, "here, on your lands?"

She pulled his head down and kissed him, sliding her tongue inside his mouth to taste him. He took her shoulders and held her away.

"Is this about anger?" he asked seriously. "I know something about that: you'd do anything to forget. I understand, but don't use *me* to forget."

Margery sat up in his lap. "Are you not using me? You don't love me, I don't love you. We're two people doing what we have to do in life, and neither of us is happy about it. If I want to snatch a moment's pleasure with you"—she ran her thumb gently over his lips— "what is to stop me?"

Gareth searched her face, lingering on her mouth. She was willful and impulsive, still certain of her ability to do what she wanted. But she ignited a fierce excitement inside him that he'd never imagined. She came up on her knees and straddled his hips, kissing him hard. The way she rubbed against him, he could have easily taken her right now.

He imagined the release of being inside her body . . . then decided against it. He was trying to woo her into marriage, not make her feel guilty over a quick toss in the grass. She was so angry at Fitzwilliam's betrayal that she would do anything to forget—even bed a man she didn't love.

She loosened the laces of his shirt, spreading it wide and placing the palms of her hands on his chest. Gareth held his breath as she pressed a kiss against his hot skin. With a groan, he lifted her head and covered her mouth one last time with his, all the while remembering the look on her face as she'd told him about Fitzwilliam. She still wasn't telling the entire truth.

He held her shoulders to push her away. "We must stop."

She sat back on his thighs and stared at him angrily. "I do not understand you. I can feel that you want me."

She rubbed her hips against his and he groaned.

"Margery," he whispered, "sometimes I can

think of nothing but wanting you. And then I remember the husband that you search for."

She stiffened.

"I imagine he wouldn't approve of this."

She scrambled off his lap and stared at him with fury darkening her blue eyes. "Why do you think I care? How can I respect a man who is only after my fortune?"

Gareth sat up straighter. He told himself he felt no remorse for his own motivations where Margery was concerned.

"Such is always the way among the nobility," he said softly. "Did not you learn such lessons in your childhood? A woman of privilege is seldom given the freedom to marry at will, as you have."

"But a man of privilege—what am I saying? *Any* man has more freedom than a woman. I am doing nothing more than a man would. I have made no commitments to a husband, therefore I am not bound in any way."

He gathered up their fishing poles, removing the fishhooks and string. "You are bound to yourself, just as I am. And I know this isn't what you truly want."

She opened her mouth to speak, then closed it. He watched the anger die away until there was only vulnerability. She sighed and rose to her feet.

"I won't argue with you anymore, Gareth. You must be starving, and I did not catch you a meal."

He watched her spread a blanket on the ground, then cover it with meat pies and cheese and berries. She broke open a round loaf of bread, and he heard his stomach rumble.

Margery glanced at him, but her smile was distracted. He was already regretting his words. At this very moment, he could have been inside her.

But he had to think of his distant goals—not the immediate ones. His vision told him he *would* have Margery in time.

In the middle of the night, Gareth woke out of a sound sleep and felt panicked. He sat up in bed, rubbing his face with both hands. Even his impending sword fight with Townsend had not made him feel like this. He was sweating, and his breathing felt labored, as the certainty of danger suddenly swept over him.

Margery.

He bounded out of bed and pulled on boots and his leather jerkin, grabbed his sword, and tore open the door. He ran down the corridor and opened Margery's door.

Her bedchamber was empty, her bed rumpled. On the edge of the sheets, he saw a spattering of blood.

Chapter 18

The shock that slammed through Gareth stole his breath. Someone had taken Margery. He was her personal guard, and he'd failed.

And there was blood on the sheets.

He could almost hear her father, Lord Welles, speak the words that had shaped the significant moments of Gareth's life. *You must protect her.*

What had he allowed to happen?

He ran back to his room, pulled on more clothing and a plated brigandine, then strapped on his sword and a dagger. He ran down the corridor, from one circle of light to the next, then took the stairs two at a time.

He already knew it was useless to search the castle. He had seen the truth in his visions, but he hadn't believed, arrogant fool that he was. Margery would be on a man's horse, heading down into the Severn Valley.

Would they cross the Severn and head into Wales, or take ship in Gloucester?

Outside, the night was moist with a misting rain that threatened fog. He didn't bother trying the gatehouse first. He could not explain the reason that he needed the gates opened and the portcullis raised in the middle of the night—not without risking that the entire household would discover Margery's abduction. Instead he quietly woke Desmond, who followed him down from the barracks and out into the ward, wearing only a long shirt.

"I'm not even dressed, Gareth," Desmond said with a grumble. "This had better be—"

"Margery is missing," Gareth said shortly as he entered the stables. "I need you to tell the gatehouse guards to let me out."

"Missing? Let me sound the alarm. We'll muster—"

"No!" He began to saddle his stallion. "What if her captor wishes to compromise and marry her? We can't let them be found together. I will go alone."

"Alone? 'Tis a foolish plan."

"Perhaps, but I know which way they are going," Gareth said, mounting his horse and trotting toward the gatehouse. "I can travel swiftly, and bring Margery back without anyone knowing."

Desmond ran alongside. "How do you know where they're going?"

"I just know."

At the gatehouse they found two soldiers unconscious, and the portcullis raised.

"They're alive," Desmond said as he knelt beside them.

"See to them, but don't let them know what happened. Lie, if you must." The horse was restless, and danced with Gareth's tight hand on the reins. "But Wallace, keep watch on the battlements for my return. I'll be back soon."

Desmond stood up as Gareth's horse entered the tunnel of the gatehouse. He called, "But how can you—right, you just know."

Gareth rode out into the night. Soon he was damp to the skin, but the discomfort was only what he deserved. Somewhere, Margery was alone with a scoundrel. She must be frightened, maybe seriously wounded, but he had no way to know.

He deliberately chose the road to Gloucester. A ship heading out to sea was the quickest way for a man and woman to escape. He prayed he'd made the right choice.

He gave the animal its head, and tried to think of nothing beyond his mission. Yet his mind whirled with thoughts he couldn't control.

How could he have been so arrogant as to think the vision of Margery on a man's horse was about him? He had paid more attention to seducing her than to keeping her safe.

He concentrated hard, trying to force his mind to show him Margery—but all he got for his effort was a headache that pounded between his eyes so hard he had to squint. The Beaumont Curse had never been his to command, only to suffer through.

An hour later, the road Gareth followed disappeared into a small forest where, beneath the trees, the darkness was almost complete. Owls hooted above him, and his horse slowed and became skittish. Not far away, he thought he heard a woman scream.

Cold fury welled up inside him, at himself and this man who dared to take Margery for his own. He slid off the horse, tied him securely, then crept forward. The sound of a voice grew slowly louder.

"Why did you make me do it?"

It was Humphrey Townsend. Gareth had never suspected him capable of such desperation. Why hadn't he killed Townsend when he had the chance?

Gareth suddenly realized that Margery wasn't answering. He held his breath, sweat making his clothes stick to his back.

"I didn't want to hit you," Townsend continued, "but you must marry me."

"I will not," Margery said coldly.

Gareth lowered his head as relief eased through him. She sounded unharmed, thank God. He got down on his hands and knees and crept forward through the brush. The rain had turned the earth to mud, which oozed between his fingers and coated his skin.

He peered through the undergrowth, wet ferns sticking to his face. He could see Margery, wearing just her nightclothes and dressing gown, sitting on a log before a small, sputtering fire. One soldier guarded her back.

Townsend stood over her, then threw his hands up with impatience and stalked away. "I don't really need your acceptance," he said over his shoulder. "If we stay here long enough, you shall be forced to marry me."

"I'd rather live with the shame."

Gareth grinned, enjoying the courage she displayed. He began to work his way around the edge of the clearing, until he was directly behind the soldier.

"Your brothers won't see it that way." Townsend squatted down before her. "I'll treat you well, I promise."

"Why do you need to force me into marriage?" Margery demanded. "Surely you earn enough to live decently. Any number of girls would—"

"Any number of girls don't have the dowry I need."

"Greedy, aren't you?" she said with sarcasm.

"No, I have sisters," he said glumly. "Sisters with no dowries of their own."

Gareth gave a grim smile. He and Townsend were not so different; both of them wanted to marry Margery for their own reasons. But this was hardly an amusing situation, what with the blood on her sheets, and knowing Townsend had been cowardly enough to hit a woman.

He waited until Townsend paced to the far side of the clearing. Then Gareth rose up and hit the soldier over the head, watching with satisfaction as he crumpled to the wet ground.

Margery gasped and whirled around, certain that a boar was charging her from the depths of the forest. But Sir Humphrey's henchman was unconscious, and Gareth stood there, muddy and wet and grinning at her. She would have thrown herself in his arms and sobbed her relief, but Sir Humphrey suddenly gave a yell and came running toward them.

Gareth stepped in front of her, shielding her. He held his sword in one hand, a dagger in the other. Sir Humphrey skidded to a stop.

"Beaumont," the man said, trying unsuccessfully to cover his dismay.

"Townsend," Gareth answered. He threw down his weapons and rushed the other knight, who fell backward with Gareth atop him.

As they rolled around in the mud, Margery stood up and peered side to side, trying to see Gareth. She winced at a particularly hard blow, then winced again as her bruised cheek began to ache. Soon Gareth was back on top, throwing punches into Sir Humphrey's face and stomach.

Margery began to feel sorry for her kidnapper when he covered his head with his arms. "Gareth!" she cried. "You can stop now!"

After one more punch to Sir Humphrey's jaw, Gareth got to his feet and stood above him. "I could kill you for this," he said with soft menace. "But I don't need to."

With a groan, the knight pushed up onto his hands and knees, then sagged against the log Margery had been sitting on.

"I can tell her brothers instead," Gareth continued.

"No," Sir Humphrey whispered.

Margery almost felt sorry for him. Her brothers *would* kill him if they knew what he'd done.

Gareth grabbed Sir Humphrey's tunic and lifted him, letting him dangle from his fist. "I will never see you near Margery again, will I?"

"No," Sir Humphrey mumbled.

"No what?"

"No, I won't come near her."

He sounded defeated, despondent, and Margery wondered how many sisters he had. Gareth picked up his weapons, and as he led her away, she looked over her shoulder to see Sir Humphrey holding his head in his hands.

"Are you sure it's safe to just . . . leave him?" she asked.

"I do not think he'll bother you again."

They reached Gareth's horse and he lifted her into the saddle sideways. When he slid in behind her, she turned in his arms and buried her face against him, regardless of the mud and water soaking his garments. She was grateful just to hold him. The horse trotted out of the forest and headed down the road that wound into the foothills of the Cotswolds.

Even now the terror of helplessness was hard to forget. Margery had thought her plan to find the perfect husband was destroyed, that she'd be married to a crude braggart. Sir Humphrey had threatened to rape her right there, in front of his soldier, if she didn't agree to marry him.

And then Gareth had come. She had not believed it possible that he could find her, yet he had. His face was hard and angry as he met her gaze.

"Are you hurt?" he asked.

"No. You came in time."

He closed his eyes briefly. "I should have known you were in danger. How did he—"

"Please, not now," she interrupted, huddling against him as the chill wind penetrated her wet clothes. "Take me home first."

When they arrived at Hawksbury, they silently entered the gatehouse and Gareth listened to the portcullis lower behind them. He rode through the tunnel, still cradling Margery. She'd been shivering uncontrollably for the last hour.

Wallace Desmond was waiting for them, his face grim as Gareth handed Margery into his arms. After Gareth dismounted, he took Margery back.

"Who did this?" Wallace asked.

"Townsend, but he won't bother her again—
and no, I didn't kill him, though maybe I
should have. How did you explain my actions
to the patrols?" Gareth asked, looking up at the
men walking the torchlit battlements.

"I told them the truth: that they'd already let
a brigand escape and were in serious trouble.
But they think this is a kitchen maid you're
rescuing."

"That was a good idea," Gareth said, eyeing
Wallace with new respect. "I had better get inside. Wallace, please see to my horse, then help
me find some hot water for Margery's bath."

"How are we going to keep *that* a secret?"
Wallace asked, wiping rain from his face.

Margery stirred. "We keep cauldrons boiling
in the kitchen," she murmured. "A few buckets
will do. I don't need a full bath."

Gareth ignored her. "We'll fill as many buckets as we can. I'll meet you in her bedchamber.
Hurry!"

Gareth carried Margery into the castle
through the garden entrance and fortunately
saw no one. In her chamber he set her in a
chair, where she hugged herself and shivered
as he dragged her wooden tub before the
hearth. He built a large fire, then lit every candle.

He turned to look at Margery, who still sat
dazed. "I'm going to get the twins," he said
firmly.

"No!" She straightened with her usual authority. "No one can know what happened."

"They will tell no one."

"Maybe not, but then I'll have taught them to live in fear. I will not do that. Gareth, you must promise me that only Sir Wallace will know about this."

"But why? Do you not want Townsend punished?"

"You have already done that. Just listen to me!" She reached for his hand and held it tight. "If the king hears that I am unable to protect myself, I'll be forced to live at Greenwich with the queen. Much as they have only my interests at heart, I won't let them supervise the decision of my husband. And if they're worried enough, they could force me to choose now!"

"None of this would have happened if I hadn't failed you." He'd never had such a shameful defeat in his life. Always he was the victor, even if he was sent away in the end. He let go of her hand and turned away. "I should have known what was happening. What is keeping Wallace?" he asked with exasperation.

"You said that before," Margery began slowly. "That you should have known. What do you mean?"

"A good soldier would anticipate problems like this," he answered, glancing at her to see if she believed him.

She looked suspicious, but she let it go.

After Wallace came in to dump the first

buckets of water into the tub, Gareth wet a cloth and began to clean her face.

She tried to push him away. "I can do this myself. I was just cold."

"Be still and let me see to your injuries." He tilted her head toward the light. "Your cheek is already starting to bruise. How will you explain that?"

"I tripped in the dark," she said immediately.

"Where else are you injured? I saw blood in your bed."

She grinned, then winced and touched her cheek. " 'Tis Sir Humphrey's."

He lowered the cloth and looked into her twinkling eyes.

"When I woke up and saw him, I punched him in the nose." She started to giggle, a little too loudly.

Gareth frowned as the giggles turned to shivering, and she squeezed her eyes shut. Each tear that fell hurt him like a knife to the chest. He pulled her into his arms, confused by his own anger and pain. He had saved her; why did he still feel so bad?

Wallace brought more hot water. Gareth wanted to help him, but Margery wouldn't let him leave.

When the tub was near full, Wallace gave a thoughtful look to Gareth, who was kneeling with his arms around Margery. She kept her face buried in his neck.

"Do you need anything else?" Wallace asked.

He shook his head. "Thank you for your help. Go find your bed."

Margery looked up and smiled. "Thank you, Sir Wallace."

When they were alone, Gareth ran his hand down her hair. "I am sure you can bathe alone. Call me back when you are finished."

She clutched his sleeves. "Don't leave. Drag the screen before the tub. Please, just . . . don't leave."

He couldn't go against her wishes if he wanted to. His guilt and his anger were so entwined, he didn't know where one left off and the other began. He tried to remember the revenge he wanted, and how much he despised her family.

But none of that mattered when she huddled against his chest and shivered . . . all because he hadn't protected her. She tried so hard to be brave and independent. To see her like this was almost too painful, and he didn't understand his feelings.

Gareth leaned down and pressed a kiss against her head. "Let me get the screen. You'll feel better in the water."

When everything was ready for her bath, Margery gave him a shaky smile and disappeared behind the screen. He tried to stay focused on his inadequacy, on what he should have done to keep her safe.

But the rustle of her clothing as it dropped to the floor seemed to echo loudly. She was naked, and there was only thin wood between them. He heard the splash of water when she entered the tub, then her groan of pleasure as she slid into the water.

Suddenly the room was too hot; he could see steam rising above the screen. Gareth loosened the laces of his shirt and tried not to imagine Margery in the tub, soapy water hiding and revealing her body. He sat in her chair, his elbows on his knees, his face buried in his dirty hands.

Her bath seemed to take forever. He heard her leave the tub and begin to towel herself dry.

"Gareth?" She sounded hesitant.

"Yes?"

"My dressing gown is too filthy to wear. Could you get a nightdress for me? They're in the chest beneath the window."

When he opened the chest, he inhaled the smell of roses. His hands shook as he lifted out a linen gown. The material was fine and thin, with lace sewn about the bodice.

What was his problem? Though he couldn't lie with Margery tonight, surely she was beginning to depend on him. She trusted no one else to see to her. Soon he would win her to wife.

He turned around and saw her standing before him, wearing only a cloth wrapped about her body. Her wet hair fell in wavy curls to her waist. She had long supple legs, delicate shoulders and arms. She crossed her arms at her waist, which pressed her breasts so high, he thought they'd spill out.

As Gareth stared at her, dumbfounded, she said, "May I have my nightdress now?"

Chapter 19

Margery tried not to smile as Gareth dropped the garment. He picked it up and handed it to her, his eyes glowing in the candlelight.

Her anger at this whole situation was returning, along with the recklessness that made her long for pleasure before she was forced to choose a husband. The look on Gareth's face just fueled the emotions that coursed through her.

She took her nightdress and disappeared behind the screen. For a moment her thoughts returned to Sir Humphrey, and she shivered at how close she'd come to forcibly becoming his wife.

Margery had needs of her own, none of which would be fulfilled in her marriage vows. She dropped the towel and pulled the nightdress over her head. Soon she would have memories of passion that didn't involve Peter Fitzwilliam.

She mulled over what she would do. Should she approach Gareth and blatantly kiss him again? He was a man; she didn't think he'd refuse her offer a second time. She imagined his shocked stare, and then his wondrous eyes would heat and—

Margery gave a little shiver. She could persuade Gareth to enjoy himself, at least this once.

Taking a deep breath, she came out from behind the screen. He stood beside the bed, his jerkin discarded, his shirt hanging loose at his neck. Her mouth fell open in surprise and rising anger. Did he think seducing her would be so easy? All right, she had meant to kiss him— but she would not be so quickly won.

Gareth said mildly, "Would you mind if I used the tub before I leave? I am covered in mud from my toes to my ears."

Her lips moved for a moment, but nothing came out. This wasn't going at all as she expected.

"Use my tub?" It came out like a squeak. "But . . . the water is dirty."

He shrugged and drew his shirt over his head, then leaned over to drop the garment on a chair. His bare chest was enough to take any woman's breath away.

Gareth smiled. "You were mostly cold and wet, not dirty—unless you hadn't bathed in months."

"I take frequent baths," she said, frowning.

She should look away, but he was half naked, and he was standing right beside her bed. He still had yellowish-green bruises from his first battle with Sir Humphrey, and there would probably be more after today.

She blatantly stared at him, at his broad, muscular shoulders, narrow hips, and heavy thighs. He wore a codpiece over his hose, and she blushed as she realized her interest.

He grinned as he walked toward her. "So may I use your tub, or would you like to stare at me for the rest of the night?"

Margery groaned and closed her eyes, knowing her face was bright red. "Forgive me. I do not normally—I mean I never—Oh, just use the tub." She turned away and covered her face.

He had the audacity to chuckle as he moved behind the screen.

She threw herself on the bed and covered her head with a cushion. But she could still hear him—the splash of the water as he entered the tub, his tuneless whistle.

She and her husband would most certainly have separate chambers. She wanted to control how much time they spent together.

But listening to Gareth splash about in the water, she imagined sitting before the fire with her husband each evening, climbing into bed together, doing . . . intimate things in that bed together. And waking up in each other's arms.

But then she would grow close to her husband, and he would sleep with a maidservant, or whatever men were wont to do. She couldn't bear to have her expectations crushed, so she wouldn't have any expectations at all beyond a civil, comfortable relationship—more like a partnership.

"Margery?"

She came up on one elbow. "Yes?"

"I hope I have not offended you by being so forward as to use your tub."

"Why, no, Gareth."

"Do not worry so. I am sure your husband would never dream of doing such a thing."

With a groan, she covered her face again. How had he known what she was thinking? She lay still, and as she listened to the sounds of him bathing, soon she was imagining touching him again.

Margery suddenly sat up. What was she waiting for? He was a man. He wouldn't refuse her—although he already had. Surely that was just on principle.

She stood up and walked slowly toward the screen, biting her lip. She put a hand on the wood and stopped, unsure of what to say. Then taking a deep breath, she stepped around the screen.

"Can I help you wash your back?"

Gareth stiffened at the sound of her voice, his back to her, his wet shoulders gleaming in the candlelight. His hair was damp, darker, slicked back. He looked over his shoulder at her with wary eyes, but didn't answer.

Silently she walked around to the front. He was almost too big for her tub. Soapy, cloudy water lapped at his bent knees. His lower body was a vague, rippling outline beneath the surface. He lifted his arms out and rested them on the edge of the tub, where they dripped water in soft spatters onto the floor.

The moment felt almost like a dream, where Margery did things she'd never do by day. Everything was forbidden, yet the intoxication of it lured her forward. At the foot of the tub she leaned over him, resting her hands on the rim. There were mysterious shadows flickering over his hips. She wanted to submerge her hands and explore.

He tilted his head back to look up at her. "Isn't this . . . dangerous?"

"Yes." Her voice was almost a whisper.

"If someone saw this—"

"They won't."

"I'm not sure why you're—"

"Shh." Margery slowly pushed her sleeves above her elbows. She glanced at the small table where the dish of soap and extra towel lay, but there was no washcloth. She spied it in the depths of the tub, next to his hip. She reached down into the water, making sure to brush along his flesh as she brought the cloth out.

He closed his eyes for a moment, and she felt wild and powerful. Did he tremble like she did? Gareth had lived many places, done many things. Surely her nearness did not affect him so much.

She wrung out the cloth, dipped it into the soft soap, then walked around to his back to kneel down. When she saw his hands grip the rim of the tub, she smiled with satisfaction.

Spreading the cloth across her hand, she murmured, "Lean forward."

There was a long pause and she thought for a moment that Gareth would refuse. She didn't know she was holding her breath until he finally did as she asked. Before she could change her mind, she began to wash his back in slow circles, being gentle where she saw bruises. His body was hard and so different from hers.

She didn't remember even having time to truly look at Peter like this. Their moments together had been quick and furtive and exciting, nothing like this slow, languorous danger that now moved through her. She dropped the cloth, lathered her bare hands, and began washing his neck beneath his hair.

He propped his head in his hands. She didn't know whether she was putting him to sleep or if he was enjoying her touch. She moved lower on his back, feeling his hot, wet skin and each muscle beneath the surface. As her hands dipped beneath the water, her fingers moving just past his waist, she felt him shudder.

Gareth pressed his fingers hard into his skull, trying to hold on to his sanity. Margery was doing her best to seduce him. Any moment now, his control would crack and he would drag her into the tub and thrust up inside her.

But he was determined that he would bed her only when she loved him, when she was choosing him as husband and they were bound together.

Women usually played coy and shy with him. He was supposed to guess their feelings and take action, so whatever they did sexually would be his fault, not theirs. All they would allow themselves was pretending to submit to his desires.

Never had a woman treated him like Margery did, like he was worth her time and attention.

He tried to tell himself that she always went after what she wanted because she was spoiled. She had her marriage plan all worked out, and it didn't include an unpredictable husband she desired too much.

He suddenly realized *he* was playing the woman's part in this seduction: flirting, responding, but not letting things go too far. He wanted her to become so frustrated that she had no choice but to marry him.

She gently pulled him back until his shoulders relaxed into her breasts, and he wanted to groan. She felt so good.

"I can see soap in your hair," she said softly,

her mouth close to his ear. "I'll have to rinse you."

"Yes." Gareth could whisper nothing else. He was pillowed against her breasts while her soapy hands slid down over his chest. Her fingertips flicked against his nipples and he jerked in her arms.

"Margery, don't do that." His voice was an awkward imitation of itself.

"Why not?" Her tongue traced his ear. "I want you to do the same thing to me."

She tilted his head back against her shoulder and covered his mouth with her own. Her teeth nibbled at him; her tongue licked him. He was wrapped in the heat of her passion, so close to surrender. When she tried to open his mouth, he gripped the last of his willpower and held her away.

"You don't really want this," he said hoarsely.

He saw fury come over her face an instant before she pushed to her feet. His head fell back against the tub, and he was suddenly alone and cold, his erection painfully hard.

"Why do you keep trying to tell me what I want?" she demanded, her hands on her hips. "I can make my own decisions."

"You're angry and frightened because of what happened with Townsend," he said. "This is the only way you think you can regain your authority."

She flung her arms in the air. "I don't know

what you're talking about!" She stalked around the screen.

He heard her flounce back onto the bed. He sat frozen, calling on all the restraint he'd been forced to develop over the years.

Rejecting Margery's advances was insane. How was this going to work in his favor? He might drive her away permanently.

Yet ... it felt like the right decision. He reached down for the bucket beside the tub, stood up, and poured it over his head. With a shudder, he let the now-cold water do its work.

Margery sat stiffly on the edge of the bed, crossed her arms over her chest, and fumed. How dare Gareth tell her what she wanted, what she needed! Every man she'd ever met had tried to influence her choices. Now she was the one in charge of her life—and he wouldn't let her do what she wanted.

"Margery?" he called.

She frowned. "What?"

"I have no garments here."

Her eyes widened as he came around the screen, wearing just a cloth about his hips, his skin damp, his blond hair tousled.

"I am sure no one will see me if I run down the corridor," he said.

"You're leaving?" Margery tried to sound confident, but only succeeded in sounding fearful.

Suddenly the thought of being alone this night brought on a wave of unfamiliar terror.

What was wrong with her? In an instant, she'd gone from desire to fright. Sir Wallace had surely searched the grounds and the castle; no one could get to her. In an hour or so, dawn would lighten the sky and she'd be safe for another day.

Gareth set his pile of dirty garments on a chair, then stood beside her bed. "I promise you that from now on I will be ever vigilant. This will never happen to you again."

Childish words spilled out of her. "I just . . . cannot be here alone tonight. Please—"

He sat down beside her and the mattress made her lean toward him.

"Your ladies could come sleep near you," he said. "I shall post guards right outside your door."

"No guards! I cannot show that I am afraid. And how could I explain all this to Anne and Cicely? Please, just . . . stay with me." She breathed her last words in a soft voice as she gazed into his eyes.

"Margery—"

"Please, Gareth." She leaned against him and rested her head on his shoulder. His skin was so warm, and smelled like soap. She heard his quick intake of breath. Now he would take her in his arms; now he would give her memories she'd grow old cherishing.

But he held her away. "I'll stay. Let me tuck you into bed, and I'll make a pallet before the fire."

She wanted to groan aloud. What did she have to do, force him back onto her bed and climb atop him?

"Margery." He said her name regretfully as he rubbed her arms. "You are not thinking clearly tonight. You have been frightened, and I'm here, and I'm . . . not so bad to look at. That is the only reason you are acting in this unusual manner."

She took a sharp breath. "What? You think I cannot control myself because of your looks? Do you think—oh! You are so arrogant." She grabbed a pillow and hit him with it.

Gareth ducked away and laughed. She came up on her knees to hit him again, then watched as he caught his towel before it fell. She had a sudden wild impulse to grab the towel away and see what he did. But he moved out of her reach.

"Do you have a spare blanket?" he asked.

She folded her arms beneath her chest and did her best to look mutinous. "In the trunk at the foot of my bed."

She watched him make his pallet. Beneath his skin, so many muscles rippled. When the thin cloth stretched taut over his buttocks, she slid into bed and pulled the blankets over her head with a muffled groan.

An hour later, Gareth stood over Margery and watched as she slept. He had wiped most of the mud off his leather jerkin, and now wore it like armor between the two of them.

Her face was calm, no longer fearful. Although his body still protested, he was glad he had not bedded her. In the morning she would have regretted her impulsiveness. He needed her to choose him, not run in fear from her feelings.

But there would be no peaceful dreams for him tonight, or visions, either, he was certain. He knew exactly what he wanted, and it was she, regardless of the secrets between them. He had even begun to think only of letting himself take her, pleasure her. At the thought of his vengeful plans, he felt uneasy.

He banished such thoughts. They would be wed; they would have passionate nights, and probably many children to keep her busy. He would never starve again, or be forced to sleep in rat-infested inns.

He tried to picture her brothers, to imagine basking in their anger while he enjoyed the contentment of vengeance. Yet Margery's smiling face had begun to replace such thoughts. Would she be smiling if she discovered the truth?

A sennight passed, and during the days, Gareth watched Margery keep herself busy with the harvest and the coming preparations for winter planting. Each evening he would come to her bedchamber to guard her. He knew she was still afraid to be alone, because she never asked him to leave.

Most nights she was asleep when he arrived. Then he would watch her, memorizing how she moved, the expressions on her face, the way her hair cascaded like a dark waterfall over the edge of the bed. He would imagine sliding under the cool sheets, lifting her night-clothes, and pulling her naked body against him.

Some evenings she was still awake, her eyes watching him intently as he closed the door and went to make his pallet. It was as if now that he'd rejected her, she would not approach him.

Night after night, the tension between them increased. If she just pressed herself against him, he would part her legs and take her wherever she stood. Instead he lay on his lonely pallet, listening to her breathe, his desire and his groin keeping him awake.

When he was in danger of forgetting his purpose, he prowled the room and made himself remember what she and her family had done to him. But those feelings were burning out beneath the lust that lay banked, waiting, inside him.

Chapter 20

One day a messenger arrived, and that night Margery waited for Gareth in her room, so excited she didn't even get ready for bed. She was no longer afraid to be alone, but she let him continue his vigil.

She was sitting cross-legged in bed, staring into a candle's flame, when he opened the door and slipped in. He never knocked, for that might awaken someone. Instead, it was always a sudden, delicious surprise when she saw him. The pleasure that moved through her kept her warm—as did the secret that she wanted to tell him.

Gareth leaned back against the door and looked at her quizzically.

She grinned.

He walked to the trunk for his blanket, eyeing her. She crawled to the end of the bed, then flung herself into his arms, making him stagger back a step. She stared up into his intent face, and her smile died as he looked at her mouth.

A shudder of pleasure, of excitement moved through her. In anticipation, she slid her hands up the back of his neck into his hair.

Yet he calmly lifted her hands away from him, and went to sit by the hearth. He didn't seem to see the room, or her, but something far away in his thoughts.

Gritting her teeth, Margery followed him and sat in the chair beside him. She tried to imagine another man, her husband, here in this room with her, but she couldn't. There were only images of Gareth—kneeling to make her a fire, changing his clothes behind her screen, standing beside her bed. She would have such wonderful memories to carry through her life, when her duties kept her alone. Yet she needed one final memory from him.

"Margery?" He suddenly got to his feet and came to her.

This was it. Her breathing was shallow; her heart began a wild pounding. *Please, let him touch me, let him take me to bed.* He leaned over her, blocking out the rest of the room, until her world was just the two of them. He lifted a hand and reached toward her.

"Margery, don't move. Your necklace has—"

As his fingers neared her chest, she couldn't help but jerk. The necklace fell in a heavy loop down her body, and beads scattered everywhere.

"—broken," Gareth finished, smiling.

She wanted to groan. He knew just what he was doing, what he did to her. She gave a reluctant laugh, and they both got down on their knees. In the dim firelight they searched for the beads. When their fingers brushed and connected near one, Margery lingered.

"Ah, ah, ah; this one's mine," she said, snatching it from his palm.

"Then this one's mine."

His fingers slid beneath her shin and she giggled. Soon they were each scrambling for the most beads they could carry. She only knew the warm breathlessness of their bodies straining, brushing. She picked up his foot to find a bead; he reached over her back for another one.

Finally they knelt facing each other, two piles of beads before them. Margery felt her breath catch as she looked up at him, and watched his gaze drop almost lazily down to her breasts. She froze, waiting, hoping, but he merely gathered up all the beads, placed the pile on her bed table, then stood looking down at her.

"Did the messenger today carry good news?" he asked.

She smiled. "My brothers will be here tomorrow." For just a moment before he turned away, she could swear that his face darkened with anger. She had to be imagining it.

"I haven't seen them in so many months. And they said Peter has already gone on to

London. This is wonderful news! I've even planned a hunt in their honor."

Gareth leaned his shoulder against the windowsill and looked out over the dark countryside. Meeting her brothers again had always seemed like a distant nightmare, far in the future, where he'd demand satisfaction and vengefully pummel them into unconsciousness.

But tomorrow they would come, and everything Gareth had worked toward with Margery would be in jeopardy. Bolton and Welles would take one look at him—a man who brutalized people at tournaments, who was followed by a murderous curse and strange visions—and cast him out of their sister's life.

But Margery was no longer a child, he thought, watching as she slipped behind the screen. She was a grown woman, with strong opinions and needs. And right now she needed him. He was her personal guard, the man she wanted in her bed before she married. He could not imagine her meekly agreeing with whatever her brothers said. She'd been a grief-stricken young girl when she'd last behaved like that.

He turned around as Margery reappeared, wearing her nightdress. Her long hair covered much of her body, but the gown was so fine that when she walked he could see the curve of her hip and the pale shadow of her nipples. She glanced at him, then stared, her face serious. He didn't know what expression he betrayed; he was beyond caring. He watched her climb into the four-poster bed and she eyed him almost warily as she pulled up the blankets and coverlet.

He should take Margery tonight. He walked slowly toward the bed, and her eyes grew wider and wider as she looked up at him. He saw the excitement, the knowledge in her gaze. She wanted him.

If he did take her, then when her brothers arrived, Gareth would have an even stronger hold over her. His seed would already be in her belly. Nothing could stop him from claiming his right to marry her.

He halted beside the bed, unlacing his tunic and shirt. She let the blankets slip down to her waist. She was breathing fast, and her eyes sparkled with that wildness that made him boil inside with need of her.

Unbidden, an image rose of her face if he claimed her as wife before her brothers. He tried to thrust the thought away, but it took hold and grew. She would be the one humiliated, not her brothers—because she would not have chosen him freely as husband.

He closed his eyes. Was this panic that he was feeling? He, who approached every battle with savage bloodlust? Her brothers loomed as vividly in his mind as cold-blooded monsters, yet they were only men. They'd been tamed by wives and children, whom they were anxious to get back to. They wouldn't be visiting Margery for long. All Gareth had to do was make them extremely uncomfortable, and then wait until they left. This time around, he would be the one with all the power.

Margery leaned back on her hands, and her nightdress slid off one shoulder. He could see her fragile collarbone, where he wanted to place his lips. But not tonight.

He sighed, kissed the top of her head, and walked toward his pallet.

"Gareth?" Her voice was quiet.

He paused, but didn't turn around.

"Why can't we?"

Over his shoulder, he said, "Because you would look at your brothers tomorrow and regret it. I will not be your bad memory."

"You are wrong," she said with conviction.

He sighed. "I've been wrong before." He stretched out on his hard pallet and flung his arm over his eyes.

In the great hall, Gareth sat beside Margery to break his fast. Though he was exhausted from little sleep, she could hardly keep still. Even at Mass she had constantly looked over her shoulder, as if her brothers would arrive at any moment. She was bursting with excitement, and he found himself more and more angry. Everything in both their lives came back to her brothers.

He left Margery to her preparations and

went out to the tiltyard. Under Wallace's tutelage, the solders and knights had become a fine fighting force. There were even a few whom Gareth thought he could take on and actually enjoy the fight.

But today he leaned against a rail and glowered at everyone.

Wallace eventually strolled over and leaned beside him. "It's been a few days since you looked this mean."

"I am not mean."

"I'll reserve opinion on that. 'Tis just that lately, you've been rather . . . jovial."

"I am never jovial."

Wallace sighed. "However you choose to call it, I thought you had been succeeding in your courtship of Mistress Margery."

Gareth shrugged and frowned.

"Ah, you've had a problem."

"Not until today."

"What happened today?"

Gareth glanced at Wallace. "Her brothers will soon arrive."

"Oh, I see."

Gareth had a strong urge to punch that grin off Wallace's face. But he contained himself.

"Do I need to reassure you?" Wallace asked. "You have won the lady's affection. Surely her brothers cannot change that."

For a moment, Gareth almost wanted to explain all of his past with Margery's family. But he'd never had a friend who remained friendly once he learned the whole sordid truth. He had become too comfortable with the man, and that was dangerous.

Though Wallace seemed different from other men, Gareth still would not test him. "I can handle her brothers. I just wanted to warn you to steer clear of Bolton if you can."

Wallace raised his eyebrows. "Just because I know him?"

"Why would you work as a captain of the guard if you're inheriting a barony? He might also be suspicious that two men from his past are both here with his sister. I do not mean for you to hide, but if you can avoid him . . ." His voice trailed off.

"I understand," Wallace said softly. "I shall do my best."

Before the midday meal, horns sounded a blast, and a dozen men on horseback came through the gatehouse. Gareth put down his blunt sword and walked to the edge of the tilt-yard. He recognized the two men in the lead as Margery's brothers, Viscount Reynold Welles, and James Markham, Earl of Bolton.

They both looked hale and fit, considering they'd just returned from defeating the pretender to the throne and his supporters. They were dark-haired like Margery, but Welles was a tall, broad mountain of a man next to Bolton's thinner build. Welles wore plain, functional garments, while Bolton dressed as if he were going to court instead of traveling from battle.

They looked around the inner ward, where Gareth stood waiting, but they didn't notice him. As the company dismounted, pages and squires ran to take their horses. The doors to the great hall opened, and Margery descended regally, followed by her ladies, wearing a smile that could have split her face. The last few steps, she gave a glad cry and ran to her brothers. They grabbed her up, passing her between them for hugs.

Gareth walked closer, needing to hear everything. His stomach roiled with anger and tension, and he was barely able to keep a fierce frown from his face.

Margery stood between her brothers, with their arms overlapping across her shoulders. "It is so good to see you both," she said happily. "I worried every day that you were with the king."

"The Irish didn't mount much of a battle," Bolton said with easy confidence. "We barely got dirty."

Welles rolled his eyes. "It was not quite that easy."

"Nevertheless, the pretender will be turning the roasting spits in the royal kitchens from now on."

Everyone laughed, and Margery's brothers turned to introduce her to the men they'd traveled with. More knights for her to consider for husband—more men Gareth would have to discredit. He was beginning to regret not bedding her last night.

Everyone trooped inside for dinner, so Gareth washed up and followed them. Margery had already seated her brothers at the head table, along with a few of their companions. Ladies Anne and Cicely were each seated between two men, and they looked flustered and happy.

Gareth almost sat at a lower table to give Margery and her brothers privacy, but he caught himself in time. What was the point of revenge if Welles and Bolton knew nothing of it?

He approached the head table. Margery's smile softened as she looked at him. "Gareth, come sit with us. You remember my brothers."

Gareth could tell that at first the younger brother did not remember who he was. Welles wore a polite smile as he rose to his feet. But Bolton had been a man when he'd forced Gareth to leave his home. He remembered. His smile died, and his eyes narrowed as he looked between Gareth and Margery.

"Gareth Beaumont?" Bolton said to Margery.

"Yes. Do you not remember? He fostered with us."

Gareth saw Welles's quick frown, and he knew how their minds were working. They were remembering his family curse, the tournaments where he had crushed every opponent, how he'd been driven from England. They took in his plain jerkin and simple boots.

When Margery gave Gareth the place beside her, Welles's eyebrows rose, and Bolton frowned. It was a good, satisfying moment.

Margery could barely contain her excitement. Her brothers were whole and well, and their service to King Henry was temporarily over. She knew their wives must be missing them terribly. And imagine, they each had a child to return to! Sometimes it was incredible how things had changed.

She suddenly felt Gareth's thigh along the length of hers, and she struggled not to blush. Things had changed for her, as well. She passed him a loaf of bread and he smiled that devilish smile at her.

"So, Margery," began her brother James, "how goes the husband hunt?"

She sighed, regretting that James was ever to the point. Every young man they'd traveled with turned his curious gaze on her. With a sinking feeling, she realized her brothers had brought these men for her to look over, like sheep at the market. She rescued her faltering smile when Gareth rested his hand on her thigh.

"James," she said, "that is hardly polite dinner conversation. I am meeting men, I am not 'hunting.'"

Everyone laughed, but she had to force her laughter. How dare her brothers assume she needed their help? They had each made a few foolish choices, and somehow each had come out happy. Why couldn't they leave her alone?

"If we cannot discuss your life, Margery," Reynold said, "then what kind of brothers are we? We are only concerned for you."

She smiled sweetly through gritted teeth. "Then let us discuss this later in private."

James arched an eyebrow as he looked at her. "We go away for a few months, and you've become your own woman."

"I've always been my own woman. And how is your new daughter?"

Throughout the meal, she kept the conversation away from herself. She knew James and Reynold watched her with concern—and watched Gareth with suspicion. Let them look. She wanted Gareth beside her, and she took strength from the comfort of his hand touching her. He was a reminder that she could live her own life, make her own decisions, even where he was concerned.

As the maidservants were carrying out tarts and pies and puddings for dessert, James pushed back his bench and looked thoughtfully at her. She braced herself; then his gaze turned on Gareth.

"Beaumont," he began, "I heard you've been out of the country these past few years."

Chapter 21

Margery held her breath as she turned to look at Gareth.

"I have most recently lived in France," he said.

James rested his elbow on the table. "What did you do there?"

It was her turn to lay her hand on Gareth's thigh.

"Mostly tournaments and mercenary work," he said.

"You could not do that here?"

Margery saw her brothers' friends eyeing Gareth, whispering to one another and frowning. She could not imagine what it must be like to be treated this way. She used to fear it, and lived her life with the worry of it, but now it only angered her. She opened her mouth to defend him, but he squeezed her hand in warning.

"I couldn't earn my living here," he said calmly, his gaze intent on James.

"And why is that?"

"Because every tournament I entered, I won. My opponents were upset by that. In fact, I am sure I remember some of your friends here." He glanced around the table pointedly, and Margery wanted to cheer.

Reynold gave James a warning look. " 'Tis good to see you in England again," Reynold said.

Margery thought even Reynold's politeness sounded forced. What was wrong with her brothers? They were usually never rude.

"So why have you come to see Margery?" James asked.

She wanted to groan. There, it was out: the question she had been dreading. She could hardly tell them she'd felt the need to hire a personal guard. "He was traveling through, and I asked him to visit for a while."

"Let Beaumont answer," James said in a low, tense voice.

Margery's fury rose to new heights. How dare James question Gareth, a man who'd saved her life and helped her whenever she needed it! As if James should even talk, considering that he used to treat his own wife with disrespect.

Again she felt Gareth stroking her hand, calming her.

"Margery," Gareth said, "it is not necessary for you to speak for me. I am not hiding the fact that I came back from France specifically to see you. Lord Bolton, do you have trouble with that?"

James got to his feet, and Reynold grabbed hold of his arm and pulled him back down.

Reynold said calmly, "Margery, we are both tired from travel and fighting, and being away from home. If we are overprotective, it is because we love and care for you. At least judge us knowing that."

Margery forced herself to calm down. She motioned for the jugglers and musicians to begin their entertainment—anything to get the table's focus off her and Gareth. She felt her brothers' disapproval as a palpable thing. Did even James and Reynold put stock in something as foolish as the Beaumont Curse?

Margery spent the afternoon preparing for the hunt, talking to her brothers about their families, and getting to know some of the friends they'd brought to meet her. She was meeting so many new men that soon she'd have to create a list. However was she to keep track of which men fit her standards?

For she was certainly not going to let the king choose one for her.

After supper, while the musicians played and couples danced, James sat alone with Reynold at the head table, watching his sister be courted by the men he'd brought for her. He'd thought it would make him happy to be helping her—but it didn't.

He sighed and swallowed more ale. He felt Reynold's amused gaze.

"Doesn't this make you feel ill?" James asked.

Reynold smiled. "Uncomfortable, perhaps."

"I always knew she would marry. I've met many a man who's asked to court her, but I never actually watched them do it."

He glowered as Margery was swept from one dancing partner to another.

"It almost makes me want to draw my sword," Reynold said in bemusement.

"Exactly." James gazed about the room until he found Gareth Beaumont. The man was dressed in the plainest brown tunic, as if he were a soldier instead of a knight. He sat alone at a table and watched the festivities. One after another, pretty serving girls approached his table, and one after another he sent them away distractedly. James knew damned well whom Beaumont watched. But Margery did not dance with him.

"You do see whom Margery is avoiding," James said as he slammed his tankard down a bit too hard.

"Gareth Beaumont."

James eyed his amused brother. "This is not funny. He never takes his eyes off her, the big ox."

Reynold glanced at him. "I think I object to that."

"Well, you're not an ox—a giant maybe, but that is off the subject."

"Which is Gareth Beaumont."

"Yes."

"Margery may be avoiding him, but she watches him."

"She does not," James quickly said.

"Oh yes. Do you not remember them as children? I know you were not around as much as I, but—"

"I was there enough. But I don't want to remember."

"He was good to her," Reynold said quietly. "He saved her life. And then we sent him away. Maybe we made a mistake."

"We had to protect her," James insisted. "I am her guardian; I will not second guess my every decision where Beaumont is concerned. His family, his lack of wealth or lands—hell, have you ever seen him fight? He can be vicious."

"But it is her choice now," Reynold said, "thanks to your friend the king."

James only grunted his response. He watched as Margery went to Beaumont's table and leaned down to speak to him. Their heads were close together, and James didn't like the way they smiled at each other. Beaumont stood up and they walked to the center of the floor.

Reynold caught James's arm. "Leave them be. We have raised her well, and she shall make the right decision."

"But he has nothing to offer her!" James said, watching with distaste as Beaumont put his hands on Margery's waist to lift her during a dance. They didn't take their eyes off each other. "I can't look anymore."

"Just sit there. It will get easier."

"Are they still watching us?" Margery asked, as she and Gareth linked hands for the dance.

"Of course they are. What did you expect?"

She sighed. "That they would realize that I'm an adult, and can make my own decisions."

"They're simply protective," he said, and she thought he sounded reluctant.

"You are my protector now."

"But you won't tell them that."

"If they thought I was in danger, they would make me return to one of their homes. I cannot live under that kind of scrutiny."

The dance separated them, and Margery watched Gareth move from woman to woman. She had never thought she'd be this angry, this disappointed with her brothers. She had so looked forward to their visit; now they were judging her friendship with Gareth, and finding it lacking.

Each of her brothers had lived his own life, and made some really foolish mistakes. So had she. But she'd be damned if she would always suffer for it.

When Gareth returned to her, Margery whispered, "You are still coming to my chamber tonight."

His eyes widened. "But your brothers—"

"I do not care. I feel safe with you there, and I will not let them change my decisions."

"I think you'll regret this," he said quietly.

"I don't regret anything I do with you. And if you try to refuse me again, guard, I will kiss you right now before all of them."

He smiled. "Then I would have to fight them."

"Just say you'll come."

His gaze dropped to her mouth and his smile died. "I will not disappoint you."

When Gareth slipped into her bedchamber at midnight, Margery was waiting for him. Before he could say anything, she pressed him against the wall and pulled his head down for a kiss. She'd wanted this all evening. When she should have been scrutinizing potential husbands, she'd only dreamed about having his arms around her. She tasted the inside of his mouth with her tongue and he groaned.

"Margery," he whispered her name against her lips, "this is dangerous."

She pressed kisses to his cheek and chin and neck. "I know. Isn't it fun?"

He lifted his head and held her away. "But as I left the corridor, I thought I heard—"

There was a brisk knock at the door. She stared at it, wide-eyed.

"—your brothers," Gareth whispered.

She nodded frantically toward the window, then followed him to make sure he couldn't be seen behind the draperies. She took a deep breath, pulled her dressing gown tighter, and marched to the door.

When she opened it up, Reynold and James stood there. They weren't smiling.

"Might we come in, baby?" Reynold asked.

"Of course, though it is rather late." She winced at his old nickname for her, and stepped back as they walked past her. She longed to run down the empty corridor, as far away as she could.

But she was stronger now. She was a woman who wanted to play the game of life by a man's rules—and she was doing it. She found herself wondering how often her brothers had had women in *their* chambers.

Margery shut the door, then gestured to the chairs before the hearth. As they sat down, she pulled up another chair from the corner of the room.

James cleared his throat. "Do you know Beaumont's true purpose for being at Hawksbury?"

She stiffened and thought of poor Gareth listening to this. "You can't even be civil before you start in with your questions? No 'how are you, how was your evening?' "

"How are you? How was your evening?" James repeated with a smile.

"Fine and fine." She got to her feet. "You may both go now."

Reynold stood up and put his arm around her shoulder. "Baby—"

"Do not call me that!" she said, pulling away from him. "You're trying to remind me that I am still your little sister. But I'm a woman now, and have been given the freedom to make my own decisions."

"We know that," Reynold said quietly. "And I only call you that name because it has good memories for me."

"It does for me as well, but I am no longer the same person."

"We can see that," James said, leaning back in his chair and stretching out his legs. "But that doesn't negate our concern. Do you know of Beaumont's past? If you did, you wouldn't have him here."

"I know everything. He is my friend, he has *always* been my friend. And if he wants to court me, like every other man I meet, then who are you to stop him?"

"But he is so unsuitable!" James said with obvious frustration.

"Did you ever think that might be one of the reasons I like him?" Margery demanded, knowing she only said it to be shocking.

Why did they have to keep insisting that they knew better than she did? For a wild moment, she wanted to rip open the draperies and reveal her forbidden dalliance with Gareth. But it would only be spite on her part, and she couldn't use Gareth just to make a point.

She longed to have this whole "husband hunt" over with. Yet then she thought of Gareth, and the pleasure of looking forward to her evenings with him. He would leave her after she married, and her nights would be lonely.

The idea of him not being in her life was beginning to hurt.

Reynold stepped between them. "I am sorry we disturbed you, sweetheart," he said, and hauled James out of his seat. "Maybe we interfere too much. Maybe we should have trusted you all those years ago, instead of sending Gareth to another foster home."

Margery stared at him, trying to remember to breathe. "You sent him away?" She couldn't stop herself from glancing at the window in horror. Gareth had saved her life and her brothers had sent him away. *This* was why Gareth was so bitter toward her family. My God, did he think even *she* was involved?

"It was my decision," James said. "Do not blame Reynold."

"We made it together," Reynold insisted. "Father had just died, and you were our responsibility."

James tried to take her hand, but she pulled away. "Margery, please, we had never been fathers. We wanted to protect you from anything unsavory, anything that could hurt you."

She turned her back on them, tears stinging

her eyes, and looked at the draperies where Gareth hid. "You yourselves hurt me. I cried for weeks, thinking that Gareth didn't want to be my friend. And can you imagine how he felt? He rescued me, and you punished him— a mere child himself."

"We cannot change our mistakes," Reynold said softly. "All we can ask is that you forgive us."

Margery turned to stare at them. They looked serious and uncertain and worried. But she still thought of Gareth, thrust out into the world at twelve years of age, with no family, no home—betrayed. "I don't know that I can," she said softly. "I have to think on it."

Reynold nodded. James opened his mouth to speak, then changed his mind. They walked to the door, but she didn't follow them. When they both turned back toward her, she looked away. The door closed.

Gareth didn't move.

Margery *hadn't* sent him away. She hadn't known. They'd both been victimized by her brothers—men who thought nothing of manipulating other people's lives on a whim.

Margery pulled the draperies back, tears running down her face. "I didn't know what they'd done," she cried.

He looked into her clear eyes and thought of all the cruel things he'd said to her. He pulled her into his arms, burying his face in her hair.

" 'Tis all right," he whispered. "You must not blame yourself."

She shook with sobs. "You . . . must have felt . . . so alone. I can't imagine what you went through."

"I survived." He took her face in his hands and kissed the tears she shed for his pain. Her lips were salty with them. She slid her arms up his back and held him tight against her. Her body sheltered him, comforted him. With a groan, he slanted his head and took her open mouth in a deep, desperate kiss.

Never had his emotions swamped him like this. Margery was the only sane thing in his world, and he clung to her now. He suckled her throat, whispered into her ear of her incredible beauty.

Then she stepped back, and Gareth's eyes widened as she shrugged her nightclothes off one shoulder, revealing the soft perfection of her breast. His mouth went dry when she shrugged again and the garments dropped to her waist. He stared helplessly at her body, his mind flooding with the shock of fierce arousal. With a final fluid movement, she sent the nightclothes sliding to the floor.

Chapter 22

With a feeling of incredible joy, Margery watched Gareth fall to his knees before her. He pulled her against him, bringing her nipple into his mouth. She gasped and arched her back, and he held her tight to keep her from falling. He sucked and licked at her nipple, then worshipped her other breast with his mouth.

She put her arms around his head and held him to her. He moved between her breasts, and his tongue against her made her feel as if she'd never known her own body before.

He sat back on his heels to look at her, his hands sliding lightly from her hips to curve around her buttocks. She didn't feel embarrassed, only proud as he looked at her with such desire, such aching need in his beautiful, golden eyes. She wanted to be everything for him.

He pulled her toward him again, his mouth against her stomach now. His hands traced light, erotic paths to the front of her thighs, and his thumbs stroked the hair between her legs. She gasped and shivered, and would have collapsed had he not held her up. His fingers slid deeper and deeper, until the unbearable tension and pleasure made her shudder and brace herself against his shoulders.

Gareth stopped moving, and she gave a little cry of disappointment. He couldn't stop now! He wouldn't—

He stood and swung her up into his arms, then kissed her passionately as he strode to the bed. She moaned when he laid her down because she didn't want to be separated from him. He stepped back and swiftly pulled at the laces of his tunic and shirt. She slid his hands aside, then separated his laces, feeling his skin beneath her fingers.

He dropped his head back, eyes closed, and stood tensely beneath her explorations. She pulled his tunic over his head, then her hands glided over his upraised arms to meet at his chest. She touched him through his shirt, then slid her hands beneath to caress his flat stomach.

"Margery, please," he whispered, pulling her face up for a kiss. "This is torture. I have to—"

"Shh," she said against his mouth, moving her hands up over his chest. "I have wanted to look at you, touch you, for so long." She took his shirt off, then bent and kissed his nipples as he had done to hers.

With a shudder, he pulled their hips together. She rubbed herself against him as she untied his hose and codpiece, then stepped back to let them slide to the floor.

Gareth was so wonderfully made. She explored his chest, his arms, his stomach with her mouth and hands, touching each scar and fading bruise. She let her fingers tease him, never quite touching his erection, but tickling the curling hair surrounding it. He was trembling, and she felt the wonder and power of what they could do to each other. She walked behind him, kissing his back, gently massaging his buttocks, before sliding her hands around his hips—and took his penis in her hands.

Before she could do more than stroke him lightly, he turned around and lifted her off the floor.

"But Gareth—" she began, laughing. He dropped her back on the bed and came down beside her.

He shushed her with a kiss. "I refuse to spill my seed anywhere but inside your body."

"You were in danger of that?" she whispered, trying not to smile.

"I want to bring you pleasure." His voice was a low rumble in his chest.

She moaned softly as he slid his mouth down to one breast, and his fingers teased the other.

"Oh, you bring me much pleasure." She arched her back and held him against her.

"Not yet enough." His lips were strangely erotic and tender, all at the same time. He licked and touched and sucked until she moved restlessly beneath him, aching for more. She wanted him inside her, filling her, making her a part of him.

Margery rolled against him and held him to her chest. "Please, Gareth, please."

He smiled into her face, looking so young, so happy. "Soon, my sweet." As he watched her, he parted her legs and cupped her body gently in his palm, rocking and rubbing against her. Her head fell back as a shudder took her, drawing her ever closer to the wonder promised by his touch.

Gareth began a gentle exploration with his fingers, sliding and circling and rubbing until her breath came in little gasps and she was pressing up against him. He lowered his mouth to her breast, and she was suddenly mindless, aching. A shuddered release of pleasure rocked her, wiping away everything in her life but him.

She wanted and needed him. He rose up above her, parted her legs with his hips, then settled against her, rocking, until more waves of sensual madness moved through her. He was hot and hard, so different from herself.

Margery leaned up to kiss him, her tongue finding his mouth, wanting to give him everything he'd just given her. Restlessly her knees lifted, and with a thrust he entered her body. She groaned, burying her face in his neck, feeling that they were a part of each other.

Gareth held still, kissing her cheeks, her eyelids, her lips. When he did begin to move inside her, he was slow and gentle in care for her. No man had ever treated her as if she was more important than he was.

He lifted himself up on his arms and looked down at where their bodies joined. "You feel incredible," he said.

"*You* are incredible."

He searched her eyes, his smile dying. He leaned down to give her soft kisses which turned gradually deeper and harder, just like the thrusting of his body. He moved faster, exciting her again to join him on the brink of this joyous release. Margery cried out this time and held him tight, as with a groan he released himself and gave her everything.

For endless moments, they just tried to breathe. Gareth never made her feel crushed, only safe and relaxed. He lifted his head and smiled into her eyes. After a gentle kiss, he rolled to one side and threw an arm across her.

When she reached for the blankets, he stopped her. "Are you cold?"

"No," she said softly.

"Then do not cover yourself. Let me look on the most wondrous sight of my life."

His words and the gentleness of his voice

warmed and soothed her. They lay with their legs entwined, their bodies satisfied.

With the drowsy pleasure of his head resting against her breasts, she closed her eyes and slid her fingers through his hair.

"Margery?"

She opened her eyes. Gareth propped himself on one elbow, and his hand gently cupped her breast.

She smiled. "That feels good."

He searched her face with a seriousness that began to worry her. "Margery, will you tell me more about Fitzwilliam?"

That name shattered their intimacy. She tried to sit up, but he held her down. She spent a long moment searching his face, feeling tense and miserable. How could Gareth spoil everything like this? Why—

And then it came to her. Feeling nauseous, she whispered, "How did you know?"

"I felt no maidenhead," he answered. He didn't look angry or disgusted, just concerned.

Tears pricked her eyes, but she refused to cry. No man would cry over a foolish mistake. She remembered the pain of her first encounter with Peter; there had been none of that this time. With her wedding night, she would have to pretend. "Say your piece and be done with it," she said angrily.

"My piece?" He reached up to caress her cheek, but she stopped him. "Margery, what did he do to you?"

"He did not rape me, if that is what you're thinking."

"I am glad to hear it." She tensed as he kissed her between her breasts, then lay his head there, still looking into her face. "Do you want to tell me?"

"Do I have to?" She felt ridiculous, defensive, while he looked at her so calmly.

"No. But you might feel better."

She closed her eyes and pressed her lips together to keep them from trembling. Gareth knew at least part of her secret, and he didn't seem to hate her. But saints above, to relive such a terrible time in her life—she didn't know if she could. She opened her eyes and a foolish tear escaped.

"Margery." His whisper was almost a groan. He moved up, still lying against her, and kissed her cheek. "Tell me."

She couldn't look at him, so she rolled away. But he pressed up against her back, tucking his legs behind hers, hugging her waist with a strong arm. He had always made her feel safe in his embrace.

"Peter told me we would be married," she said softly. "I loved him, and I thought he loved me. So I let him . . . I let him . . ."

" 'Tis all right." He kissed her neck.

But it wasn't. She just couldn't bring herself to tell him the humiliation of Peter's rejection merely because she didn't conceive. "A few weeks later, he said he wouldn't marry me."

"That is all? He did not give you a reason?"

"It concerned his family." That wasn't a lie.

"All you had to do was tell your brothers. Fitzwilliam would have had no choice."

"Do you think I want a forced marriage, with no trust, no respect? That would hurt too much."

He was quiet for a moment, his breath soft across her hair. "Margery, now I've hurt you, too."

"No, you haven't!" she insisted, rolling on her back to look up at him. "This was my choice. I wanted this pleasure, just as you did. I don't want marriage from you, just a wonderful memory." At least she thought she did. She was confused and lonely and hurting, but Gareth made all of it go away.

She pulled his head down and kissed him, gently at first, then with increasing ardor. They were both breathing heavily when he lifted his head.

"I'm not sure this is the right thing to do," he said, but his gaze was on her mouth, then her breasts.

"I'm sure." She rolled until he was on his back, then rose above him. Up on her knees, she considered his long body. "Can I . . ." Her words trailed off, and she felt herself blush.

He gave her that devilish smile that melted her. "Can you what?"

"Can I touch you however I'd like?"

She literally saw the shudder move through his body. "I am yours, my lady."

She laughed. "I am no one's lady."

He caressed her knee as his smile faded and his gaze grew serious. "You are my lady."

"For tonight," she whispered, letting her hand rest on his hip.

He didn't answer, just watched her.

Margery stared at his wondrous body, at the many differences between them. Then she started to touch the sloping muscles of his stomach, his nipples, so much smaller than hers, the soft skin of his elbow, the hair leading down from his chest. It was empowering to know that she could make him tremble, that he trusted her enough to lie vulnerable to her. There was a strange, gratifying tenderness in the pit of her stomach when she looked on him.

But then it changed into something more demanding, more primitive. She straddled his hips, and heard his strangled groan as she settled herself against his penis.

"Does this hurt?" she asked.

"No; God no," he half-gasped.

Feeling wicked, she rubbed against him, and felt him grow even larger. She had never thought nudity could be so enjoyable. She kissed his chest, his stomach, his mouth, never letting him penetrate her body.

Knowing he couldn't take much more of her sensual exploration, Gareth grabbed her arms. "Come here."

"But I'm already—"

"No, up here." He raised himself up, and took her breast into his mouth. As she stiffened and moaned, she brought his erection even closer to the depths of her body. She was hot and wet, as if she was made to be this way only for him. Never had he known such incredible, deeply felt pleasure as having Margery writhe in his arms.

He rolled on top of her, hushing her disappointed cry with his lips. He kissed his way down her body, nibbling between her breasts, trailing his tongue in a long line down her stomach. He spread her trembling thighs and felt her stiffen.

"Gareth—"

"Shh."

He kissed the most intimate part of her. She gave a hoarse cry, then shuddered in his arms. When his own body ached beyond all his restraint, he buried himself inside her, pillowed his chest against hers, and cupped her face in his hands. He looked into her eyes as he moved ever deeper. Memorizing the passion on her face, he closed his eyes and tumbled with her into the brilliant abyss they'd made together.

Margery remained awake as Gareth slept beside her. She nestled in the crook of his arm, her hand caressing his chest, her gaze lingering on his face. His beauty made her ache inside, but she could not let that sway her.

She had succeeded in this one quest. She had incredible memories of Gareth—and they would have to last her forever. She thought again of the list of husbands she was composing, but couldn't imagine lying beneath even one of them.

That didn't matter, though, she told herself. What mattered was living her life the way she wanted, and never, ever being hurt again.

She rose up on her elbow to caress Gareth's cheek. He slept on, undisturbed. Even with all her careful plans, the sorrow of leaving him would be hard to escape.

An hour before dawn Gareth was wide awake, with Margery sleeping against his side. He tried to tell himself that everything had gone according to plan, yet he still felt sick inside.

What had he done? He'd used her to assuage a life's worth of loneliness, just as he'd meant to use her against her brothers. He'd been manipulating her as her brothers had done to both of them.

He was no better than Peter Fitzwilliam.

She'd been so hurt. Gareth kissed the top of her head, caressed her bare shoulder. He would have cruelly married her regardless of her feelings, regardless of the fact that he hadn't loved her.

When he looked on her wondrous, innocent

face, he ached for what she'd suffered, for what he'd done to her. He'd seduced her for his own purposes, for money and revenge.

He couldn't hurt her anymore. She deserved a world of happiness, and that meant a good, honest husband. That would never be he.

A sudden sharp stab of pain in his skull made him shudder. Margery stirred, and he was able to slide his arm out from beneath her before another pain overtook him. He stood up, and the room whirled as the colors of a vision formed in his mind.

This time Margery appeared, looking happy and in love. She wound her arms around a man and kissed him.

But it wasn't Gareth. It was a stranger, someone who would make her happier than Gareth ever could. The vision faded, leaving him with a pounding head and battered spirits. Even God knew that he didn't deserve her. He dressed quickly, and allowed himself only one last look at her face, then left her chamber before the castle awoke.

When Margery opened her eyes, the pale light of dawn flooded her room. Gareth was gone. She hadn't expected anything else; he was always gone by morning to protect her reputation.

She dropped her head back on the pillow. She was tired of always being protected, like a fragile doll people set on a shelf and didn't play with. Last night she had determined her own destiny, and it felt . . . good . . . maybe.

Or did it only remind her of everything she'd never have?

As she dressed she told herself it would be easy to face her brothers; they never had to know that she had needs like any man.

Yet lying to them made her feel ill, even though they'd lied to her for years. Gareth had suffered because of them, so why should she feel guilty over her secrets?

At Mass, James and Reynold sat with Margery, and she noticed Gareth far back in the chapel. They all went into the great hall to break their fast, and again, her brothers were near her, and Gareth far away. She didn't know what to say to any of them. Her brothers seemed soft-spoken, abashed at their mistakes. And they *had* apologized. When she finally gave them a strained smile, they looked relieved.

Margery tried to meet Gareth's eyes, but he never lifted his head. What was he thinking? Surely he didn't regret their night together. Or was he worried that he'd reveal too much by simply gazing at her?

She felt uneasy sitting apart from him. She enjoyed his wit, the way she'd finally gotten him to laugh, how safe she felt near him.

She enjoyed him too much. Maybe it was better if they remained apart for a while.

An hour later, her guests and household met

in the inner ward for the coming hunt. The houndsmen restrained the greyhounds, who barked and strained at their leashes. People were armed with bows and swords. A crossbow hung on her own saddle, and a dagger rested in its sheath on her belt.

The servants departed the castle early: the grooms to drive the boar and deer toward the hunting party, and the kitchen servants to set up pavilions and food for the meal. Soon the hunting party set off on horseback for the journey to Margery's forested land—the same woods where Gareth had rescued her from Humphrey Townsend.

Reynold and James rode on either side of her, talking about their children, their wives, the army, anything they could think of. They still seemed uncertain of her and themselves, but she didn't have the time to worry about their feelings. She had to coordinate the hunt and all the men who ogled her and talked to her—and still try to keep Gareth in her sights.

But he eluded her. Why was she allowing herself to feel hurt? She had gone into their relationship knowing it would be brief and only physical. But suddenly she didn't know if she wanted to behave like a man, if that meant pretending their night together was meaningless.

Horns sounded for the start of the hunt. The dogs were finally unleashed, and with a riotous barking they dashed into the forest. The hunting party spread out and entered the line of trees.

Margery left her brothers behind, following the same path Gareth took. She heard the barking of the hounds before her, inhaled the cool earthy smells of the forest, and rode as if no root or tree could trip her horse.

The forest grew darker, quieter, and somehow it seemed ominous. She pulled her horse to a halt and listened. The hunting party must have veered farther west than she had.

And then she heard the squeal of a boar. Her horse shied and danced. Margery grabbed her crossbow, which was already cocked, and swiftly urged the horse forward. When she dodged a last stand of trees, she came out into a clearing and saw the boar, dark and tusked and angry, about to charge toward her.

A man knelt on the ground between them. He pushed himself to his feet and staggered. He turned toward her, and the sun suddenly shone across his blond hair.

It was Gareth—and he was injured.

Chapter 23

Margery didn't think of the fright or the danger; she just did what her brothers had drilled into her from childhood. She stood up in the stirrups and rode toward the boar, lifting her crossbow to aim. She heard Gareth shout her name, but it was as if he were far away.

With a hoarse squeal, the boar charged toward her. At the last second, she veered to the side and released the crossbow's trigger. The boar crashed to the ground, her bolt firmly in its chest. It twitched once, twice, then lay still.

Breathing rapidly, she slid off the horse's back and raced for Gareth, who limped toward her, his face pale and angry. She saw no blood on his tunic, and relief brought tears to her eyes. She would have thrown herself against him, but he grabbed her arms and held her away.

"What were you thinking?" he demanded,

giving her a shake. "You could have been killed!"

"It was charging you! I couldn't let you die. Oh, Gareth!" She flung her arms around his neck. He staggered and went down on one knee.

Off balance, she dropped down beside him. "You *are* hurt!"

Blood dripped from a wound in his thigh, seeping through his hose.

"It barely touched me," he said gruffly. "It startled my horse and I fell. As the boar charged, the horse fled, and left me with the consequences."

"Be still." She tore his ripped hose open, and saw that the blood had already slowed. "You are fortunate. You'll live."

"Are you happy about that?" he asked softly.

She unsheathed her dagger.

"I guess not."

"Be quiet." She cut strips of her linen smock into bandages, and began to wrap his leg. "Do you want to bleed to death?"

After she finished, Margery sat back on her heels to inspect her work. If the boar had gouged him any deeper, he could have lost his leg—or his life. She began to shake.

"Margery?"

She put up her hands. "I'm fine. But you were almost killed."

They stared at each other, and suddenly there was more at stake than his wounded leg.

She realized she would never have this connection to another man. With the husband she envisioned, she'd be safe, but never alive. She could make all the decisions, but none would be shared.

She had a sudden moment of clarity as she looked at Gareth. She thought of his strength, his kindness, his passion. A tentative, fragile thread of hope wound through her chest. Could he be the answer to all her problems—the husband she so desperately needed?

He didn't care about her relationship with Peter; only that she'd been treated badly. He had no family to manipulate him; no one would use him to get to her money. Because of the Beaumont Curse, maybe he wouldn't mind if she couldn't bear him children.

Most importantly, he would not have to worry that she expected undying love from him. She refused to think about love, because it left her too vulnerable. She would think about trust and friendship, and helping each other in a time of need.

She told herself that she wasn't being selfish. He could use her aid as much as she could use his. He would never know poverty again. Together, they could manage all her lands.

Oh, why hadn't she thought of this before?

Gareth continued to watch her, his gaze wary. She wanted to spill out her proposal, to see his face alight with joy. But now was not the time. She needed to care for his wounds, and deal with her brothers.

She smiled and leaned to kiss him. "Let us rejoin the hunting party. You can ride with me."

He didn't return her kiss, and she attributed that to the strain of being wounded, and the nearness of her brothers. There could be no other reason, she told herself.

Gareth got to his feet without Margery's help and mounted the horse behind her, trying to stay as far away as possible. Her fleeting, happy kiss haunted him, left a pain in his gut that wouldn't go away. He wished she would hate him, and be ashamed of the sin they'd committed. It would make leaving her more bearable.

But she looked over her shoulder, giving him a sultry smile rife with sensual promise.

He *had* to see her married to someone else— quickly. He was too much the coward to tell her of his betrayal.

There wasn't a cowardly bone in Margery's body. He still felt the horror that had invaded his heart when she'd charged the boar alone, armed with only the lightest crossbow. She had been determined and skillful and brave, and his admiration only made him feel lower than any scoundrel. She had risked her life—for him.

They reached the clearing, with its bright pavilions and streamers and colorful blankets scattered with food. Margery sent a few grooms back for the boar, then tried to help Gareth dismount. He brushed her aside, but before everyone, she slid beneath his arm to help him walk. He couldn't pull away without embarrassing her, so he used her capable shoulders for support just as he'd used her body for revenge.

He wished she would stop looking so concerned, so vulnerable. It would be apparent to everyone that they had been intimate.

And then she'd be stuck with him, when she could have had a good life with a man who deserved her.

Her brothers stared hard, their faces closed, emotionless. They had spent their whole lives concerned about their sister, trying to do what was best for her. At least they'd had a decent motivation for the mistakes they'd made.

Gareth had only selfishness and greed for his.

Margery knelt beside him while Anne and Cicely stood behind her looking concerned. As she checked the bleeding in his leg, her brothers sat down on either side of him, like armed guards.

"So what happened?" Bolton asked, eyeing him suspiciously.

Before he could answer, Margery said, "A boar attacked him."

Welles peered at the wound. " 'Tis not bad.

Since you are here, I assume you killed it?" he asked Gareth.

"Your sister did." He saw her blush. "She came riding into the clearing like an avenging angel." *For me, a man who doesn't deserve her concern.*

Bolton scowled. "I don't think I appreciate your—"

Margery knocked her brother's foot aside, and he closed his mouth.

During their dinner Margery did her best to ignore her worry for Gareth, and her excitement about asking him to marry her. The suitors who surrounded her blurred into faceless men whom she no longer had to consider. She had found her solution, and she *still* couldn't believe her future showed promise!

She knew her brothers watched every move she made. Let them. They had no say in her decision; why should they care if she married a man who had nothing? She had more than enough wealth—she only needed to satisfy herself and the king.

They spent the rest of the day outdoors, eating and drinking, dancing and laughing, except for Gareth, whose wound seemed to be bothering him. She wanted to sit at his side, but that would only attract suspicion.

She joined in the frivolity, nervous with anticipation. The celebration continued when they returned to Hawksbury. In each dance, she was passed from man to man. She took extra time with her brothers, knowing that they would be leaving in the morning.

Gareth sat with his leg up, his face unreadable. She didn't know what he was thinking; she only knew that she would make him happy. They would solve each other's problems.

That night Margery tried to stay awake until Gareth arrived, though she had barely slept the night before. When she heard the latch raise, she opened her eyes to smile sleepily at him as he came through the door. He didn't meet her gaze.

"Gareth?" She sat up and patted the bed beside her. "Come sit with me. I need to talk with you."

He hesitated. "My leg has grown stiff this day. I'd rather stand."

She felt an inkling of worry, but dismissed it. She rose to her feet and watched his gaze drop down to the sheer nightdress she wore. When he looked away, expressionless, she almost faltered. What was wrong?

"Gareth, you know I've been searching for a husband." She walked slowly toward him, then stopped and rested her palms against his chest. He was warm, solid, capable. She wanted to lean against him, to absorb his strength.

He didn't embrace her, and the room suddenly seemed too hot. Something was dreadfully wrong. She talked faster and faster, like a fool, as if by sheer volume of words she could make everything work out.

"I have more than enough wealth," she said, "so I do not need to choose for that reason. I was looking for a man whom I could get along with, whom I enjoyed. I thought of—you. Would you marry me?"

His face remained blank, like a stranger's—like he'd been when he first arrived at Hawksbury Castle. Margery's hands started to tremble. She wanted to clutch his doublet and shake him, demanding that he act like *her* Gareth. Why didn't he speak?

He finally sighed and closed his eyes for a brief moment. His voice sounded strained. "Margery, you knew I could not stay here. I must return to France. I've never wanted the responsibilities of a wife. I am sorry if you thought otherwise."

Margery's throat seemed to close up, and no other words would escape. He didn't want a wife; he didn't want *her*. She had never expected rejection—not after the intimate things they'd shared in her bed, not after the easy way they'd had with each other.

What had she expected? She had pursued him, not asking for promises or love. She had wanted one last reckless, passionate evening to remember forever.

And that was all she got.

Her last chance at a decent marriage withered and died, taking with it the scattered remnants of her girlhood dreams.

Though the strain almost broke her, she smiled. "I understand."

Frowning, he reached a hand to her, then stopped. "Margery—"

"No, 'tis all right. I knew we didn't love each other. I knew you were not a man to marry." She backed away, wearing her ridiculous grimace of a smile. "There are still plenty of men to choose from. I've even begun a list, you know." She suddenly could take no more, and turned back toward her lonely bed. "Good night, Gareth."

She would have sobbed if he attempted to touch her. He didn't, and that was worse. He simply made a pallet of blankets before the hearth and turned his back on her.

Margery lay down in bed, fighting tears, then fighting to keep them silent. What was wrong with her, that every man she thought she loved, rejected her?

Gareth could hear her crying. The sound was like broken glass being raked through his heart.

He told himself it was better this way. She wouldn't know how he'd used her for revenge, for his own gain.

Even forgetting all his sins, how could he make her the wife of Warfield's Wizard, a man scorned for visions he couldn't control? Sooner or later she would know he wasn't like everyone else, and she'd hate and fear him.

At least she'd already begun to hate him. Maybe that would help her in the end. He closed his eyes and tried not to hear the pain he'd caused.

Before Mass the next morning, Margery stood in the inner ward with James and Reynold, who were mounted and ready to leave with their company of men. She understood their urgency. They had wives and children they hadn't seen in months; they had people who loved them.

She felt so alone, drained of the emotions she'd cried her way through. For her husband, she would have to choose a man she'd barely known, and share the intimacies of marriage. Her chance at the happiness her brothers had was gone.

She heard a sudden clash of steel coming from the tiltyard. Through the mist of an early fog, she saw Gareth and Sir Wallace practicing. She steeled herself against the ache of pain, but it came anyway. Gareth worked his partner hard, driving him back slowly and steadily. His limp from the boar's wound was barely noticeable. Even when Sir Wallace stumbled, Gareth didn't let up.

"What a fine display," James said dryly.

Margery glanced up at him. He leaned on

the pommel of his saddle and watched the battle with narrowed blue eyes.

"Only by practicing does one get better," Reynold offered, but James paid him no heed.

"Are you watching him, Margery?" James asked softly.

She bit her lip, but turned toward the combatants. She heard the grunts of labor as Gareth sliced and thrust until he drove Sir Wallace against the wall.

"Look how Beaumont treats a training partner."

She had seen Gareth practice with Sir Wallace many a time. He had always been fair and honorable; today he looked like a man possessed. Was he angry that she had turned their *affaire* into something more serious? Was he even now desperate to get away, but unable to, out of a sense of honor to his oath?

"James," Reynold scolded softly. "You know nothing of the man's mood."

She turned her back on the tiltyard and smiled resolutely up at her brothers. She didn't want to discuss Gareth again. They each leaned down to give her a kiss.

"Say hello to Katherine and Isabel for me," she said. "You will both come to Greenwich to hear my decision, won't you?"

"Of course." James's gaze lifted to the tiltyard again and he frowned. "But as for husbands—"

"Godspeed, James," Margery interrupted.

He gave her a reluctant grin. "Very well. Make a good choice."

They lifted their hands in farewell, then guided their horses toward the gatehouse.

As they rode slowly away, she heard James say, "That man Beaumont was training with—did he look familiar to you?"

Reynold shrugged. If he spoke, Margery heard none of it. She watched her brothers until they entered the gatehouse, then she looked blankly at the ground and hugged her cloak tighter against the chill.

She went to the chapel for Mass, and prayed to God for help. But with all the sins she'd committed, she didn't believe she deserved any.

During the fortnight until the Cabots' tournament, Margery barely spoke to Gareth. But she felt his presence in everything she did, watching over her, protecting her. She was miserable.

Every night she pretended to be asleep when he entered her room. She heard each movement as he made his pallet and lay down, as far away from her as he could get. Every night she wondered if he'd come to her bed, and if he did, what she would do.

She could never again welcome him for mere pleasure's sake. The recklessness that had invaded her soul had burned to ashes. No longer was she shaking her fist at the heavens, determined to behave like a man. She was only a tired, lonely woman, with a decision to make that seemed to have no more consequence for her.

What did her choice matter, if it couldn't be Gareth?

She even wrote that list of all the men she had to consider, and tried to find the one with the most promising traits. But they each had some flaw, and soon all their faces blurred together.

She found herself writing Gareth's name, over and over. When she realized what she'd done, she scratched it out so hard she put a hole in the paper. Then she buried her face in her hands and wept.

Five days later, they traveled in a small caravan for two rainy days to reach the Cabots' tournament. The Cabots' home was more a sprawling, welcoming manor house than a fortress, and Margery usually felt at peace there. But now she kissed Sarah's delicate cheek, and congratulated her on her coming child, all the while feeling so remote and distant it was as if she watched another person acting as her.

Across rolling meadows, as far as the eye could see, tents and pavilions flew the pennants of their owners, and grassy stretches of fields had been roped off for various competitions. Peddlers and villagers sold their wares from booths. Ladies and their servants cheered as their men trained for the tournament.

By twos and threes, men started to surround Margery before she'd even had a chance to escape inside. There were men she knew, men on her list, men she'd never even met. They enclosed her, suffocated her, and she wondered frantically where Gareth was. Would even Sir Humphrey be in attendance, ready to kidnap her again?

Then the noise of the crowd hushed to a murmur, and as they parted, she could see the manor house. King Henry descended the stairs, resplendent in his royal blue silks, his long, pale face slightly smiling. While all her suitors bowed, Margery sank into a deep curtsy.

She had not known the king was coming. Her stomach roiled at the thought of his questions.

She lifted her head, and then felt as if she'd been punched in the stomach. For standing at the king's side was Peter Fitzwilliam.

Chapter 24

G areth dismounted and watched Margery
become swallowed up in a sea of eager
men. He flung his cloak back and kept his hand
on his sword hilt, almost wishing one of them
would try to take her away.

Yet he could not be so spiteful. He wanted
her happiness above all else, and if one of these
men could bring the sparkle back to her eyes,
so much the better.

When the king stepped out into the sun-
shine, Gareth bowed like everyone else, but he
couldn't keep his head down for long. He had
seen the man at the king's side before. He was
of middling height, obviously appealing
enough to women, with curling brown hair
that shined as if he took extra care with it. The
vanity of noblemen never ceased to amaze Gareth.

It took Gareth a moment to remember why
the man was familiar. He was overcome by a
vague feeling of sickness, and he realized it

was the memory of his most recent vision. This was the man he had seen kissing Margery. Through the mists of Gareth's mind, they had looked into each other's eyes, destined for a lifetime of happiness.

As the man descended the stairs at the king's side, Gareth told himself it was for the best, even as the pain in his chest felt like it was constricting his breathing. Margery deserved a normal man, one who could move with her from court to country, at home anywhere. A man without visions or curses, a man who wouldn't use her for his own selfish purposes.

The nobleman approached Margery, and brought both her hands to his lips.

Did she already know him, or would this be the first meeting that swept her away with wonder and the beginnings of passion? Gareth found himself walking numbly forward, as if he had to see it all for himself. He deserved every last bit of torture.

Then he saw Margery's face. She had gone chalk white, her mouth sagging open.

He stepped closer, pushing aside squires and pages.

When the nobleman lifted his head to smile at her, bathed in the approving gaze of the king, Gareth saw her tremble.

"Who is that?" he asked one of Margery's knights.

"Viscount Fitzwilliam," the man answered, his dour face transformed with speculation.

"Seems like his interest in our mistress has re-kindled, eh?"

Margery's first lover—who had taken her virginity and cast her away without regard to her feelings.

Gareth shouldered aside anyone who stood between him and Margery. The anguish she so desperately tried to hide made him burn with a fury he had never felt before. He wanted to bury his sword in Fitzwilliam's body and watch his guts spill.

Instead Gareth took Margery's arm. She stared wide-eyed at Fitzwilliam as if Gareth wasn't there.

"Mistress Margery," Gareth said near her ear, "let me see you to your chamber."

She didn't react.

"I am sure you would like to settle in, perhaps rest before the evening's festivities."

Fitzwilliam gave them a jovial smile. "Margery, we haven't even had time to talk. Come sit by the hearth with me and tell me all you've been doing."

Gareth eyed him coldly. "It has been a strenuous trip. I will see her to her room."

Margery suddenly seemed to will herself into awareness. She lifted her chin, and some of her color returned. She gave Fitzwilliam a perfunctory smile, even as she grasped Gareth's arm with abnormal strength.

"Lord Fitzwilliam, it is good to see you again," she said coolly. "I look forward to speaking with you later this evening. Sir Gareth, how kind of you to escort me to my chamber."

But they could not pass the king without a bow and a curtsy. Gareth prayed that their sovereign did not ask his name, because he could very well be ordered from the tournament, leaving Margery defenseless. But King Henry's gaze remained speculatively on her.

"Mistress Margery." The king's voice was soft, as if he knew he had no need to raise it. "We have missed you at court."

"Thank you, Your Majesty," she said. "Is the queen with you?"

"Alas, she had to remain at Greenwich, but she has been anxious to hear of your decision. Have you met the fine young man who is to be your husband?"

Gareth saw her blush. For someone who just a moment before seemed paralyzed with fright, she had recovered with amazing poise. "I am still considering, Your Majesty."

He laughed, but he was already looking beyond her to the noblemen who waited for his attention. "We shall talk, mistress. I have been spending much time with young Fitzwilliam. You could do worse than consider him."

"Yes, Your Majesty," she murmured as he and his entourage swept past.

Gareth watched her with concern, but she never looked at him, nor did she push his arm away. Together they entered the Cabots' home and were escorted to the chamber set aside for her. The maidservant left them alone in the corridor.

Margery released his arm. Her gaze never rose higher than his chin. "Thank you, Gareth. Have a good evening."

"Margery, if you need to talk—"

"Talk?" she repeated in a brittle voice. "I knew I would have to see Peter eventually, and now it has happened. What is there to talk about? After all, he is just another man I have given myself to."

She closed the door in his face, and Gareth stood frozen, anguished, his hand flat against the wood that separated them. Was the vision of Peter and Margery kissing meant to warn him of their past, or predict the future? He was sick of always feeling helpless—useless.

And who was he to judge Fitzwilliam, when he had used Margery just as poorly?

Margery stood at the window and stared blankly at the tournament pavilions below.

She had finally seen Peter, but the pain of caring for him had fled, leaving her only sad and bewildered.

Yet there was always the constant worry that he would tell someone of their secret indiscretion. She had to talk to him, find out what he wanted.

And find out why the king had recommended him as a husband.

During supper, Margery knew Gareth lingered near, watching over her. She had never doubted that he worried about her safety—after all, he said he'd sworn an oath to her father. Fine comfort that was.

Still, she'd made sure his bedchamber was near hers, for even now she did not want to be surprised by a greedy man.

Peter sought her out after the meal and drew her aside to a window seat, which overlooked the darkening sky and the multicolored patches of pavilions. She felt safe enough, with hundreds of people in the hall, and Gareth standing sentinel nearby.

She just wanted to have this conversation over with. The suspense had to be worse than knowing.

For a moment she stared into her lap, where Peter's hand held hers. She removed her fingers from his, then shivered when he let his hand rest on her knee for a moment too long.

Enough with cowardice, she told herself, and raised her gaze to his. She expected to feel the anguish of love lost. Instead she felt . . . tired.

His smile, once full of promise, was now only patronizing. "My dear girl, it is so good to see you."

She nodded once and said nothing.

"Did you receive my letter?"

"What do you want, Peter?"

"Want?" He lowered his voice, then looked about to see if anyone was near. "Margery, you already gave me everything I could want."

Her worst fears were about to become reality. He would tell everyone what she had done. She braced herself to feel terror and anxiety, but she could barely work up the strength to be nervous.

Gareth was watching them, his beautiful face inscrutable as he waved away one eager serving maid after another. He didn't want her himself, yet was he making sure no one else could have her?

She knew such thoughts were unfair. He was her personal guard, trying to see his task to completion. He had not asked her to throw herself at him. He had given her exactly what she wanted.

It was not his fault that sexual intimacy was no longer enough for her.

"Margery!" Peter sounded annoyed. His brown eyes, which had once seemed so warm, now regarded her with calculating intent.

She gave him a weary smile. "Yes?"

"I have been thinking of our last parting."

She tensed, but refused to look away.

"Perhaps it was a bit . . . abrupt."

"What do you mean?"

"That I have changed my mind." He took her hand and this time squeezed enough so that she couldn't pull away. "Margery, I cannot imagine my life without you."

Once she had lived to hear those words from him. Now all she could think was—*liar*.

"Peter, do you need money?" she asked. "Does my enlarged dowry draw you more than before?"

His eyes glittered and his smile faded just a bit. "So we are being blunt, are we?"

"I prefer it that way."

He reached up and caressed her cheek. "Money does increase your desirability—and it makes up for your barrenness. Who knows, you might even yet have children. Or maybe I will give you children we can raise together."

Margery felt ill. It was as she suspected: he only told her she was barren to be rid of her. And like every other man, it seemed he would have his dalliances outside their marriage, and she would be the one to live with the results. She would have slapped him if he hadn't chosen their meeting place so well.

She said, "I no longer want to marry you."

He grinned. "We are already married before God. Should I tell your brothers that?"

She could stand up and walk away; she could argue—if only he didn't make sense.

She had no illusions that a marriage between Peter and her would ever be a love match. Maybe he'd even spend most of his time in London, and leave her in peace.

Margery glanced at Gareth. He looked as

fierce as his Viking ancestors, as if he had a personal stake in his duty as her guard.

But he didn't.

She glanced once more at Peter.

He was looking at Gareth speculatively. "And who is that, my dear?"

"Just another of my suitors," she answered with careful indifference.

"He seems . . . protective of you."

" 'Jealous' would be a better word."

Peter glanced back at her, but before he could speak, she said, "I shall give your proposal consideration, Peter."

His smile brightened. "I can be patient."

"You will have to wait until I present my decision to the king."

He took her hand again and she allowed it, with a sad resignation that she knew would forever be part of her life.

As Gareth watched Margery and Fitzwilliam, he knew only too well that he had no right to feel angry, frustrated, and worried. Whom she married was none of his concern.

Yet it hurt to think she might go back to a man who had used her so cruelly. Could Fitzwilliam have changed? Not much, by her sad expression.

She rose and left Fitzwilliam, and Gareth fell into place beside her. He wanted her to confide in him, to trust him with her secrets, to seek his advice as she had once done. He so badly wanted her happiness. But she said nothing, and he no longer had the right to ask.

For the rest of the week, Gareth watched Margery from afar. She kept to her large circle of friends wherever she went, but her face looked strained as one man after another took turns approaching her.

She was remote and polite to Gareth. The sparkle of laughter that used to linger in her eyes when they were together had gone out.

In a lifetime of disappointments, never had he felt this lost, this discouraged. For Margery, he had destroyed all the walls he'd used to keep people away. Now his heart felt battered, unprotected—and it was his own fault. He tried to remember what it was like to despise her and her family, but all he felt was a profound loneliness. He didn't understand his own confusion. He ached as if everything worth living for had gone when he'd lost Margery.

Fitzwilliam never strayed far from her side, and after a few days, she ceased to look miserable. She was not happy either, but Gareth hoped that would come with time. His vision had shown him that Margery and Fitzwilliam would be together.

What made it worse was that she continued to look out for Gareth. When he entered the tournament there were grumbles of anger from his opponents, but she smoothed things over with King Henry.

She had been proclaimed the tournament's captive princess, and the final champion would win her release and perhaps her favor. King Henry made great sport of this playacting. Margery went along with the game amiably, but Gareth knew she only concealed her suffering.

Soon he was competing in archery, horse racing, and especially the joust. He won good sums of money at everything he did, but there was no satisfaction or joy in victory. It was only money to survive on after he'd left Margery. He couldn't imagine that day. It was as if his true life had begun with her, and when he left, it would all be over.

The final joust for Margery's favor was between Gareth and Fitzwilliam. Gareth had continued to play the suitor, and he knew Fitzwilliam considered him his main rival.

At his end of the lists, Gareth sat on his stallion, fully armored and carrying his lance, waiting as Fitzwilliam rode past the crowd for their adulation. The king had seated Margery beside him, and then obviously urged her to tie her scarf to Fitzwilliam's lance.

It should have been a terrible moment for Gareth. But as he looked across the tournament field, past the crowds cheering for Fitzwilliam and booing him, an incredible calm descended over him.

He loved Margery.

She made the best of every situation with a

courage he could never begin to imitate. She had intelligence, and a gift for enjoying life to its fullest. She cared for other people more than herself. And he finally understood and accepted that he would do anything for her happiness.

Fitzwilliam was obviously the king's favorite, and Margery would have a better life with a man such as he, of her own class. Gareth and his problems would only make her miserable.

The rest was easy. As his horse thundered down the lists, Gareth let Fitzwilliam's lance hit his shield. He let go of the reins and tumbled backward onto the ground. The impact stunned him for a moment; then he rolled over and sat up. He'd have new bruises, but nothing was broken. After removing his helmet, he got to his feet.

The cheers were deafening as Fitzwilliam approached the royal stand. The king brought Margery to Fitzwilliam and put their hands together, and Gareth turned and went back to his tent—alone.

Margery had been home at Hawksbury for a sennight. No matter what task she was performing, the image of Gareth falling from his horse constantly flashed in her mind. The terror had lodged so deeply in her throat that she thought she'd never breathe again. She had barely noticed Peter or the king or the cheering celebration. Only when Gareth had gotten stiffly to his feet had life returned to her heart and soul with a wave of relief.

As she lay in bed late one night, she still didn't understand why Gareth had done it. Only she seemed to realize he had fallen deliberately. It was as if he was releasing her back to Peter. What did it matter to Gareth who she chose?

Something wasn't making sense, but she couldn't figure it out.

There was only a week remaining until she met again with the king. Margery had gone over her list of potential husbands, and realized with dismay that she could either choose a man she was uncertain about, or she could choose Peter—who held no illusions for her.

There was really only one choice. Peter had threatened to tell everyone her sins, knowing that she couldn't embarrass her family that way. She was trapped.

Everything was made worse by the fact that Gareth was avoiding her. At night he assigned a guard to her door, and came no more to protect her himself.

Her bedchamber was no longer a haven. In her mind she saw Gareth before the hearth, behind the draperies, above her in bed. None of it could ever again be real.

The loneliness of her life was overwhelming—all because she loved Gareth.

With bittersweet irony, she could finally admit it to herself. Her marriage proposal hadn't been about helping each other; she had been desperate not to lose the one person in life who made her happy, made her feel whole.

Gareth.

Even his name made her bury her face in her pillow and cry. How would she get through her days without him? He was drawing farther away from her, and she didn't know what to do to stop it.

As the days sped by Margery abandoned her list of suitors. She had no choice but to marry Peter, or cause a huge scandal.

Other men still continued to appear at the castle to court her, but she didn't turn them away. What did it matter anymore?

She sat before the hearth in the great hall, her embroidery untouched in her lap. Gareth sat at a nearby table, a book opened before him. She tried not to look at him, for the pain was nearly unbearable. Yet she glanced at him occasionally, and he never seemed to turn the page. What thoughts moved through his mind? Was he anxious to leave? Even glad that the king's celebration was almost upon them?

Her latest suitor, Sir Bradley Palmer, had arrived just that afternoon. He must have barely twenty years, and seemed so young to her. Sir Bradley was eager to face life, while she felt only old and tired.

Sir Bradley came into the hall, walking by Gareth, who looked up. When their gazes met,

Margery watched in amazement as Sir Bradley stumbled back, fear widening his eyes. Gareth calmly closed the book, waiting in what seemed like resignation.

Was this yet another man Gareth had defeated in tournaments?

Sir Bradley approached her with haste, looking over his shoulder repeatedly at Gareth. "Mistress Margery, I am sorry to be so bold, but do you not realize what man lies hidden here?"

"Hidden?" she asked with incomprehension.

"That man!" He turned and pointed at Gareth. His voice was loud, and soon he had the attention of the entire hall. "Surely you do not know his true identity."

Gareth watched Sir Bradley with an impassive gaze.

"He is Sir Gareth Beaumont," she said, knowing she'd done all this before.

The man's eyebrows rose. "He does not even change his name. His gall astounds me. I am from Sussex, mistress, and there we all know who he is. Beaumont acquired another name when we squired together—Warfield's Wizard."

Chapter 25

All eyes turned to Gareth, and Margery felt panic take hold of her. "Warfield's Wizard? Surely you must have the wrong—"

"No!" The young man's voice rose through the hall. "I worked my way from page to squire at his side—always, he was different. He knew things others didn't. Beaumont made Lord Warfield's son ill, and foretold it with a vision. We knew to run in fear when his eyes would look far away, and his face darkened with a frown."

A chill of recognition moved through Margery. She met Gareth's calm eyes, remembering his blank gaze, his frown of pain. Always, he knew when she needed help, even knew where she'd been taken by Sir Humphrey. She wanted Gareth to deny it all, but he said nothing, just watched her with grim resignation.

She suddenly understood everything: from his unexplained knowledge of events to his belief in the Beaumont Curse. He thought himself

345

some kind of monster, and by his silence, he invited the crowd's condemnation. In fact, he seemed to want it.

Margery felt suddenly as if a great weight had been lifted from her soul. Gareth didn't think he deserved her hand in marriage! She closed her eyes to hide her tears of relief. She hadn't been wrong about him—the way they enjoyed each other's nearness, his gentleness and passion in lovemaking. He had been hiding a secret he thought too terrible for her to hear.

Instead, it only made her love him more. How horrible to feel so different from everyone, to be condemned and hated for something he had no control over. Yet he had gone on with his life, and kept his burden private.

She couldn't look at him, for worry that her admiration and love would shine from her eyes. Now was the moment she had trained her whole life for; to keep her people calm and secure in the knowledge that she was the ultimate authority at Hawksbury Castle.

The hall buzzed with whispered voices and a dangerous undercurrent. Everywhere Margery looked, servants and soldiers moved away, as if they'd never seen Gareth before. She had to stop this now, before the cry of "witch" ruined his life forever.

She did the first thing she could think of: she laughed. It was so easy to let peals of her laughter ring through the hall. She laughed at her mistakes, at her foolish pride, at the ignorance that allowed her to believe Gareth's words instead of his heart.

"Oh, Sir Bradley, please forgive me. Do not think I mock you, but I have known Sir Gareth since we were children. Never could I believe such things of him. He has cared for me and protected me. If he was a wizard, do you not think I would have seen the signs?"

"Mistress, men such as he are too cunning for a mere woman," Sir Bradley said.

Margery's smile lessened at his stupidity. "Just a few weeks ago, Sir Gareth was gored by a charging boar. Do you not think if he was a wizard, he would have stopped the animal?" she scoffed.

The voices were dying down, and one or two of her knights were starting to smile. "At the Cabots' tournament, I watched Sir Gareth get knocked to the ground in the final jousting match. He could have won a fortune. Do you not think a wizard would have stayed in the saddle?"

Sir Bradley's face was growing red. He looked about, trying to marshal any supporters. "But, mistress—"

"I must admit, it saddens me to think you would believe such nonsense. His family has had a tragic history, but that is all." She turned away from Sir Bradley, as if she had already dismissed him from her suitors.

She glanced casually at her servants and

friends, who had been near Gareth for months now. Surely they wouldn't think ill of him.

Her knights laughed together and turned away, resuming their game of dice. Anne and Cicely bent over their embroidery. A serving maid shyly approached Gareth with an offer of ale, and soon his usual parade of admiring maidservants fell into line.

Margery gave a shaky sigh—it had worked. She signaled for her minstrels to begin a dance, then walked over to Gareth. He slowly looked up at her, his face unreadable.

"Sir Gareth, I believe I still owe you a dance."

She knew she had left him no choice. He rose to his feet, his golden eyes gazing deeply into hers. What did he see in her, what did he know? The possibilities were endless, and she suddenly wanted to explore everything with him. She put her hands in his, and his warmth flowed through her. Though he didn't smile, he studied her with an intensity that left her flustered and yearning. As they whirled past Sir Bradley, she made sure to show a happy, joyous face. It wasn't difficult; she was in Gareth's arms.

Gareth held Margery's hand through the dance, grief and gratitude waging war in his mind. She knew everything about the curse. He'd been able to tell from her face that she believed Bradley Palmer.

Yet instead of sending him from her in fear,

she was saving him from certain banishment, perhaps even death. Her unselfishness humbled him, but it only made him resolve to leave her the moment he could. She did not deserve the scandal of having him in her home.

That night, Gareth sat alone in his bedchamber before his bare hearth. He felt relieved that the truth was out, and that Margery had accepted it gracefully. Now she would understand why he had to leave.

In his mind he saw the grounds of Hawksbury Castle. Not since his fostering had he stayed in one place long enough to know people. He would miss the soldiers and knights; he would even miss Wallace's friendship. He'd never thought he'd learn to trust a man, but Wallace had changed his skepticism. Wallace could have courted Margery himself, but he would never betray their friendship.

Yet he would be a much better husband than Gareth.

The door suddenly opened and Margery slipped in. She leaned back against the wall and gave him a speculative look. "I had to come. I think you need protection from Sir Bradley."

She smiled, but he couldn't smile back. He just looked at her across the room, and felt that they were farther apart than ever.

"You know what I am now," he said simply.

She walked toward him, her gown swaying

with the motion of her hips. The heat of un-
fulfilled desire was almost painful. As he remembered all he'd done to her, he knew he
deserved every pain and more.

"I've always known what kind of man you
are." Her voice was low, sultry.

She was so naive.

"You only think you do," he countered angrily. "You don't know why I came here; you
don't know the things I'd planned."

She stood above him, her hands on her hips.
He leaned back in the chair and gripped the
arm rests.

"Gareth, you came here to protect me. Is that
a lie?"

He looked away. "That was only part of it."

"How did you know I needed protection?"
she asked softly.

He clenched his jaw. How could he answer?
How could he prove once and for all the sick
things that went on in his mind? "I just knew."

"How did you know?"

He stood up to tower above her. He needed
her fear, needed to drive her away. "Do you
want to hear it all, how I see things before they
happen? How I saw your face in my dreams
and visions after all these years?"

"You swore an oath to my father," she said
calmly. "When you . . . saw me, was it me you
came for, or my father?"

He wanted to say "your father," but the lie
wouldn't leave his mouth. "I came for you

both." He gripped her arms when a pleased smile curved her mouth. "I did not lie to you about that. I lied about everything else."

"Everything?" she asked in a weak voice.

If this was the only way to drive her from the chaos of his world, back to the privilege and safety of hers, then he would tell her every ugly truth and be damned in her eyes. "Since I was twelve years old, I have spent every moment of my life hating your family. I rescued you, and you banished me."

"But I didn't know!" she cried.

She tried to wrap her arms about his shoulders, to press against him. It took everything in Gareth to keep from holding her, to remain as cold and remote as a statue.

He pushed her away. "I understand that now. But back then, since you didn't try to stop it, I thought you were just as guilty. And when I arrived here and saw how good your life was, I was furious."

"You had a right to be."

By the saints, nothing was getting through to her! Must he spell out his every sin and watch the pain in her eyes? "Did I have a right to get close to you, to try to persuade you that I was more than your friend?"

Her eyes glistened. "What do you mean?"

"While pretending to be your suitor, I was seducing you in truth. I was lying to you, and I set out to use you."

"But why?"

"Because it would have been my final revenge on your family. I wanted to make you fall in love with me, to choose me as your husband."

"And I did." Her voice was barely a whisper.

He whirled away from her and covered his face against her anguish. "You would have chosen me—a man cursed through life, Warfield's Wizard, a poverty-stricken knight. I wanted all that for you." He turned back toward her. "Now do you see what kind of man I am?"

Margery hugged herself as tears ran down her face. No matter how he'd come to Hawksbury, no matter his motives, he wasn't the same man now. The pain in his eyes and in his voice told her that.

And she loved him. But she didn't think he was ready to hear that.

"You have never trusted anyone," she said slowly. "Life—and my family—has taught you that. You were right not to trust me. I was using you, too. Every moment I pursued you, every time I tried to bring you to my bed, do you think I had marriage on my mind?"

He looked at the floor, not at her. She wanted to put her arms around him, to take all his pain away and bury it inside her.

" 'Tis not the same thing," he said in a low voice.

"Is it not? I wanted you as my last good memory before an awful marriage. Did I care that I might hurt you? At least you wanted to marry me. I just wanted to selfishly use your body for my own pleasure."

"Do you not see?" Gareth said, obviously scoffing at her sins. "It worked right into my plans!"

She stalked into his line of sight, then held his arms when he would have turned away. "Listen to me! Even my marriage proposal to you was selfish. You were the solution to my plans. I was not thinking about love, or even your feelings. I just selfishly assumed that I was the answer to all your prayers. But of the two of us, who was the one to do the noble thing?"

"Margery, don't do this."

He looked deep into her eyes, and she saw all the pain and anguish he had spent a lifetime learning to hide.

"It was you!" she cried. "You refused to marry me; you saw what I was doing."

"How could I marry you after everything I'd done, everything I was?"

"Tell me about the visions," she whispered suddenly.

He tried to pull away, but she threw herself against him and put her hands on either side of his face. "Tell me about the visions."

"There is nothing to tell," he said, and his misery hurt her. "They aren't even useful most of the time. I usually see minor things, like someone getting sick, or something lost. I get so nauseous that I want to understand none of it, and I pray to God to take them away from me. But He never took them away from my father or my grandfathers, and they went mad."

She held her breath for a moment, fighting tears. This was the true Beaumont Curse. "Oh, Gareth. Don't tell me that you've worried your entire life that you would be next to go mad."

"Me? My arrogance protects me from madness. I'm so foolish that even when the visions warned me you'd be riding away with a man, I thought it was I!" His laugh was full of self-hatred. "I let you get kidnapped. Do you not see, Margery? You don't deserve this."

She tried to kiss him, but he wouldn't lower his head. She leaned against his chest and pressed her lips to his throat. "But you found me. 'Tis all that matters."

"Fitzwilliam wants you back," he said coldly. "You should marry him."

She looked up into his remote face. "You want me with a man like *him*? Last spring, he told me he wouldn't marry me because I hadn't conceived his child. He told me that I was barren, worthless." The words tumbled from her lips like the tears from her eyes.

Gareth stared at her, wide-eyed. "You had only lain with him twice. Surely you know his words meant nothing."

"I had no one to ask," she whispered. "I know you think I'm a fool. But I had not only dishonored myself with him; I hadn't conceived."

"Margery," he whispered, wiping away her tears with his thumbs. "Some women take a long time to have children."

"But you would not care, would you?" she asked hopefully.

"Of course not. If I were your husband, I would love you no matter—" He stumbled over his words as he saw the trap. "But I will never be your husband."

"Gareth, please—"

He disentangled himself and stepped back. "If you cannot choose Fitzwilliam, choose Wallace Desmond. He's a good man. Now go back to your bed before someone discovers you here."

For a moment she wanted to melt into his arms and press kisses to his face. He loved her, he had almost admitted it. And she loved him.

"This isn't finished between us, Gareth," she said fervently.

He turned away.

Somehow, Margery would convince him that they were meant to be together. She was too close to happiness to accept less.

For the trip to Greenwich Gareth packed all his belongings, since he wouldn't be coming back to Hawksbury. At dawn he loaded his saddlebags, and as he stuffed the garments down as far as he could, his fingers encountered a small bulge. He pulled out a balled piece of leather.

Slowly, he unwrapped it, and found his half of Margery's crystal stone, which reflected the lantern light in a scattered pattern across the wall. He almost threw it away—then closed his fist around it tightly. It was all he would have left of her.

Someone entered the stables behind him, and he quickly shoved the stone into the pouch hanging from his belt. He tightened the saddle, then turned and found Wallace watching him.

"Is something wrong?" Wallace asked softly.

Gareth shrugged.

"You haven't seemed yourself these past few weeks. In fact, you have stopped your pursuit of our fair mistress."

"I'll be leaving as soon as she chooses a husband."

Wallace put a hand on his shoulder and Gareth stared at it in surprise.

"What made you change your mind about Margery?" Wallace asked.

"You were right. I couldn't lie to her anymore."

"I think there's more to it than that." Wallace lowered his voice. "That knight who came here accusing you of wizardry—tell me about him."

Gareth knew he should keep lying; Margery had preserved his secrets with her laughter. But as he looked into Wallace's face, he could not break the trust they had begun to build between them.

"Some of it is true. I . . . see things other people don't see, though I wish I didn't. In my mind, I saw Lord Warfield's son taking ill. Then I simply forgot it hadn't happened yet, and asked after his health."

Wallace watched him solemnly. "That is how you knew Margery was in danger."

"I've always known, even when we were children. I don't know why."

"I do," Wallace said, beginning to smile. "Fate. Love."

Gareth turned back to his horse, resting a hand on its warm flank. "But that isn't enough."

"Why not? I heard her defend you. I have seen the way she looks at you. She loves you; you love her."

"Love isn't enough," Gareth said in a soft, sad voice. "I lied to her, I used her against her family. Even my past is too difficult to overcome. I told her to find another man."

"I think you're wrong."

"Perhaps. But at least I'll be able to live with myself, because I've finally done the right thing."

Chapter 26

At the end of September, the palace at Greenwich came alive to celebrate the return of the king from the battle of Stoke. Hundreds of candles blazed throughout the presence chamber, where the golden thrones of King Henry VII and Queen Elizabeth were elevated. Tapestries and multihued banners of cloth were strung from the walls.

Margery stood beside her brothers, dressed in a pale blue brocade gown that shimmered with cut glass and pearls, wearing a decorated cap with the sheerest veil covering her long hair.

She knew she should be nervous, but a calm determination had come over her. Both James and Reynold eyed her with suspicion, but she merely continued to smile with confidence—and answered none of their questions.

Instead she looked over her shoulder, searching for Gareth. She had made Wallace promise to keep him in the presence chamber. She spied

Gareth in the second row of the large crowd, looking grim. Their gazes caught and held until he looked away. He shone with that savage, bright beauty that almost hurt her eyes. In his royal blue doublet, he glimmered as a jewel among common stones. She offered a silent prayer that she could make everything work out.

The king and queen had not yet entered. The musicians played, and the smells of a feast wafted through the air. Margery left her brothers and moved through the crowd, searching for Peter Fitzwilliam.

She spotted him leaning close to a blushing young woman, though he straightened when he saw Margery coming.

"Mistress Margery!" he called, with the joviality of true confidence.

"Lord Fitzwilliam," she said, smiling coolly, "I would like to speak to you."

"By all means."

He walked away from the poor girl without even a farewell. His conceit sickened her, but she wouldn't have to bear it for much longer.

She led him to a window alcove hung with gold draperies and flowers. They were in sight of the hall, yet their voices would not carry far. Margery saw her brothers watching with concern. Perfect.

"You do not need to prepare me," Peter said conspiratorially. "I'll look quite pleased and surprised when you call my name."

She gave him a polite smile. "I won't be calling your name."

His smile faded. "Pardon me?"

"I won't be calling your name, Peter. You will not be my choice for husband."

He looked almost petulant, like a little boy who wouldn't be getting a new pony. "But Margery, I don't wish to tell your brothers what you and I did together. It would be such a shame to anger them."

"I won't stop you," she said, gazing calmly into his face. "Go ahead and tell them what you did to me."

He hesitated, and she held her breath. "They'll name you a harlot."

"But they'll blame *you*." Margery felt suddenly liberated in the face of his unease. She had been such a fool to allow this man to ruin her life. "Go ahead, they're already watching us. Tell them."

Peter glanced toward her brothers, and bless them, they were frowning darkly. And she hadn't even prompted them. If only they'd put their hands on their sword hilts . . . but it was too much to hope for.

Peter sighed and shook his head. "We could have had an interesting marriage, you know."

She didn't trust herself to speak, so just continued to smile politely. In a moment he left, chasing after the girl she'd taken him from.

Margery closed her eyes and tried to absorb her victory without giving in to tears. She had nothing left to fear from Peter. She could now put her mistakes with him in the past, where they belonged. It was time to turn her attention to the next challenge.

"Margery!"

She recognized Anne's breathless voice as the twins came to take her hands. Margery kissed each of their cheeks, and smiled. How she would miss them when they returned to their parents.

"Oh, Margery," Cicely said, her face a study in worry, "will you not tell us whom you have chosen?"

"How can you keep us this anxious?" Anne added, her gaze still following Peter. "Is Lord Fitzwilliam the one? What about Lord Chadwick, or—"

Margery raised both her hands, laughing. "How can I tell you and not my brothers?"

"Then tell us all!" Anne cried with exasperation.

"In a few moments, I will," Margery said. "Trust me."

Cicely looked around the hall with shining eyes. "This is so exciting. Perhaps I, too, will get to choose my husband."

Margery took her hands, and grew serious. "It is a great responsibility. I still don't know if it will all work out in the end. Pray for me."

She returned to her brothers in time to curtsy as the king and queen and their courtiers paraded into the room. The light reflected from their glittering garments like the sun off a rippling brook. Margery returned the queen's pleased smile, then watched as they sat on their thrones.

James leaned closer to her. "Are you ready, sweetheart?"

"I hope so." She gave him an excited, happy smile.

"Are you sure you don't want to tell me whom you have chosen?"

"It has to be a surprise."

James playfully scowled, and Reynold winked at her. How she adored her brothers, she thought, as silly tears once again pricked her eyes. Even if they'd made mistakes along the way, she was truly blessed.

King Henry rose from his throne, and as if on cue, the music and the conversations stopped. A ripple of excitement and curiosity made people surge forward. Margery saw the king search the crowd until he found her, then he motioned for her.

The courtiers parted and she forced herself to walk slowly, smiling at the people on both sides. This was the moment, and she was nervous and excited and breathless.

Gareth watched Margery walk through the king's noble guests, and he couldn't help but feel proud of her. She looked radiant, composed, confident—how had he ever thought her spoiled or selfish? She would make her family proud.

And she had been right about him. He'd spent his whole life afraid to trust people; had pushed away any who sought his friendship. He didn't know if he would ever become used to the loneliness again, now that he'd spent so many nights in her company.

"Mistress Margery Welles," the king said, gesturing to her as she came to a stop below him. "Come stand next to me, my dear. You have provided our court with months of speculation, gossip, and true enjoyment. But it is now time for you to reveal your choice in husband."

Gareth watched Margery and the queen share a smile, before Margery turned and faced the multitude of people in the hall. Flames from hundreds of candles and torches gleamed in her eyes. The skin above her neckline glowed with a mellow, creamy light that set off her rich, dark hair. She was a stunning beauty who could have any man she wished. She deserved only the best, and he could trust her choice.

"My dear friends," she began in a clear, strong voice, "earlier this year, I was given a great honor by their royal majesties: the freedom to choose my own husband. I met many worthy men in the next few months, and I hope I have gained several new friends. But alas, I could choose only one man."

Gareth's chest ached. He could not witness Fitzwilliam's smug victory. Besides, Margery no longer needed him—she had her brothers, and soon her betrothed. Saying good-bye would only prolong both their pain. He eased his way backward through the crowd, toward the entrance. But he couldn't take his eyes off her sweet face, couldn't block out her melodic voice.

"I have chosen a worthy man," she said, her face alight with pleasure. "He is gracious, and always kind to me, yet strong enough to defend my lands and my people. We have loved each other for a long while."

Gareth nodded to the soldiers guarding the doors, and reached for the door latch.

"Although he is not of noble lineage, he will always be my only lord. I choose Sir Gareth Beaumont."

He froze with his fingers clutching the latch. He couldn't turn his head, couldn't look at her. What had she done? Why had she embarrassed herself like this?

He heard the shocked murmurs, then the rustle of garments as the crowd parted. He looked over his shoulder to find Margery's brothers walking toward him stiffly.

Giving him no choice, they escorted him toward the royal dais. He wanted to protest, to say it was all a mistake, but they drew him forward with a combined strength he could not hope to overcome.

Bolton leaned near and whispered, "We have some talking to do."

When they stopped before Margery, her two brothers backed away and left Gareth standing there alone, beneath the frown of the king and the scandalized whispers of the court.

She smiled at him with a radiance that was breathtaking. Then she knelt down before him and bowed her head.

"My lord," she murmured.

He stared down at her in shock. "Do not do this to yourself, Margery," he whispered.

"But I love you," she said in a clear voice that could be heard to the back of the hall.

Gareth didn't know where to turn, whom to appeal to. The king's frown was starting to fade, and the queen wiped a tear from her cheek. No help there. He would go to her brothers, tell them—

What could he tell them? Margery had just proclaimed her choice before the entire land. She had destroyed her chances with any other man—all for him.

"You should not have done this," he said with a shaky voice.

Margery took his hands in hers and pressed her lips to his knuckles. "You're everything to me, Gareth. I want only you."

He pulled her to her feet. He had to find a private place to talk some sense into her, to make her see that she'd be ruining the rest of her life.

She drew his head down and kissed him. He had never thought to feel her lips again, and for a moment he was caught up in the incredible magic of her kiss. From somewhere far away he heard cheers and applause. By the saints, what was he doing?

He gripped her shoulders and held her away. "We have to talk," he said in an urgent voice.

King Henry raised his arms for silence. "Sir Gareth, what is your answer?"

There wasn't a sound as Gareth swept his gaze over the crowd and saw Wallace grinning. This was all too overwhelming.

"Why are you doing this?" Gareth demanded of Margery, regardless of the waiting king.

"Because I love you and I can't be happy with anyone else."

"I have no land, no lineage that isn't tainted." Even his pride fled as he looked into her hopeful eyes.

She cupped his cheek. "I am not marrying your lineage. Do you not trust my feelings? I will not abandon you, as so many others have done. Do you love me?"

He closed his eyes. "Margery, please."

"Do you love me?" she repeated.

"God help me—yes."

With a glad cry, she threw her arms around him. "That is all I've ever wanted. We will make each other so happy!"

Gareth held Margery tight against him, amazed that he'd somehow won her love, despite his sins and his foolish mistakes. They would spend their days together, their nights in each other's arms. And if God didn't bless them with their own babies, they would find other children in need of a home. Margery had enough love for dozens of children.

"Silence!" The king's voice echoed through the noisy hall. "Mistress Margery has not had her answer yet."

Margery stepped away from him. Holding her hands, Gareth looked deep into her eyes, then dropped to his knees. He kissed her hands as she had done to him, then said in a loud voice, "I will take this woman as my bride, and I pledge that I will make myself worthy of her."

King Henry sighed. "Very well. The queen tells me we'll find some sort of title for you."

Margery laughed and fell into Gareth's arms, spreading kisses over his face as he stood up. "I knew it," she whispered. "I knew you wouldn't refuse me."

"I couldn't—especially after I found this." From the pouch at his belt, he removed the crystal stone and held it up to the light. "I feared I'd lost it. You'd think it was the most precious jewel, the way my heart grieved for it."

Margery closed her eyes and a tear escaped. She smiled and would have wiped it away, but he grasped her hands and leaned in to kiss her tears.

"My lady, I promise you'll never have cause to shed these again."

"Except in joy," she said, fumbling in her purse. "Be warned, I cry very easily when I'm happy." She held up her own half of the crystal stone. "I've kept this with me since childhood, and never have you been far from my thoughts."

With their lips together he murmured, "You've been in my dreams. We shall never be parted again."

They shared a deeper, more joyous kiss, oblivious to the cheers resounding through the hall.

Epilogue

A month later, Gareth, Margery, and her entire family were gathered at Hawksbury Castle. It was a brilliant, cool autumn day, perfect for endless feasting. Margery hadn't imagined that she could ever again feel this excited about every day of her life. This afternoon, she would finally be married to the man she loved.

She looked around the table as all her friends and family gathered for the morning meal. Gareth sat across from her, talking with her two brothers. Although it had taken a few weeks, the three men had finally begun to have conversations that didn't involve angry scowls and clipped words.

Margery sat between her two sisters by marriage, Reynold's wife, Katherine, and James's wife, Isabel. Both women were so different, yet so perfectly completed their expanding family. Margery had never had sisters before them, and it felt wonderful to be able to share her every thought and feeling. The three of them had spent endless hours talking about every facet of the wedding day. Isabel, who had not had a proper marriage, seemed to most enjoy learning how to plan one. She'd said she needed to be prepared, since their first child was a daughter.

Margery couldn't stop smiling. She gazed on Gareth with wonder, still unable to believe she'd be spending every night in his arms.

He glanced at her with a warm smile, then his gaze sharpened and his face grew serious.

Before Margery could question him, Katherine looked back and forth between them. "What is wrong with your bridegroom?"

"Men," Isabel said, rolling her eyes. "He is just anxious to get the day over with, and move on to the important matters."

The women laughed as Gareth rose to his feet and came around to her side of the table. He examined Margery almost quizzically, then a small smile turned up one corner of his mouth.

"What is it?" she asked, reaching up to take his hands.

"Nothing. I just think it is definitely time to be about this wedding."

Margery stared up at him with bemusement. His eyes weren't looking into her face, but lower. She blushed furiously before she realized that he was staring directly at her stomach and smiling with pride.

Awareness came over her in a rush of joy and tears. She gasped and spread her hands across her stomach. "A baby!" she blurted, forgetting where she was.

There was dead silence.

Gareth grinned. " 'Tis a boy," he said confidently.

As tears gathered in Margery's eyes, both her brothers sprang to their feet, hands on their sword hilts, their faces wearing identical angry scowls as they glared at Gareth. Smiling, their wives tugged them back down again.

Gareth gave her a silly, satisfied grin. She brought his hand down to her stomach, and together they touched the miracle of their child. He was right—this one would be a boy. But there would be others . . .

Margery met Gareth's smile with one of her own, feeling loved and cherished, and very, very blessed.

Coming in July from Avon Romance
Two historical love stories that will capture
your heart

WOLF SHADOW'S PROMISE
By
Karen Kay

He was a wounded Native American warrior.
She was the woman he could never have. But
together they made a promise of love that
could last forever . . .

NEVER KISS A DUKE
By
Eileen Putman

Emmaline Stanhope knew better than to fall in
love above her station, but she had never
encounted a man like Adrian St. Ledger—a
duke who was no gentleman!

Dear Reader,

If you have enjoyed the books you've just read, I know you'll want to take note of what's in store for you next month from Avon romance, beginning with a historical romance you won't want to miss, Tanya Anne Crosby's *Lion Heart*. Set in the romantic Scottish Highlands, this Avon Treasure is filled with passion, adventure—and has an unforgettable love story that will sweep you away.

From the Highlands to the American West . . . If you love Native American heroes and bold western settings then Karen Kay's *Wolf Shadow's Promise* is the story you've been looking for. Karen's characters always jump off the pages, and in *Wolf Shadow's Promise* you'll meet a hero and heroine who challenge each other in the most spectacular ways . . .

Never Kiss a Duke . . . unless you want to be compromised in front of the entire *ton*. In Eileen Putman's newest Regency-set historical a pert miss learns that you must be very careful about who you associate with—lest you get a reputation. Eileen's dialogue is sheer perfection, and you'll remember this delicious love story long after you've read the last page.

Contemporary readers, don't let the month end without reading Eboni Snoe's *Wishin' on a Star*. Not only is Ms. Snoe a rising star of romance, she also brings an exciting touch of magic to her romances. Here, a heroine discovers an extended family she didn't know she had . . . and finds the kind of love she's only dreamed about.

Enjoy!

Lucia Macro

Lucia Macro
Senior Editor

Avon Romances—
the best in exceptional authors and unforgettable novels!